THE WANDERERS

THE WANDERERS

CHARLES SAMUEL BETTS

authorHOUSE®

AuthorHouse™
1663 Liberty Drive
Bloomington, IN 47403
www.authorhouse.com
Phone: 1-800-839-8640

© 2011 by Charles Samuel Betts. All rights reserved.

No part of this book may be reproduced, stored in a retrieval system, or transmitted by any means without the written permission of the author.

This is a work of fiction. All of the characters, names, incidents, organizations, and dialogue in this novel are either the products of the author's imagination or are used fictitiously.

First published by AuthorHouse 04/14/2011

ISBN: 978-1-4567-6519-4 (sc)
ISBN: 978-1-4567-6518-7 (hc)
ISBN: 978-1-4567-6517-0 (ebk)

Library of Congress Control Number: 2011906976

Printed in the United States of America

Any people depicted in stock imagery provided by Thinkstock are models, and such images are being used for illustrative purposes only.
Certain stock imagery © Thinkstock.

This book is printed on acid-free paper.

Because of the dynamic nature of the Internet, any web addresses or links contained in this book may have changed since publication and may no longer be valid. The views expressed in this work are solely those of the author and do not necessarily reflect the views of the publisher, and the publisher hereby disclaims any responsibility for them.

The Brig O'Dorcas Savage

THE WANDERERS

It matters not how straight the gate
How charged with punishment the scroll
I am the master of my fate
I am the Captain of my soul
William Earnest Henley

CHAPTER 1

It was in May, 1833, when Geri and her three year old son, Robert, arrived to the pier at Belfast, Ireland. It was just two years ago that Pat Hogg had died suddenly. They were living near Dublin, Ireland, and Pat was doing well in his work as a stone mason. She would never forget that day when Ian, Pat's foreman, came to their small cottage. It was too early for him to be away from his work. At first Geri was just puzzled, but quickly she felt a deep fear in her heart. Ian stood painfully before her and stuttered out that Pat had been killed on the job . . . Geri just stood there at the door, and her face lost all of its color. Big tears rolled down her cheeks. Without saying a word she turned, closed the door and walked to their small kitchen. She picked up baby Robert, her one year old baby boy, and held him close to her breast. The baby nudged her breast and made sucking sounds. She guided his mouth to her breast and nursed him until he went to sleep. After putting him into his crib, she went into their bedroom and began to cry. It was a bitter despairing cry that would last for over an hour.

She had just fallen asleep when there was a knocking on the door. She slowly got up and staggered to the door. On opening the door she saw three ladies standing on the stoop. She did not know them as Pat and she had just moved into this small village called Tain. The first to speak was a tall, elderly woman. She said, "I am Effie McKay, and I am on the grief committee of our village. Ian McGregor just notified us of your loss. None of us have known you and your husband, but all of us have lost our spouse. We know how brutal it is to be suddenly left alone in a strange place. We want to help you any way we can as we know how desperate your feelings might be at this point in your life." Geri didn't feel desperate, but the kindness of Ms. McKay's voice comforted her. She didn't say anything at first. Slowly tears flowed down her cheeks, and Effie embraced her and comforted her. The other ladies went about the cleaning, cooking, and taking care of Robert. Slowly Geri relaxed and started talking about herself and Pat.

She said, "Pat and I were born and raised near Copenhagen, Denmark. We were childhood sweethearts and married when we were just eighteen. We were only married one year when Pat came home and said we were moving to Ireland. His sister had written him a letter telling him that they were immigrating to Nova Scotia, and he could have their house if he wanted to come to Armagh, Ireland. We said yes and immediately packed up our belongings and came to Armagh. It was a wonderful house, and we were very happy. Over the next two years Pat became a master stone mason. They were building a large Cathedral in Dublin and invited Pat to come and work on this project. They said he would have work for at least ten years. We liked Dublin and planned to live there. A few months ago, Pat heard of this small cottage that was on ten acres of land. He had always wanted to own land, and we decided to buy it. The cottage is only two miles from his work so here we are." She started crying again.

The next two years were difficult for Geri. She had a baby and no way of earning a living. Her first thought was she could sell their house in Armagh. She wanted to stay in their little cottage as long as she could. Effie became a good friend and helped Geri. She worked at various jobs, and Effie took care of Robert. Geri was just 22 years old, but all during those two years, she was not able to find a husband. There were many married men in the village that wanted her to be their mistress, but no one was interested in marriage to a widow with a baby boy. She was despairing of her situation when she received a letter saying there was a person that wanted to buy her Armagh House. In March, 1833, she finally sold her house in Armagh. The money she received for the house opened new opportunities for her. Pat's sister had written frequently. In one letter she said, "Geri, you are a young widow woman with a baby boy. There are many single men here, and you will have a good chance of finding a husband in Nova Scotia. You should come here." At first, this seemed like a farfetched idea. One night when she was unable to sleep she decided that she had to move on, and the idea of going to Nova Scotia seemed like a good idea.

Chapter 2

She immediately wrote Tabitha, Pat's sister, telling her she wanted to come to Nova Scotia. Two months later she got a reply saying come on and gave her their address in Halifax. It took only a short time to sell her cottage, and she began searching for the next ship going to Nova Scotia. The only one available sailed from Belfast on the northeastern coast of Ireland. This was about 106 miles from Dublin. It took almost four days by coach to reach the Port of Belfast. All of the steerage bunks were taken, and only one cabin was available. Geri had the money from the sale of two houses and without thinking bought a first class ticket.

    The purser didn't think she was able to buy such an expensive ticket as she was shabbily dressed, but to his amazement she paid for her ticket with gold. He found himself warning her to be careful how she showed her gold filled purse. Geri replied, "Sir, I have worked hard all of my life, and I learned how to handle a pistol when I was twelve years old. I pity the person who tries to take my gold from me." With that she walked proudly aboard the ship and went to her cabin.

    With the evening tide the sailing ship, Brig O'Dorcas Savage, set sail for Canada. The first night at sea went well. The winds were coming from the east and they were traveling due west. All sails were up and full pushing the ship at a speed of eight knots. The next morning came, and there were red clouds in the east. When Geri and Robert came on deck, they were greeted with cold winds. The winds were from the north, and the waves were rising to swells of four to six feet. This excited Geri as she had sailed in the Baltic Sea and loved to sail with a brisk breeze. Captain John Limon was walking the quarter deck when he noticed Geri and her son. They were walking the deck as if they were veteran sailors.

As he was noticing this, his purser walked up and said, "That woman and her son are the ones I told you about who paid for first class passage with gold." The Captain didn't say anything and continued to observe his barometer. The shifting winds concerned him, and he feared that they were moving into a storm. In the next hour the winds increased to a near gale force. The Captain ordered that all loose gear be stored, and he sent the crew aloft to reef the topsails.

As the crew was securing the main deck, they were also checking the lashing of the lifeboats. A lifeboat near midship had its tarp in slight disarray. They had to take it all off in order to lash it down tightly so that it would not fill with water from the bad weather. When they stripped it off they found a stowaway. It was a young red haired girl with flashing defiant blue eyes. They hauled her out of the boat and brought her before the Captain. In a gruff voice he inquired what was her name. She replied that her name was none of his business, and she had no intentions of telling him who she was. Her anger irritated him, and he told her that this ship did not tolerate stowaways, and she would spend the voyage in the brig.

Geri had witnessed this and interrupted saying, "Captain, I have need of a servant, and if this young lady will bond herself to me until she has repaid her passage fee, I will pay for her a ticket in the steerage." Captain O'Rourke replied, "Mrs. Hogg we have no room in the steerage; we just have room in the brig." Geri replied, "I know that there is no room in the steerage, and I will let her stay with me in my cabin, but I will not pay first class for her to stay there." The Captain looked at his purser and said, "I will accept the stated conditions."

So Geri would have a companion and a servant for the rest of the voyage. Geri, Robert, and their new servant went to her cabin. The first thing Geri asked, "When did you last have any food?" She didn't answer but said, "I am very thirsty. I have not had water for two days." Geri immediately got her water and encouraged her to drink slowly. When she had satisfied her thirst she said, "I haven't eaten for three days." Geri left and went to the galley and asked for some food. The galley cook knew about the stowaway and had prepared some food for her. When Geri returned with food, she found Robert playing with his new friend. Nothing was said until all of the food was eaten.

The wanderers

The stowaway had been eating so intensely that she was completely unaware of her surroundings. When she finished eating, she looked up and felt embarrassed. She was a proud girl and was ashamed about her behavior. She said, "I know that I must appear that I have no manners, but I was so hungry I couldn't control myself. You have been so kind to me, and I want to tell you why I am here under these conditions. I come from an important family in Ireland, and we have come under hard times. My father was just barely able to feed us, and he told me that he must bond me to a rich merchant in Belfast in order that I might have food and shelter. I was to be a house maid, and I would be given some education. I agreed, and I was a maid all right, but I was to have other duties. My master wanted me to sleep with him. When he told me this, I knew that I had to escape that very day. He sent me on an errand, and I went down to the dock. It was mid day, and the crew of this ship was not on deck. I slipped on board, and I was in the lifeboat for two days before they sailed. I remembered hearing a policeman coming by asking if they had hired any new people. They said no, and inquired about whom were they searching. They said a bonded girl had run away, and her master had offered a large reward if she was found and returned to him. Her name was Amy MacMoyre. You can see why I didn't want the Captain to know my name."

Robert said, "Mommy, I like Amy. I don't want her to be taken away." Geri felt sorry for Amy, and she wanted to help her. She told Amy that she was a person of limited means and was immigrating to Nova Scotia. She had no relatives there, but her sister-in-law was going to help her get started. She continued saying, "I am determined to make my own way. I know I am a good sailor, and I hope to be able to start my own fishing business. I can use you as a member of my crew and any other activities that may come about. There is a severe storm coming up. I am going to see how well I can handle myself in this storm. I intend to stay on deck as long as I can. I will need you to take care of Robert during this time." Amy was very excited. She was to have a job and maybe a family.

After talking to Amy, Geri got up and put on her oilskin clothing. When she appeared on deck, there was a remarkable change in Geri. She was no longer a shabby, depressed woman who looked like she was thirty years old and worn out. She looked like a twenty-two year old young woman who had a strong vibrant look. She said nothing to anybody and started performing deck duties with the skill of a master seaman. She could reef sails, secure the main deck and did all of this efficiently and professionally. Captain Limon thought that she was one of the crew and asked the First Mate who was that sailor. The First Mate didn't know and went over to Geri and was surprised to find that it was a woman, their new passenger. He didn't say anything to her and reported back to the Captain who the sailor was. Both were surprised and taken aback by what they had discovered. The Captain decided to say nothing and wait and see how long Geri would continue to work. By now the storm was in full force. The waves were ten to twelve feet high and water from the waves and the strong wind washed the deck and made it hard for the crew to keep their footing. Amazingly, Geri was weathering this very well. In fact she seemed thrilled to be on deck. At eight bells the deck crew was replaced and Geri worked on. It wasn't until second crew was replaced that she went to her cabin.

CHAPTER 3

Amy had gotten some hot food from the galley and helped Geri get out of her wet oilskins. Geri fell on her bunk and went to sleep. She slept for two hours and got up and ate the now cold food with relish. Amy went to the galley and got a pot of hot coffee, and Geri slept for two more hours. By this time it was about 6:00 p.m. The night was closing in, and she got into her oilskins and appeared on the deck. The storm was still strong, and the crew was getting very tired. She didn't need to be told what to do as she sensed where she was needed and continued to work thru two four hour periods. It was 2:00 a.m. when she retired to her cabin. Amy and Robert were sound asleep, and she just barely got off her oilskins when she collapsed into her bunk. At eight the next morning, she awakened and found a warm breakfast by her bunk. Amy had gotten up early and gone to the galley and had gotten breakfast for Geri and Robert. Amy and Robert were becoming attached to each other.

Geri got up slowly and began stretching and flexing her arms and legs. After loosening up her muscles she sat down and ate a hearty breakfast. She asked Amy how things were going with her, and Robert. Robert answered by saying that he and Amy were friends. They talked a little longer, and Geri started putting on her oilskins. She was on deck and working by 9:00 a.m. The ship was in disarray. The storm had broken some of the lashings on the lifeboats and Geri went immediately to work. After securing all of the lifeboats she started securing the random items that had broken loose. The Captain and First Mate marveled at her competency. The First Mate said she was the best one of the deck crew. The Captain wondered if she was skillful at piloting. The main pilot was having trouble maintaining the ship's point of sail. The beam wind was coming from the north and the ship was going due west. He was having trouble keeping the ship on course as the ship wanted to turn to the direction of the wind.

The First Mate approached Geri and said that the Captain wanted to talk to her. She went immediately to the quarterdeck and approached the Captain. He said, "With your work on the main deck, you have helped us immensely, but now we have a serious problem. Our pilots are having a hard time holding our ship on course. They need help in order to steer the ship. Have you had any experience with piloting?" Geri replied, "Captain, I sailed with my father on the Baltic Sea from the age of ten to the time of my marriage which was eighteen. In my last two years of sailing, I was his chief pilot. I am aware of the trouble the pilot is having, and I know that I could be of help." The Captain replied saying, "We need you to help our pilot; would you be willing to do this?" She responded in nautical terms saying, "Aye, Captain" and went aft to the pilot. She told him she was there to help him steer the ship and immediately got into a position that relieved a lot of the pressure he was experiencing holding the ship on course. As they progressed the pilot experimented with Geri's skill. He would ease up on what he was doing and see how she responded. To his surprise the ship kept its course and there was no slack to the wheel. Geri knew exactly what he was doing and acted as if nothing had happened. He tried other maneuvers, and he was surprised at how quickly she could respond to the change. When he was relieved, she stayed on with the next pilot and went thru the same testing. When she had been at the wheel for sixteen hours, the First Mate relieved her and was pleased there were no objections from the pilots as to her skill.

Geri went to her cabin and collapsed in her bunk. Amy slowly took off her oilskins and covered her up. She slept for two hours and got up. Amy went immediately to the galley and got food for her. While she was eating, the Captain knocked on the door and came into the cabin. He said, "Mrs. Hogg, we are in a precarious position. The hull of our ship has sprung numerous leaks and much of my crew is manning the pumps. Our carpenter is working to stop the leaks, but in the mean time, we need as much help as we can get. Will you take over pilot duties eight hours on and eight hours off?"

Geri said, "With Amy's help, I can keep the ship on course, but I need somebody to take care of my son, Robert." The Captain said, "I will get a woman passenger in the steerage to come to your cabin and care for your son." Geri replied, "Before you go Captain, Amy will need some oilskins as it is very wet topside." The Captain was walking away as she was talking saying, "I will get the oilskins quickly; please relieve the pilot as soon as possible!"

As Geri was helping Amy dress, she had a memory of the times when she and her father experienced late winter storms. They were very fierce, and they had to make port as soon as they could. She knew that no ship could survive more than three days in these storms. Her father told her that these storms usually occurred in the upper latitudes, and if he was in such a storm in the Atlantic, he would immediately turn the ship southward and get as far south as he could and as rapidly as he could. When she was going topside, she detoured to the bilge to see how severe the leaks were. There were numerous small leaks and the pumps were just barely controlling it. The Captain and the First Mate were struggling. She quickly told him what her father had said, and since this seemed to be the only hope the Captain had for saving the ship, he said, "I want you to turn the ship to the south, and I will instruct the Second Mate to take orders from you as to how the sails are to be furled."

She went quickly to the quarterdeck and assumed the control of the ship. She turned the ship to the port side and put the beam of the ship in line with the wind coming from the north. She then ordered a slow unfurling of the main sails. The ship was now going with the wind and was rapidly picking up speed. She wanted the ship to be going fast enough so that the trough of the wave didn't pull the ship backward. In other words she wanted to sail on the top of the waves. The speed of the boat became so fast that the water passing the hull was creating a sucking action, and for the first time they were getting ahead of the leaks. This change allowed the carpenter to be more effective in his caulking. Things continued to be precarious for the next twelve hours. The Captain sent a message to Geri when she completed her eight hours and asked her to stay piloting as long as she could. On the fourteenth hour the wind was shifting to the east and the waves were lessening. By the sixteenth hour, conditions had so improved that the Captain relieved Geri. Amy had collapsed near the twelfth hour and the Second Mate had relieved her. Geri struggled to her cabin and collapsed on her bunk. She didn't take off her oilskins and slept for the next 10 hours.

CHAPTER 4

When she awakened, she could feel the ship was sailing in much calmer waters. She slowly got up and was surprised that the cabin was empty. She took off her oilskins and tried to take a sponge bath. She was almost dressed when Amy and Robert came into the room. Robert ran to his mother and hugged her crying in relief as his mother was back and well. Amy said that the Captain had ordered the cook to prepare a fine meal for her, and Amy was to bring it to her as soon as she was awake, but Amy was so excited about her adventure with Geri that all she could do was to talk and talk. She mostly wanted to talk about the thrill of being at the wheel and guiding the ship during a storm. She marveled at the strength of Geri and couldn't understand how she could stay at the wheel for so long in such violent weather. She said, "Geri, do you know that the crew thinks you are the one who saved the ship from sinking?" Geri replied, "Amy, that is flattering, but it took everybody to keep our ship afloat. This was the most violent storm I have ever been in. Now let's stop talking and go to the mess area and get some food."

As they walked to the galley they could feel the smoothness of the ship as it sailed, but Geri was aware of how sluggish it sailed. This meant to her that there was still a serious problem with a leaking hull. When they arrived at the galley, the cook brought a fine meal. He served ham, potatoes, and seasoned beans with hardy biscuits. For dessert, he served rice pudding. When Geri finished, she thanked the cook for such a fine meal. It pleased him, and he saluted her saying, "Ms. Hogg, I thank God that you were on board this ship, for I fear what might have happened to all of us if you had not been here." Geri felt embarrassed by his praise and in a low voice thanked him again.

She, Amy, and Robert went top side. She was appalled by the damage that she saw. The main deck was littered with debris. The backstay was sagging, and the mount on the chain plates were loose and in danger of pulling out. The main sails that she had used in driving the ship were torn. To her she felt that the ship was in need of major repairs, and she wondered where the nearest port was.

As she looked around, she saw that the First Mate was working on the main deck, but she could not see the Captain. She asked Culum Rafin, the First Mate, where was the Captain. He replied, "He was here a few minutes ago. He must have gone to his cabin." With that Geri went immediately to his cabin to offer her services. She knocked on his cabin door and heard him say, "Enter." When Geri entered the room and the Captain saw who it was, he got up from his chair and went over to Geri and thanked her for all she had done to help save his ship.

They talked about the storm, and the damage the ship experienced. Both felt that they should go to the nearest harbor to get the ship repaired. When they went to the charts, they realized that they were not close to any land. The storm had pushed the ship almost 700 miles off its course. The Captain was considering going to Bermuda for repairs. Geri had no experience with the Atlantic and did not comment. As they concluded their conversation, Geri said she would be available to any ship duty he might need for her to do. The Captain replied. "After all the work you did during the storm, I have listed you as a Second Mate with all its privileges. That means your fares will be returned, and you will receive the salary of that position. I want you, Amy, and Robert to eat at the Captain's table. As far as duties, I feel that you have already done enough. Try to relax and be with your family." It was obvious that Amy was now a part of Geri's family

Geri was not willing to sit aside when there was so much work to do. She said, "Thank you for your appreciation of my services, but you must understand something about me. I have always carried my own weight, and I can't sit by when there is so much work to be done. My father and I had a small boat building and repair business so I have experience in boat repair. With your permission I could evaluate the damage to the ship and tell you what I think could be done while we are at sea." The Captain was surprised by what she had said and for a few minutes was silent. Finally he responded saying, "Ms. Hogg, you continually amaze me. Your piloting skills and your stamina impressed me, and now you are saying that you have had boat repair experience. It is almost unbelievable. I can't understand how I could have had so much good luck in having you as a passenger. Of course, I would want you to inspect the ship and give me your ideas of what can be done while we are at sea." Before she left his cabin he asked her if she had any experience in sailing in the Atlantic. She said, "No." He continued saying, "We are 700 miles off our course. The closest land is Bermuda. Are you familiar with this island?"

Geri said, "My father mentioned this island to me many times. He had sailed all over the Atlantic during his younger years and had helped supply the British army when they stopped there on their way to attack the United States in the War of 1812. He said that the British had a naval base there. I don't know the present state of this base, but I suspect that since it has been only twenty years since the navy base was there that they still have some ship repair services." Captain Limon thanked her and dismissed her. She left to go about her duties.

Captain Limon was a tall, slim man about six feet in height. His brown hair was graying along his side burns. He had deep blue eyes that he could turn into a blazing blue when he was intense. He was broad shouldered and had strong muscular arms. He had been at sea since the age of twelve. He had worked up through the ranks and had been a Captain for the last ten years. He was part owner of this ship, and his partner was a wealthy merchant located in London, England. His partner was also his father-in-law. He had three children, and his wife was insisting that he leave the sea and stay more at home. This was to be his last voyage, and the plan was that Culum Rafin would take over his position. Culum was overqualified for being a Captain and was eager for this opportunity. During the storm both had commented that maybe their plans were going to be for naught. Both felt that Geri had a lot to do with their now being still afloat.

When Geri left the Captain, she went immediately to her cabin. She related what had been said, and they both were concerned about going to Bermuda. The man Amy had run away from was an Englishman, and Amy felt that he was very powerful politically. The fact that he had offered a large reward for her return scared Amy. As they were sharing their concerns about this, Geri said, "Amy, I want to adopt you. Would you be willing for me to do this?" Amy's answer was by her going over and hugging Geri. "Oh, Geri, I was so frightened and alone when you offered to help me. I have seen how strong and courageous you are and being with you on the quarterdeck and with Robert has made me feel safe and loved again. Yes, I want to be your daughter, but first, I want you to know who I am."

Chapter 5

She started off by saying, "I come from an old Irish family. Have you ever heard of The Book of Armagh? This is the only book that contains the confessions and letters of Saint Patrick. This book was moved about, and it was feared that it would be damaged or lost. In 1004 A.D. it was decided to appoint keepers of the book, and my family was chosen. I am from the MacMoyre family.

My father has had a hard time maintaining this responsibility and supporting his family. I am the oldest child in a large family. As you know, many people in Ireland are starving from the failure of their potato crops. My father had work other than farming, but times were very hard. I have no book learning, and I can just barely read and write. I want to be able to read and write well. Geri, I am a good girl. I will work hard, and I will be loyal to you and Robert."

Geri looked at Amy for the first time. She saw a red headed, blue eyed, trim lass who was just beginning to express her womanhood. She was about five feet 2 inches tall and was obviously going to be taller. She thought that she was going to be a beautiful woman when she matured. As Geri was looking at Amy in a different way, so was Amy looking at Geri. Her slipping onto the O'Dorcas Savage, being discovered as a stowaway, Geri helping her, and the violent storm had kept her from looking at who Geri really was. She saw a very pretty, well formed, slender, brown haired, blue eyed woman. She figured that she was over five feet tall by several inches. She didn't look strong, but she knew that she was because of her abilities during the storm. She seemed to be well educated, but she didn't know how much. She thought if only she could teach her to read and write well. Geri interrupted her musings by saying, "We must go to the Captain and tell him of our fears about going to Bermuda and tell him that I want to adopt you so that your name will be Hogg."

That night when they finished their dinner with the Captain and his First Mate, Geri brought up the subject of the fears she and Amy had about going to Bermuda. Geri told the reason why Amy ran away from her bond agreement. Both men were sympathetic about Amy's problem and indicated that they would change the passenger records to show Amy as being Amy Hogg. Culum Rafin, the First Mate, suggested that she be reported as being the younger sister of Geri. This pleased both Geri and Amy and that night was the best sleep of the voyage.

The next day Geri hired a steerage woman to take care of Robert so that Amy could help her repair some of the equipment. Her main concern was the damaged lifeboats. She had the deck crew to pull the boats one at a time onto the main deck. It was there that she and Amy proceeded to repair them. During the day she noticed that First Mate Culum was always finding a need to inspect her work. After the third meaningless inspection, Amy said, "I think that the First Mate is interested in you." Geri had noticed the same thing, but she said nothing. The day went well; the seas were calm, and there was a warm southeasterly wind. They were able to make long tacks, and at the end of day they had gone 240 knots over the last 24 hour period. At mess that night, Culum had the steward place him next to Geri. They had a pleasant conversation, and Geri found Culum telling her all about himself.

He started off by saying that he was born in Hellerod, Denmark, but his father moved quite early to Copenhagen. He said, "My father was a Captain of a ferry boat that went from Copenhagen to Landskrona, Sweden, and back. He made that round trip two times a day. When I was old enough, I would go with him every chance that I got. On these trips my father would mention his sea adventures in the Atlantic. He gave up deep sea sailing when he met my mother. Father told me mother wanted him to come home every night and insisted that he find a job that allowed that to happen. She told him that her mother and she never had a husband and father at home for any length of time. My mother died with my birth. When she died, my father became bitter, and for the first six years of my life I rarely saw him. We didn't get along. I left at 12 to get away from him, so I am here today because my father quit deep sea sailing. He has told me many times that he loved my mother and missed her terribly as she was the best wife that a man could ever have and seeing me reminded him of his loss.

Geri interrupted his story telling and said, "I am sorry about your loss, but right now I just want to take care of my family. Please just let us be friends. This storm has been brutal to my son as I have not been with him during its most frightening times." Culum said, "I see that you thought that I was being too personal in my storytelling and wanted to bring me back to reality. Yes, that storm was brutal, and we almost lost our lives. All I wanted was to know more about your life, and I felt if I told you mine then maybe you would tell me yours and—."

Geri could sense that Culum was trying to get more intimate with her, and she had no desire to connect up with any man at this time. She said, "Oh, I had an ordinary life and nothing as glamorous as yours happened to me. If you will excuse me I need to go to bed as I am very tired." With that she got up and left with Amy and Robert. As they walked away Captain Limon said, "Well, Culum, you didn't make much headway that time." Culum replied, "The voyage is just beginning, and I have lots of time to change that." With that they both retired to their cabins.

As Geri and Amy were walking to their cabin, Amy said, "I think that Culum likes you. He seems to be a nice man. Why did you shut him up?" Geri replied, "Amy, my life right now is very complicated. I am going to a strange place, and I have limited funds. I must put all of my energy in getting us settled and working at a productive job before I can consider romancing. It is easy to tell that Culum is lonely, but now I must think of our survival."

The next day Geri and Amy were working on their second lifeboat, and Amy was asking a lot of questions about sailing. Her first question was, "Why did the Captain choose Bermuda as a place to get the ship repaired?" Geri said, "First, let's talk about distances at sea. You know in Ireland we use the British mile to describe how far a place is from where we are standing. When you are on the sea we use the nautical mile. This mile is about eight hundred feet longer that the mile you are used to." Amy wanted desperately to be educated, and she felt the only way this could happen was for her to ask questions.

The first thing that came to Amy's mind was why the difference, so she said, "Geri, that seems strange to me to have two different ways of telling the distance." Geri replied, "When we were in the Captain's quarters did you notice the maps on a large table?" Amy replied, "Yes." Geri continued, "Well, those maps are called charts, and they have lines up and down and sideways. The up and down lines are called longitudes, and the side to side lines are called latitudes. Sailors use these lines to tell them their position on the sea. Now think of dividing these lines into smaller units. You know like a gallon is divided into quarts, pints and cups. Well for some reason and I do not know why, they chose minutes and seconds as a way of dividing up the longitudes and for latitudes degrees, minutes and seconds. They then decided that one minute of latitude would be a nautical mile and that one minute turns out to be about 800 more feet than the British mile." Amy looked puzzled and said, "Gee, Geri, I asked what time it was, and you told me how to build a watch."

They both laughed just as Culum walked up for his unneeded inspection. He asked, "What are you laughing about?" Geri didn't want to engage with Culum and said simply, "Oh, nothing of importance," and continued to work on their lifeboat. Culum was not to be shut up and continued to talk. Getting no response from Geri he eventually left. When he left, Geri said, "Well, going back to your original question, the Captain said that we were blown off 700 miles from our original course. This distance would be on the same latitude as Bermuda, and it would be shorter to go there for repairs than Nova Scotia. You know, Amy, our ship is still very damaged, and we need to get to a port as quickly as possible. Our ship would be very vulnerable in another storm, hence Bermuda."

The rest of the day went without incident, and they finished repairing the second lifeboat. As they were finishing, the Captain inspected their work. He was pleased by their work and complimented them. He said, "You should consider being in boat repairing as your occupation when you get to Nova Scotia." Geri had already thought of this, but hearing it from the Captain encouraged her to put the idea firmly in her mind. When they finished their work that night, Geri said to Amy, "We are going into the boat repair business. I would like to try learning about fishing the grand banks for cod, and ultimately I want us to own a ship that would carry freight from Halifax to Boston."

Amy was shocked by all of these ideas. She had no idea about these places and wanted to ask Geri many questions, but Geri had other things to talk about.

She said, "Amy, it is important for us now to consider becoming expert sailors. I intend to learn more about navigation, and I want you to learn more about actually sailing a boat. I will talk to the Captain about being with him when he is determining the position of the ship and setting the compass for the new direction of the ship. I want you to start working with an accomplished sailor learning all of the terminology of sailing as well as learning how to manage the sails and do whatever is necessary to do on main deck duty.

I will engage Culum and find out who is the best sailor on the ship. I will try to get him to take you on as an apprentice. We are probably three or four days out from Bermuda. I am not sure how long we will stay in Bermuda, but I suspect it will be one to two months as this ship is in bad repair. I hope you will use these months and those few days on the sea to become acquainted with sailing as we will need that experience in Nova Scotia."

CHAPTER 6

That night at the Captain's table Culum, as usual, sat next to Geri. He started trying to engage in conversation. Much to his surprise, she responded by saying, "Culum, I have not wanted to engage you in your searching conversations with me, not because I found you unattractive, but because I am dealing with my future, and I am only recently becoming sure how I am going to live the rest of my life. I find myself needing help from you as you are a more experienced sailor than I am. I intend to develop a business in Nova Scotia which will include ship repair, fishing the great banks and carrying goods from Halifax, Nova Scotia to Boston, Massachusetts. Amy is going to be an important part of my business, and she is totally ignorant in the business of sailing. I would like for you to recommend an older person on the ship that might be willing to teach her sailing for the rest of this trip."

This was the first time that Culum had had a chance to be more than casual with Geri. He was very excited and said quickly, "I know just the man for you. His name is Joseph O'Rourke. He is in his mid 50's, and this is to be his last trip. He has been a boatswain mate on many ships. He is a patient man, and I think he would respond well to Amy." Geri said, "I would consider it a great favor if you would ask him to help me in this regard." Culum thought to himself, "Finally, I have some way to get close to Geri."

When they were leaving the Captain's quarter, she turned to Captain Limon and asked, "Would you be willing to let me observe your taking a position of this ship tomorrow? You know, yesterday you remarked to me that I had skills in boat repairing, and I should seek that out as a job for myself when I get to Nova Scotia. I have given this some thought and realized I want to do something more than just repair boats. I want to be able to navigate and do coastal carrying of goods to various communities along the American coast. I realize that I would not necessarily need to have the navigational skills required to go across the ocean, but I do want to have a more working knowledge of how you navigate this ship and make me more skillful in this regard." The Captain was pleased to hear this from Geri and immediately gave her a book on navigation and how to locate one's position at sea. He said to her, "You may keep this book, and if I am able to get any other books on navigation when I go back to Ireland, I will send them to you."

When they got back to their cabin, Amy was filled with questions. She said, "You stopped me from asking questions when you mentioned all those strange places. Now it is important for me to ask you about some of the things you just told me." Geri said, "What did you want to know?" Amy replied, "First, I want to know all that you know about Bermuda." Geri said, "Well, Amy, I know very little about Bermuda except it is one of a group of many islands in the north central Atlantic Ocean. I know it was discovered by the Spanish and was originally called something different than what the English called it. The English first called it the Somer Islands but only later in history did they change it to what we call Bermuda which is really the larger island of this group of islands. This island has been a British naval base, but we know people on this island in the past have built and repaired ships. I am hoping to buy one of their famous sloops when we are there. They are made from cedar and are very fast. I know you have a lot of other questions, but I want to tell you what I think is necessary for you to do over the next several months.

At first you and I will be the main people sailing our boat. I am competent to pilot the boat and can give the appropriate commands for the sailing of the boat, but I need a significant person on deck to see that my orders are carried out. I want you to be that person. We would begin our business in Nova Scotia. We will not have enough money to hire a crew so we will have to do a lot of things ourselves. You heard me talking to the Captain about navigation and to Culum about finding a sailor on board who could teach you sailing. I hope that we can accomplish all of this because I desperately need you to be a competent sailor." Amy wanted to continue the conversation with more questions, but Geri said she was very tired, and they should sleep because tomorrow was going to be very busy.

When they came on deck the following morning, Culum was waiting for them, and there with him was Boatswain Joseph O'Rourke. Culum said, "I have talked to Boatswain O'Rourke about what you wanted, and he is interested in this particularly because he is planning to leave the sea and live on land when we arrive at Nova Scotia. He was hoping that you would be able to hire him on arrival to Nova Scotia." Geri replied, "Yes, I would want to hire you." She then turned to Culum and said, "Thank you, Culum. My life is so complicated now, and I know you have been interested in me, but for now I can't consider any new relationships. Maybe some time in the future things will be different."

Amy quickly went with O'Rourke, and he started instructing her immediately. He said to Amy, "The one thing you do to learn sailing is by having hands on experience. You learn by doing. You may think that climbing the rope ladders is simple, but you will find when you do this that it is difficult, and you will be very clumsy. So, I will be teaching you more by doing than by explaining. It will be your doing that will make you a competent sailor." All day long he was working intensely with Amy, and by the time they quit for chow in the evening, she was exhausted.

Geri continued working with repairing the ship, and when the Captain was going to get his sightings for the ship's position that day, they went to his cabin and got his equipment and came back to the quarterdeck. The Captain took his sextant, and measured the position of the sun at noon and recorded the angle from the sun to the horizon. They went back to their charts and were able to plot their latitude. By using dead reckoning they were able to determine the approximate longitude. Geri was familiar with much of this. The Captain said, "The best way I can help you is to quiz you about what you have studied in the book I have given you." They both agreed this was a good way to proceed and he said, "Tomorrow I will let you take the sighting with the sextant and then go to the chart and determine the latitude we are in. I will then give you the information of our dead reckoning and see if you can come to the same figures as I have."

After this session with the Captain, Geri did not return to the deck to continue her work. Instead she went to her cabin and started reading the book that the Captain had given her. She would do this for the next couple of days. During those days Amy was actively involved with training, and Culum was trying to find out where Geri was. At the night mess of the first day after she had decided to spend her days with the navigation book, she told Culum what she was doing. He immediately said, "I can help you with this." She replied, "Culum, I appreciate your offer, but I am afraid we would be too distracted with each other for me to do any deep studying." Even though she was in a way telling Culum no, the use of the terms "we would distract each other" encouraged him to think she was thinking of him more than just the First Mate on the ship she was sailing. It was twenty days before they cited Bermuda. Each night Amy would come to bed exhausted and could hardly do anything but fall asleep.

What she did talk about was how much she enjoyed being with Boatswain O'Rourke. She said, "In many ways he reminds me of my father, and he is so gentle, yet firm with me. He is a great teacher, and I feel I am learning a lot about sailing." Geri was having a different experience those last few days. She was finding herself getting more involved with Culum than she wanted. She hoped that when they arrived at Bermuda he would be confined to the ship and its repairs, and she would be free to find out the possibility of buying a sloop and learn how they set up their repair facilities. Bermuda was surrounded by reefs, and it was somewhat of a problem to maneuver the boat to anchorage. But after this was accomplished, she went ashore with Amy.

CHAPTER 7

When they went ashore, she was able to have more time with Robert, her son. He had been under the care of a woman from the steerage for the last 15 days, and she had been too exhausted to play with him because of the storm and the other activities of the boat. Now, all of this was passed, and she hoped that they would have at least a month or two away from the boat, so they could be more like a family. Her first task was to find some place to stay. She could have stayed on the boat, but she felt like it would be too confining, and she wanted to spend much of her activities around the island and, also it was too hard to be with Amy and her son in such confined circumstances.

She liked being away from Culum because he was becoming more interested in her than she in him. He had asked her where she was going to stay, and she said she didn't know and made a point of not telling him when she did find that place. She quickly left the boat and went ashore to St. George. This was on the island north of the larger island which was called Bermuda. Most of the repair facilities were on Bermuda. She had to ferry from St. George to Bermuda and there you walked or rode a carriage. It was about 18 miles from where she landed to where she eventually found a place to stay which was near one of the major repair stations in Bermuda. Near this repair station was also a ship building area where the famous Bermuda sloops were made out of cedar. It took all day to get settled in, and all three were exhausted that night. Geri said as they retired, "From here on we all will be together." Robert was excited about this statement.

The next day she asked Amy if she could find her way back to the ship. Amy said she could, and Geri gave her some money in case she got into any difficulty. She told Amy she wanted her to find Boatswain

O'Rourke and ask him to come back with her as she wanted to talk with him.

Amy left and was able to catch a wagon going to St. George. When she got there, she saw the ship was still anchored off shore. Much to her surprise she found Boatswain O'Rourke talking to some people on the dock. She waved to him, and he came over to her. It was obvious that he was pleased to see her as he had begun to think of her as his daughter. He was proud of how quickly she would respond to his instructions. Amy quickly told him why she was there, and he said that the Captain had given him shore leave, and he could go with her right now. As usual, Amy had lots of question to ask Joseph. When she had left the ship, he had told her he wanted her to call him Joseph and not Boatswain O'Rourke. This pleased Amy as she was very fond of him.

What interested Amy most was how much damage did he think the ship had and how long would it take for the ship to be repaired. Joseph said, "They really won't know until the ship is pulled on land." He had heard that they would be on the island for about two months. He said, "I think it will be longer as I think our ship is seriously damaged. Some of the sailors are thinking of leaving the ship as they want to go to sea and not stay in port for a long time. It is likely that the Captain will have to let some of the crew go as they will have no duties while the ship is being repaired. I don't know how much money the Captain and his partner have, but I think that cost of the ship's repair will be considerable." It took three hours to get back to Amy's quarters.

Culum Rafin was very disturbed when he learned that Geri had left the ship. She had left without talking to him about her plans. He went to his friend, the Captain, and expressed his despair over how Geri was not including him more in her life. Captain Limon said, "It is obvious that you are more interested in her than she is in you. I know this is disappointing for you, but if she really is important to you, it seems to me you need to be more aggressive with her and make it plain your intentions concerning her. I know from my experience to want someone who doesn't want you in the same way is very discouraging. With anything that is worth while you must be willing to stick out your neck. I don't think that Geri will be cruel if you do decide to express your feelings for her, but you know by now that Geri is a straight forward person. She says what she thinks and doesn't flower it up.

This morning before she left she came to me, and she had a list of the items concerning what she felt was the damage to our ship. She had written by each item what she thought would be a fair cost for its repair. She told me that she realized that Bermuda is different, but this might help in my bargaining with the repair facility. After I thanked her, she said that she was going to try to acquire a Bermuda sloop and sail the rest of the way to Nova Scotia in her own boat. She asked if I could give her the money she had earned as Second Mate and the return of the money she had paid for the voyage as agreed. I did as she requested, and she left. I have removed her, Amy, and Robert from our passenger list." Culum asked if she said anything about where she was going to stay. He replied, "All she said was that she was going to locate close to a ship yard and a repair facility."

When Amy left to find O'Rourke, Geri dressed Robert and went to the Wilbourne Boat Repair Facility. She walked into the main office and asked to talk to the man in charge. She was addressing a medium height, gaunt, white haired, middle-aged woman. To Geri she looked half starved. She had large brown eyes and a warm friendly smile. She replied, "You are looking at the boss. What can I do for you?" Geri was taken aback by this and said in an atypical voice, "I have just arrived to Bermuda on the Brig O'Dorcas Savage. We survived a severe storm and put into Bermuda for repairs. I was going to Halifax to start a boat repair facility, and I now find myself shore bound until I can get another ship or buy a Bermuda sloop. If I can find a Bermuda sloop that I can afford, I will sail it to Halifax."

Abby Wilbourne smiled and said, "That is quite a story and what an ambition for a good looking young lass with a cute little boy." Usually when someone would talk to me like that I would become defensive and make a sharp retort, but you had such a kind looking face." Geri replied, "Yes, it is quite a story but let me explain. I was raised in a boat repair facility in Denmark, and I sailed the Baltic Sea for six years. The last two years of that six, I was the pilot and First Mate to my father. We were sailing a schooner, and I consider myself an excellent sailor and thank you for thinking my little boy is cute. I have had to neglect my boy on this trip as I had to help the Captain of the Brig when he was short handed during the storm that nearly sunk us. I am here now because I want to see how your facility works. If you need a competent workman, I want to earn as much money as I can before I leave Bermuda."

Abby smiled and said, "What an interesting way to apply for a job. If you hadn't said you came from Denmark, I would have sworn that you came from Ireland as I have never heard such blarney." Geri laughed and said, "Well, I can see that I am not going to get anywhere with you, but I want to say I have really enjoyed your warm smile, and I regret that you are going to lose an opportunity to have a very skilled worker." With that she took Robert's hand and turned and went to the door. Just as she was opening the door Abby said, "Hold on, lass, what is the big hurry? All we were doing was just getting acquainted. Come, let's you, me, and that cute little boy look at my operation." Geri replied, "That cute little boy's name is Robert." As she was saying this Abby brushed pass her, and all Geri could do was to follow her.

They walked all over the yard and Abby asked her many questions about what Geri was seeing and what the men were doing. When they finished touring the yard, Abby was convinced that Geri was in fact knowledgeable about boat repairing and was surprised when Geri said, "I want to talk to you about some problems you have in your yard." She then related to Abby all of the problem areas that Abby had been trying to correct and stated clearly how she would go about correcting them. This time Abby did not smile or indicate that she thought Geri was a wind bag. She grabbed her by the arm and hurried her into her office and said, "Please, sit down, Geri, I see now what you meant when you said I was going to miss an opportunity. Let's talk business. If you can straighten out these malfunctioning areas, I will sell you at cost that Bermuda sloop that you see over there." Geri said, "What will you pay for that service?" Abby replied, "I will give ordinary laborer's wages." Geri replied, "Abby, you must be thinking you are talking to an idiot. You know that your yard is failing, and you are not getting the business you need. I can restore your yard to its past glory and probably get you a big job restoring the ship on which I came to Bermuda. All of this and all you offer is labor wages. Good day to you."

She took Robert's hand and walked to the door. Abby hurriedly said, "There you go again walking away while I am talking to you. Can't you just settle down for a minute and let me figure what I can do to keep you here." Geri turned around and said, "Abby, I have been pushed around for two years by people that did not respect me, and I told myself that I was not going to tolerate it ever again. I am a capable person, and if I work for anybody, I expect them to show me respect. Your offer was insulting." Abby replied, "Hold on, Lass, I was just trying to get the best deal that I could get. What would you need to fix up my yard and get me some business?" Geri said, "I will work for labor wages, and if I get your yard functioning well, and I get Captain Limon to use your facilities for his ship repair, then I want that Bermuda sloop in good repair as the reward for my excellent services." This time Abby knew not to argue and she agreed. Geri continued saying, "I want this agreement to be in writing, and I want it notarized and witnessed. I will start work tomorrow at seven o'clock, and I want the men working in the yard to understand I am in charge." Abby nodded and Geri left.

The next day was spent convincing the men that Geri knew what she was doing. The second day they were still resentful about having a woman as boss, and a young one at that. During that day they ran into a problem that none of them knew how to handle. Geri took over and solved it quickly, and all were amazed. It wasn't just this incident that impressed them, for she was able to show them easier ways of doing their jobs. At the beginning of the day they were grudgingly giving her the boss job, but by night they were commenting how much she was helping them. They went to Abby and said, "For God's sake don't run off this Geri because she is the best boss we have ever had."

When Joseph and Amy arrived to where Geri was staying, Geri was greatly relieved as she was fearful for Amy. When she saw that Amy was accompanied by Joseph O'Rourke, she was thrilled. She said, "Joseph, I am so glad that Amy was able to find you. I don't know if Amy has told you of our plans." He replied, "It took three hours for us to get here, and you know how talkative Amy is. Yes, she told me your plans, and Amy and I are hopeful that we can get an agreement. You probably don't know it, but the Captain will probably be stuck ashore for at least two months. I had already told the Captain that this was my last trip, and I would try to find another ship as I wanted to get to Nova Scotia as soon as possible. Your plans fit well with mine as far as getting to Nova Scotia. Do you have any other plans that might include me?"

Geri said, "I want to start a business in Halifax, Nova Scotia. I plan to use my Bermuda sloop as carrier of goods from Halifax to Boston, Massachusetts. As I acquire money, I intend to acquire a fishing boat and have a crew that will fish off the grand banks. I know that salted cod is sought for in the European markets. I intend to search out whatever market that is available. I see you fitting into all of this. As you know, Amy is far from being a competent sailor, and she considers you as the best teacher in the world." Joseph smiled and looked at Amy and said, "I know that is an exaggeration, but I love Amy for it." He blushed as he said this since he had not used the love word in a long time.

He continued, "I know that I could be an asset for you, but you can see I am getting old, and I have to look for some security in my old age." Geri responded, "I can't promise what the future will be for you or me, but I would think in two years you would know how secure my business is and what possibilities it will have. In the beginning you will have the same security that I and my family have. We will work hard and only get food and lodging. When business is going better, you will be given a salary or a percentage of the business profits. I am an honest person, and I wouldn't think of cheating you or robbing you of your future."

There was silence and Joseph said, "Forty years ago I left my family and became a cabin boy. I had no education, and I could just barely read and write. I have sailed many seas. When I was gone from my family for five years I returned and found all were dead. There had been an outbreak of the croup the winter before, and all became very sick and died. So at the age of 15, I was all alone. I have always longed for a family. I was never able to find a wife, and I regret that. I know I am in my mid fifties, and it is unlikely that I will ever marry, but marriage is one of my hopes. As you outlined your situation and how I would fit in, I felt like you were offering me a family. Is that so?" Geri responded, "As far as Amy is concerned, you are already part of our family. I will let Amy talk for herself. I have admired your ability and your firm kindness. You did not abuse your men, and they respected you. At this point, I don't have an emotional attachment to you, but I certainly respect you, and I need you to be a part of my business." Joseph thought for a moment and said, "I will leave tomorrow and resign my position. I will cast my lot with all of you." Amy squealed with pleasure and rushed over and hugged Joseph. There were tears in his eyes.

The wanderers

When Joseph left the following morning, Amy and Geri sat silently together and were in deep thoughts. Amy broke the silence and said, "I don't see why Joseph thinks that he can never find a woman that would love him. When I look at him I see a tall, well kept man. His hair is gray, but even though his face is wrinkled, and there are deep wrinkles on the outer side of his eyes, he is still a handsome man. I particularly like his eyes. They are a gentle brown, and they twinkle when he smiles. Yes, if I were a woman his age, I would put my hat in the ring for him." Geri smiled at Amy, and her analysis of Joseph amused her. Amy's eyes were blinded by her love for him.

CHAPTER 8

Geri had been thinking about Culum. She was aware that he was a good looking man. He was tall, at least six feet, slim, and broad shouldered with a face that was pleasing. His eyes were gray, and they sparkled when he was with her. She thought the best way to think of his face was to say it had a strong rugged look about it. He didn't look at all like her first husband. Pat was about five feet seven and was square built. He had very large muscles in his arms and his legs. What really sold her on Pat was his tenderness and caring. Her father had been a hard man. He never showed affection to her or her mother. It was only when her mother died that she saw how much he cared for her. It troubled her that he never was able to express affection to her. Even when she left to go with Pat to Ireland, he didn't show any feelings as they both knew they would never see each other again.

She paused in her thinking and asked herself why was she thinking like this?. Her thoughts went back to Culum. Was she really beginning to think seriously about him? She must feel lonely and alone with many decisions to make and no one to lean on. Why would that bother her now? She had more money than she had ever had, and she had her son, Amy, and now Joseph. There was no logical reason for her to need Culum. With that she put all of it out of her mind and started planning her next day's activities.

When Joseph O'Rourke left to return to the Brig O'Dorcas Savage, he found himself happy. He knew that now he had a daughter, and he liked the honesty and capability of Geri. He had not belonged to anyone since he was twelve years old. Now he felt that he really belonged.

He made fast time to St. George and caught a boat to his ship. He went immediately to his quarters and started packing. With his duffle bag over his shoulder, he went to the Captain's quarters. He said, "Captain, sir, I am leaving the ship for good. I don't want to stay in Bermuda for whatever time it will take to get this ship repaired. With your permission I would like to receive my pay." Captain Limon didn't want to lose O'Rourke, and asked if he increased his salary would he at least stay for the rest of the trip to Nova Scotia. He replied, "Captain, I am through with the sea, and I am very lonely. I want to find a home and place where I might find a wife and settle down. I need to come to a warm home and a good meal. You know I am fifty-five years old, and the sea is a hard place to make a living."

The Captain was curious as to where he was staying. He said, "Captain, I met up with Amy and Ms. Hogg when I was ashore, and she is going to establish a boat repairing business in Halifax and wants me to work for her. This was a blessing for me as you know I was planning to make this my last voyage and getting off the ship in a strange place without a job was not appealing." He received his back pay and turned and left. Outside the door of the Captain's cabin he ran into Culum. Culum had heard O'Rourke say Geri's name and stopped Joseph and asked him where Ms. Hogg was located on the island. Joseph said, "I don't know the address, but I can show you if you have the time as I am returning there at this very moment."

Culum quickly made arrangements, and they left the ship at the same time. When they got ashore, it was 3:00 p.m., and Joseph told Culum it would take up to three hours to get to where Geri was staying. At that time of the day it would be hard to get back to the ship. Culum said, "Don't worry, I will be ok." As they were riding from St. George, Culum was seeing Bermuda for the first time. The tall cedar trees impressed him. He could see evidence of agriculture that had been abandoned. He saw several ship building places, but mostly the island was poorly inhabited. He asked many question about Geri and her proposed business and found that O'Rourke was reluctant to talk about what she was doing. They finally arrived at the house that Geri had rented.

When they walked in the house, it was warm and filled with odors of cooking. Amy ran up to Joseph and hugged him, but Geri was not in sight. After saying hello to Amy, Culum asked where Geri was. Amy knew why Culum was there and said, "She is at the Wilbourne's boat repair facility working as foreman." Amy assumed the role of a hostess and invited them to sit down and insisted that they stay, and when Geri came home, eat with them. The days were longer and, Geri didn't come home until 7:00 p.m. When she opened the door, there sat Culum. He was the last person she wanted to see. She made no effort to hide her displeasure of finding Culum there. Almost rudely she said, "Culum, what are you doing here?" Culum was not dismayed and tried to kiss Geri with a hello kiss. She turned her head and pushed him away and said, "Culum, you will behave yourself if you plan to stay for supper." He grinned happily and sat down and said, "I was so excited at finding you again that I couldn't restrain myself. Whether you like it or not, I am crazy about you, and if you think you can escape me, think again." Geri was flattered but turned away saying nothing.

Captain Limon had spent the whole week trying to find a boat yard that would be able to start working on his boat. The storm had created much business for Bermuda, and it looked like he would have to wait his turn. While he was pondering this, Culum came and said he was going with O'Rourke and visit Geri. He said O'Rourke told him Geri was trying to get work at a boat repair yard. As Culum was leaving Captain Limon said, "Check out the repair yard where Geri is working and see if you think it is capable of repairing our ship." Culum yelled back that he would do as the Captain asked.

When they sat down for supper, each started talking about their day, Robert started off first by saying "Amy and I went to a market, and Amy bought some fish and potatoes and vegetables." Amy said, "Yes, and Robert helped me carry them home, and we cleaned the house, and I am teaching Robert how to cook." Geri related about her work, and to O'Rourke and Culum it sounded like she was the boss.

Culum was the first to comment about this. He said, "Geri, to hear you talk I get the impression that you are the boss." This irritated Geri and she said, "Oh, you think that I am not good enough to be a boss of a repair yard. I will have you know that I worked in my father's yard for ten years, and I have helped build schooners and repaired all types of boats. Ms. Wilbourne is satisfied with my first two days, and we signed a contract today, and if I am successful, I will own a Bermuda sloop."

Culum said, "Calm down, Geri, I meant no harm. I was just surprised that you had done so much in such a short period of time. Captain Limon has not found a place to get our boat repaired, and I was wondering as you were talking if possibly your yard would have the time to take on our ship." Geri was stunned by this information. She had been wondering how she was going to talk Captain Limon into getting his ship repaired in her yard. She replied, "Culum, if you want to, I will be glad to show you the yard tomorrow, but I would really like for Captain Limon to come and see what I think we are capable of doing." Culum was very pleased that Geri needed him to help her. He said, "I will go back to the ship the first thing in the morning and get Captain Limon to come and inspect your yard." They finished supper and went to the area around the fire place. They sat and talked for about two hours and Geri said, "I must go to bed. Culum, you are welcome to sleep on the floor in O'Rourke's room. I will fix a pallet for you and that might help with the hard floor." They all went to sleep, and Culum got up early and left before Geri awakened.

As Culum was walking down the road, he was able to get a ride to St. George and arrived there about 11:00 a.m. He went immediately to the ship and reported to Captain Limon what he had discovered. The possibility of being able to start the repair of his ship excited Limon, and he insisted that they go ashore and hire a carriage to take them to Geri's repair yard.

They arrived about 3:00 p.m. and went to the repair yard, and entered the main office. Abby was sitting at her desk, and they asked if this was the ship yard where Geri Hogg worked. Abby said, "Yes, why do you ask?" Captain Limon spoke up and said, "Mr. Rafin was visiting Geri last night, and he was impressed by what Geri was doing in your yard. I want to meet with her, and the owner to discuss the repair of my ship." Abby said "I am the owner, and I will get Geri, and we will discuss your ship's needs." Limon continued and said, "Before she left my ship, she gave me a detailed description of the repairs needed for my ship. She also told me what to expect as to the cost for these repairs subject to local conditions."

This was the first major job Abby had gotten in a long time, and she told them to wait, and she would find Geri. As she was walking thru the yard, she was muttering to herself could this really be happening. When she found Geri, they went back to her office, and Geri was excited at seeing Captain Limon. Captain Limon got down to business and said, "I have had experience of what Geri's skills are in repairing ships. She had a lot to do with the securing of my ship during the storm and after. What we need to discuss is when you can start on the repairs, and what it will cost." Abby didn't know anything about estimating costs and turned to Geri. Geri said, "I will check into the cost for the materials. If it is agreeable with Ms. Abby, we can start immediately. We will try to complete the repairs in at least two months." Abby was shocked by this but said nothing. Captain Limon said, "I will move my ship to your yard tomorrow, and I want you to start as soon as possible. If you finish earlier, I will give you 100 pounds for each day that you are earlier." Abby said, "When Geri estimates the cost to you, I will draw up the contract for your approval." With that Captain Limon got up and prepared to leave. Culum wanted them to stay overnight, but Limon insisted that they return to the ship and get it prepared to sail to the yard. Abby remarked to herself that Geri had already filled one part of their contract.

Chapter 9

After Culum and Captain Limon left, Geri assembled her repair crew. She divided them into groups of four and showed them what she had determined were the necessary repairs of the Brig O'Dorcas Savage. She had grouped the repairs into four groupings. She asked the divided groups to choose what repair groupings they felt they were best qualified to work with. After this was decided, she asked who was the person that procured supplies. Bill Jones raised his hand, and she requested him to come forward and examine the supply list she felt she would need to repair the ship. She then turned to the whole crew and said, "The Brig will arrive in the early afternoon tomorrow. I want all of you to be prepared to pull it ashore, and by closing time, I want all groups to be working on their assigned repair groupings." With that she turned to Bill Jones, and they went into her office and studied what supplies were needed. She said, "Early tomorrow we will go with our list of these supplies to at least three suppliers and see what price each supplier gives for our list." Geri didn't get home until late that night.

They had all eaten, and Amy served Geri. As Geri was eating she related what had happened. She told Joseph that she wanted him to be her foreman. She wanted him to be sure that the men did a superior job with their tasks. With that she went to bed and slept an exhausted dreamless sleep. At 5:00 a.m. she was awakened by O'Rourke, and they went to the yards. When the men arrived at six she informed them that O'Rourke was their foreman. When she wasn't around, he was in complete charge. At 7:00 a.m. she was in her office talking to Abby. She said, "Abby, I intend to finish the repair of the Brig two weeks early. That means that there will be a bonus of 1400 pounds. We need to determine how that is to be divided." Abby, by this time knew that Geri had already decided how it would be divided. She said to Geri, "What do you think is fair?" Geri replied, "There are two issues that we need to clarify. One is the money and the other is the Sloop. For the money I think that 20% of the bonus should be given to the crew to share alike. We should split the rest fifty/fifty. The second issue is the sloop. Abby, you know that sloop is in need of repairs before it can be put to sea. I will furnish the supplies needed to repair it, but I expect you to furnish the labor, and this is to be done as soon as we finish the repair of the Brig." Abby was afraid that Geri would want the entire bonus and was so relieved that she immediately agreed and had a contract drawn up stating all of these conditions. Geri did nothing else until the new conditions were met by the signing of the additional contract.

By noon Geri and Jones were getting bids from three different suppliers. The one Jones had been using was the largest in Bermuda. They were very proud of their products and reflected this in their prices which to Geri were outrageous. She complained about the prices but received nothing but cold haughty looks with the statement take it or leave it. They left and went to the second supplier. On the way over she asked Jones if this was the way they had always treated him. He replied, "Yes, many times our boss had no cash, and they would extent her credit at a high interest." This was the first time Geri had a clue that Abby had limited funds and probably could not pay for the supplies. She said nothing, and they went to the next supplier. They didn't stay long as that supplier's materials were inferior. The third supplier was not used much by the boat repair people for they felt he was too expensive.

Geri immediately liked the place. The supplies were superior, and the proprietor was friendly. He totaled up the bill, and she found it was cheaper than the first supplier. She asked if he would discount the bill if she paid in cash. This shocked him as no repair facility in Bermuda did business that way. He thought for a minute and said he would discount it ten per cent. Geri said, "I will come with a wagon in early afternoon, and pick up the supplies." Jones was surprised by what had happened and said, "Where are we going to get the money?" "Why, from Ms. Wilbourne," replied Geri. Nothing else was said, but from this exchange Geri knew Abby was broke.

When they got back to the yard, Geri went to Abby and presented the bill which stated that it was to be paid in cash. Abby blanched and didn't say a word. Geri said, "I am in a hurry as I need to get the supplies to the yard as soon as possible." Abby continued to be silent. Geri waited and Abby finally said, "I don't have any money, and I don't know how I am going to make my next pay roll." Geri was boiling inside and said, "Why didn't you tell me your situation?" Abby said, "If I had, would you have come to work here?" Geri replied, "I honestly don't know. My own situation was in flux, and I was looking for a way to get to Nova Scotia, and I saw getting experience in a repair yard as positive but that is irrelevant. We face a serious problem of money. Abby, do you have any other resources that you can fall back on?" Abby said, "A year ago my husband died. We were in good shape then, and I was able to continue with the yard for a while without too many problems. My husband's foreman was the one that really ran the business, and one day he came to me and wanted to buy me out. He offered very little for the business, and I refused. He left and took the best of my workers with him. Those buildings next to our yard are his.

Since I could only hire less skilled men, he soon stole all of my business. When you came I was just about ready to move on. I had decided that I could not compete with him. I later learned that my main supplier was a silent partner with him and had really been the one that encouraged him to break away. I have been furious and felt betrayed, but up to now I could do nothing." Geri listened silently to Abby's story and pondered what she could do. She had enough money to finance this project, but it would deplete her funds and this was a risky situation. She finally said, "Abby, our contracts are worthless. You cannot perform your side of the bargain. The only thing I can think of doing is to have you deed your yard to me. I will take over the financing of this project, but you will have nothing to do with the business. If I am able to finish the project ahead of schedule then I will give you 200 pounds of the bonus. You must also deed that sloop to me. At the end of this project I will try to sell the business, and if I am successful then I will share the profit of the sale fifty/fifty with you.

Abby was silent for a long time. Big tears were flowing down her cheeks, and she was trying to hide them. She finally said, "I know you are being fair with me, but it is hard to give up what my husband and I had worked so hard to build. What really angers me is that I now have no way to get even with that bastard, Brian Douglas, and his partner Robert Coles." Geri replied, "On that score I might have a solution.

If we handle this project well, I will try to find a good competitor to buy us out. What you don't realize is that your location is one of the best in Bermuda. I feel sure that I will be able to get us both a good return, and your enemies will have some serious competition." With this Abby began to smile and hugged Geri. Abby gave Geri a quick claim deed to Abby's property. She was living in a large house on the property, and she suggested that Geri move from her little house into her big house.

Geri had much to do. She paid for the supplies with her money, and when the Brig arrived, she had it immediately pulled from the water. Captain Limon and Culum met with Geri in her office, and they noticed that Abby was not present. They inquired about where she was. Geri said, "I have bought the yard." She shifted the conversation to the supplies that she had bought for the ship. She said, "It is my policy being the owner that ship owners pay for the repair supplies as soon as they are presented with a bill stating paid in full. Here is this bill." She handed it to Captain Limon, and he studied it carefully and was surprised by how well she had acquired the supplies at such a good price. He said, "I would like to inspect the supplies before I give you any money as I want only superior materials put in my ship." He and Culum left with his carpenter and inspected all of the supplies. Two hours later he returned with the money.

That night when Geri went home, she arrived early enough to eat with the family. She told them of what had happened that day. She said that tomorrow they would move to Abby's house which is much larger and is closer to our work. Joseph O'Rourke was surprised at Geri's ability to deal with major changes. He said, "Geri, I have a lump sum of money from my work on the O'Dorcas Savage, and I want to contribute this to our welfare." Geri was impressed by his offer and said, "Thank you, it is nice to know that you are willing to invest your hard earned money with us."

The next day went well, and Amy was able to make the move. When Joseph and Geri arrived, they could smell hot food cooking. Abby was helping Amy, and they sat down to a fine meal. During the meal it was obvious that Abby was very hungry. She ate seconds on everything. This was surprising because she was not a large person.

When they gathered in the large room as they called it, Abby started the conversation. She said, "I want to have a new beginning with all

The wanderers

of you. Before my husband died I was an honest and fair person. I respected others, and I think they respected me. After my husband's death, things changed drastically. I could not run the yard, and when I lost my foreman things went down rapidly. I began to lie and cheat and do anything to keep my yard. In fact, as I have told Geri, I was to the point of closing down the yard when she appeared. I was not honest with Geri then, and I am still not being honest with her and the rest of you.

As conditions worsened I tried to sell my house. There was no market for it, and I was about to sell it to Mr. Coles, the owner of Coles Supply, for practically nothing. This is the Coles Supply place where Geri was treated so shabbily when she was purchasing supplies. When I signed over my yard to Geri I implied that the house was separated from the yard. This was a lie. The house is a part of the yard properties. Geri had been honest with me, and I am still finding it hard to be honest with her. I am sure that you noticed how hungry I was at supper. I haven't had a decent meal for over a week. I am not a gaunt person, but over the past year I have lost over thirty pounds. I want to be a part of your group, but I can't think of any reason why you should accept me."

All were silent for a while, and Amy was the first one to speak. She said, "Abby, I ran away from a bond agreement which my father had made with a merchant in Belfast, Ireland. I am sure I caused my father much trouble. I put Geri in a position of danger by her taking me in and preventing them from putting me in the brig. If I had stayed in the brig, I would have undoubtedly been returned to my master. Geri not only kept me out of the brig, but she has accepted me as her sister and has taught me many things. She has found me a dear friend, Joseph O'Rourke. In other words she has changed my whole life. I love her. I, for one, want to have you as a part of our family, and if we vote on it, I will vote for you."

There was silence, and all were waiting for Geri to respond. Geri looked at Abby, and said, "Yesterday, we had a long conversation about how our relation was to be. The only change in that conversation was that I didn't know I also owned this house. I am by nature a forgiving person, but you have lied to me two times. I am sorry about your starving, and I know you will need shelter and food, but as far as my trusting you, I will not at the present time. I am willing for you to stay here on probation. I will expect you to help Amy, keep house, and what other duties that may come up. Now let me warn you, if there is any other lying, cheating, or any devious behavior, you will be out of here and on your own." Abby looked straight into Geri's eyes and said, "I have told you everything, and I am thru with lying and cheating. I will do as you say." With that they all went to bed.

CHAPTER 10

Brian Douglas and Richard Coles were talking about the new ship in Wilbourne's Yard. They could not understand how it was possible for her to get this job and have such an efficient crew. They were terribly disappointed as they thought they were about to acquire the yard, and the house that went with it for practically nothing. The only clue was that a young woman had come into Coles Supply and had refused to buy at their prices. That woman must be connected with the changes that are happening at Wilbourne's. We need to find out all about this person and see what we can do with these changing conditions.

Captain Limon and Culum didn't want to stay on the ship while it was being repaired. They came to Geri and asked if she knew of any quarters that they could rent that were close to the Yard. She said, "I have rented a house near here, and I paid two months' rent for it. I have used it for less than a week. I will be willing for you to use it." "What will you charge us for it?" asked the Captain. Geri replied, "Just what I paid, ten pounds." They agreed and moved in. They kept the steward with them and insisted that the crew stay on board and establish a twenty four hour watch on board the ship. As we will see this was a very wise move.

The intense activity of the repairs kept Culum too busy for him to get much contact with Geri, but he used every opportunity to be with her. At first, this irritated Geri, but as time passed she began to expect it, and when it didn't occur, she found herself missing Culum.

As work progressed, Geri began to realize that she was dependent on just one supplier. Abby's telling her of the viciousness of Douglas and Coles troubled her. One day this gnawing concern was so bothering that she decided to do something about it. She left the yard and asked

Culum to go with her. They drove into St. George and visited with her supplier. She asked him if he had been approached by Coles or Douglas about stopping supplying her. He said, "Yes. They have come two times threatening me if I continue supplying you. So far, I have refused, but they can hurt me badly if I continue." Culum asked, "How is it possible for them to hurt you?" "One way is politically, and the other is by blocking my goods from being unloaded." Culum continued exploring this problem with Grady Burns, owner of Burn's supply store. Grady said, "Coles comes from an old Bermuda family, and they control much of the political structure of this Island. He threatens this, but I don't know just how this could affect me." Culum said, "We have our boat in Geri's yard, and she is doing an excellent job. We will not tolerate any interference with our repair." He turned to Geri and asked how much more supplies will she need to complete this job. Geri had made out this list and presented it to Culum. He told Grady that he wanted him to fill this order now, and that he would see what he could do to stop this threat of Coles. They spent the rest of the day getting these supplies to the yard. When Culum reported to Captain Limon what had happened, he immediately released funds for the supplies and said, "I will not tolerate this kind of behavior. I know the Governor of Bermuda, and I will speak with him tomorrow."

The very next day found Captain Limon in the office of the Governor. He had to wait several hours in order to see him and was somewhat put out by the fact that he did not get prompt attention. When he went into see the Governor, he was somewhat irritable and said, "Governor, my company is owned by me and Lord Dalhousie. I believe you will recognize that name because it was in the history of Bermuda. It has come to my attention that my company has been challenged by a person who is a citizen of Bermuda. His name is Robert Coles."

The governor knew the Coles family and quickly became alert to what he was saying. Captain Limon continued, "This person, Mr. Coles, owns Coles Supply Company located in Hamilton. For some reason he has chosen to interfere with the procuring of supplies for the repair of my ship. My ship is being repaired at the Wilbourne Yard and it's being handled efficiently by Geri Hogg. Yesterday when she started getting her supplies from Grady Burns Supply Store in St. George, she was informed that Mr. Robert Coles had threatened to close down

Grady's Supply Store if he continued to supply the necessary goods that she needed to repair my ship. He claimed that he had political pull with the Governor of Bermuda. Governor, am I to understand that you are willing to interfere with my getting my ship repaired?"

The Governor had been sort of bored with the preamble of Captain Limon's complaint until he heard that he was interfering with commerce. He cleared his throat in a very dignified way and said, "Are you saying, Sir, that Mr. Coles said that he was going to use the power of my office to put one of my citizens out of business? I'll have you know, Sir, that I do not do these kinds of actions, and I am offended by the implication that I can be influenced in this manner. I will take it up personally with Mr. William Coles, and you shall have an answer about this from me in a very short time. If what you say turns out to be true, I can assure you that you will have no more difficulty with the Coles family."

William Coles, the father of Robert Coles was sitting leisurely at his breakfast table. He was looking out across the bay at his Estate and muttering to himself saying, "What a wonderful life it is to be on this beautiful island and to have no problems." As he was musing in this way, there was an abrupt interruption of his thoughts, and a messenger of the Governor's office presented him with a summons. This was very unusual as the Governor has always been very respectful towards him. He lost all of his tranquil feelings, and anxiety arose in his chest. He got up and hurried to his carriage and rushed to the Governor's office. The Governor had been doing some investigation about the accusation of Captain Limon and found that all of the allegations were correct. When the secretary announced that William Coles was in the waiting room, the Governor said to his secretary, "I will make him wait an hour before I will see him."

William Coles had never been delayed in seeing the Governor and was even more anxious about this as he sensed that there had been some transgression that was concerning him. Finally, he was ushered into the Governor's office. He was greeted with a gruff voice and told to have a seat. There were no pleasantries or anything to indicate that there were any kind feelings towards him. The Governor took over the conversation and said, "Mr. Coles, do you own the Coles Supply Company?" "Yes, Governor," replied William Coles, "but, it is run by my son, Robert Coles." The Governor continued, "Are you aware that your son, Robert Coles, has been stating to a Mr. Grady Burns, the owner of Burns Supply Company that you have the authority to influence me, your Governor, in such a way that it would ruin his business?" William Coles was shocked. He had no idea that Robert had been involved in such activities. His face blanched, and all of his feelings of security vanished. He stuttered and stammered and finally said, "Governor, I have no idea what you are talking about." The Governor responded, "Mr. Coles, I have sent an investigating team to talk to Mr. Burns and others about the activities of your company, and I have learned that your company has been bullying my citizens for a number of years. I am incensed by this behavior, and I will not tolerate it. I am now pursuing with my counsel about what criminal action I can take against you. As of now, I have not issued an arrest warrant for you and your son, but I want you to consider yourself under house arrest until this issue has been settled. I don't want you to consider leaving Bermuda." William Coles was struggling to respond to these accusations and the restrictions that were being imposed upon him and was unable to utter even a word. He was summarily dismissed, and he staggered out into the courtyard and got into his carriage.

His mind was confused. He had gone from the sublime to the ridiculous in such a short period of time that he could not organize his thoughts, but his feelings were in sharp focus. He was enraged. How could his son have done this? How could he expose the family to such severe charges? He could not think of the words to express this rage. He was gagged by his emotions. His face became red, and he could feel the blood pounding in his head. He thought, "If I don't get control of this anger, I will have a stroke." With this he directed the driver to take him to his home.

When he arrived, he regained control of his thoughts and with a cold, steel voice, he said to his secretary, "I want you to get Robert Coles and his partner, Brian Douglas, in my house in the next hour, and I don't want any excuses." His secretary had never seen him so angry and rushed out of the house. Instead of taking the carriage, he went to the stables and got a horse and rode all the way to Robert Coles' office. When he arrived, Robert and Brian were laughing with each other because they felt that they had really scared the socks off of Grady Burns, and they were going to stop this Geri Hogg cold in her tracks. As they were expressing glee over their apparent success,

The wanderers

the door burst open and in came the secretary of Coles' father. The secretary said, "Mr. Coles, your father is enraged and is insisting that you be at his office within the hour. It has taken me twenty minutes to get here, and I assure you that if you are late, terrible things will happen, and they might happen even if you do get there on time." He had forgotten to include Brian Douglas All of the joy that Robert and Brian had been expressing towards each other suddenly vanished. Neither one had any idea why Coles' father was so angry, but it must be very important, and it seemed that it must have involved Robert's and maybe Brian's, activities. Robert didn't stop to discuss this with Brian, he just rushed out and rode as fast as he could to his father's house.

When he went into his father's office, he had never seen the rage that was in his father's face or heard in his voice. His father said, "I have just come from the Governor's office, and I have just been accused of abominable deeds. I have been accused of trying to manipulate and destroy businesses thru supposedly my influence with the Governor. The Governor outlined several people who stated that I, William Coles, have threatened to ruin their business, and furthermore I threatened I have the power of the Governor to do this. I have never done that, Robert, but, apparently, you have. I have put up with you and Brian as you both tried to destroy the Wilbourne Yard, and I regret that I allowed you to do this.

If you hadn't been such an egotistical ass, this never would have happened, and you probably would have accomplished your goal. Your idea of using the Governor's power to threatening people is utterly despairingly ridiculous. Your actions have done much damage to all of the good will that I have built up on this island. As of now, you no longer are running Coles Supply Company. I have been restricted to my house because of the accusations that have been directed towards me, so I am restricting you to no longer have any salary, and if you weren't my son, I would see that you were removed from this island. Get out of my sight."

Robert Coles was stunned. He just stumbled down the steps and got on his horse and slowly went back to Coles Ship Repair Company. He went slowly into the office, and Brian was anxiously waiting to see what had happened. For a long time he couldn't say a word. Finally, he said, "Brian, I have been discharged as the president of this company.

I have been restricted to my house, and I will have nothing to do with the company. I suspect you too will have some difficulty from all of this." "For God's sake, Robert, what happened?" exclaimed Brian. Robert responded, "Apparently someone complained to the Governor about our pressure on Grady Burns to stop supplying the Wilbourne Ship Yards. This led to an investigation of other people that we have pressured this way, and the Governor has now put my father under house arrest, and my father has told me that I am no longer president of our company and have no salary and as far as he is concerned, he doesn't want to see me. He hasn't yet discovered that you are a part of this, so I fear for you, also."

Brian came from a different background than Robert. He had lived in a world of dog eat dog for years, so he didn't become afraid with all of these changes that were now being imposed on them. All he thought was how do I fight back. He didn't think in terms of trying to pacify the Governor. He thought in terms of how he could destroy the Wilbourne business.

He realized for the first time that Robert Coles was really a weak person and got his strength from his association with his father. He saw him now as sort of a whining kid and not as a person who would stand up and fight. In fact, he felt contemptuous of him. He said, "Robert, I am not afraid of the Governor. He can huff and puff, and maybe he can do us a little damage, but I am still organized on how to defeat the Wilbourne Ship Yard. Even if I can't do it through legal means, I will do it by other means. I am determined to own that property, and nothing is going to stop me." Robert knew exactly what he was proposing and said, "I don't want to know anything about it. As far as I am concerned, I am out of here." He left abruptly, and Brian was relieved to be rid of him. He knew that he would eventually have to deal with William Coles, but for now, most of the anger was directed towards the Governor. He still had some time to pursue his own interests.

He asked his first assistant to contact Luke McGinty. His assistant was startled by this because everybody knew that Luke McGinty was a person who did bad things to people. Luke McGinty was a hired hoodlum. He would disrupt people's lives, and he was so clever in doing this that neither he nor the person who hired him were ever blamed. Later that afternoon Luke McGinty came to Brian's office, and they had a long discussion about how he could be disruptive to the Wilbourne Ship Yard. At the end of this discussion, McGinty said, "I will start tonight on this project."

As Luke was leaving Brian, he had to go past the Wilbourne Ship Yards. He decided to take a look at the yard during the daytime. He went to the main office with idea of appearing that he was applying for a job. Geri happened to be in the office at that time, and they talked. She asked him about his qualifications, and he replied, "I am a jack of all trades. I can do just about anything." Geri replied, "What for example?" He said, "Look at that man out there; the one that is trimming that timber. He obviously knows very little about that type of work." Geri interrupted him and said, "And you do. I would like for you do a better job right now. If there is anything that I despise is a braggart. So, Mr. Luke McGinty, let's see what you can do."

The last thing Luke wanted to do was to call attention to himself. Now he had gotten himself in a bad position as he had no choice but to do as he had bragged. He muttered to himself, "That damn woman; now I have got to do this in a hurry and get out of here. Why did I do this? I am a man that doesn't like exposure, and now everybody will be looking at me. I think I will flub the job and get away as soon as I can." He walked briskly to the timber and took the axe from the man. He said to himself, "What a mess that man has made of this beautiful piece of wood."

Without thinking further he started to work on the timber. As his axe cut into the wood, memories came to his mind. Memories of the past flooded in. He was a young man and working with his dad, and he loved working with wood. The smell of the wood as his axe bit into it excited him and filled his mind of the good times with his father. He found his mind drifting back to his dad and that terrible time when the sheriff came and took his father away. He was about seventeen, and he dearly loved his father. His father was a convict who had escaped from prison ten years ago. This was the only time in his life that he had ever cried. The whole episode changed his life. The community he lived in condemned him for his father's crimes, and he was ostracized. This led to his wandering and his eventually becoming a criminal. He ended up in Bermuda just one step ahead of the law. When he came out of his meditations, he found that he had finished trimming the timber. He looked at it and was pleased about how it looked. Without saying another word he walked off the yard before Geri could talk further with him.

Geri looked at the timber and realized that she had been talking to a craftsman. "Why did he walk away?' she pondered. That night she talked about this incident with her family. Abby spoke up and said, "If it is the Luke McGinty that I know, he is nothing but a hoodlum, and I am suspicious about why he was on the yard especially since he didn't really want a job."

They were now in the fourth week of the repair of the ship, and Geri felt that they were well ahead of schedule. She had begun to relax and was spending more time talking with Culum. She found herself liking being with him. One day she said, "Culum, do you remember the day on the ship when you were telling me about yourself, and I abruptly shut you up?" Culum said, "Yes, and I have been trying to impress you ever since." Geri replied, "Culum, stop that blarney. What I wanted to say was that I want to know more about you as I am becoming interested in you." Without thinking Culum reached over and kissed Geri firmly on the mouth, and Geri did not resist. They both drew back and looked at each other and wondered if they had started a new beginning. They sat quietly together and said very little. Each was in their own thoughts.

Culum was thinking that finally he was getting somewhere with Geri. Geri was worrying about his leaving. She realized that he had saved her from a big threat by his handling of the Coles affair, but now he was about to leave, and she had a serious problem with Amy. Amy was a runaway bonded servant, and they were in an English colony and under English Law.

She shook her head and got her thoughts into the present and said, "Culum, I need your help. You know about Amy's situation. She will be living under English Law for a long time, and I don't want Amy to be harassed or taken away from me. I have been wondering how I can change things for her. I know that a bonded servant can buy out their bondage, and I want you to do this for me. You will be sailing back to Belfast after you unload your goods in Halifax. I want you to look up this Mr. Reginald Brown and buy Amy's bond so that she can be free." Culum said, "Of course, I will do that, but I was thinking of other things. I was thinking how I was going to get back to you. If I accept the Captaincy of this ship, I will be committed to return to Halifax and not here." This troubled them both.

When Luke McGinty hurriedly walked away, he realized that he had not inspected the Wilbourne Yard. He was uneasy about this mistake, and wondered if he should give up this job as he was being so unprofessional. It was that Geri Hogg that confused him. Her calling his bluff had started things in the wrong direction. She was a pretty woman and maybe that is what distracted him. After a while he settled down and began planning his sabotage of the Wilbourne Yard. The best way to hurt them was to disrupt their work. He knew just what to do. He would weaken some of the supports of the ship and leave them in such a weakened condition that any hard blow would turn the ship on its side. He would do it this tonight and by tomorrow, while they would be doing their work, disaster would happen. He usually was pleased by his planned work, but this time he didn't feel any pleasure.

That night when the yard seemed asleep, Luke slipped into the yard. He knew that the ship had guards posted on the main deck and only walked around the base of the ship every hour on the hour. What he didn't know was that Geri had alerted Captain Limon of the possibility that Luke might try to sabotage the ship. Captain Limon doubled the guards and had them making rounds around the ship every thirty minutes. Luke arrived at eleven ten, and there were no guards present. He felt that he had almost one hour to do his sabotage. When he was trying to loosen the braces, he stumbled and fell and was knocked unconscious. His head had struck a large rock, and he had received a severe concussion.

He was still unconscious when Geri arrived the next morning and discovered him. She could see what he had been trying to do and knew that he had been hired to harm her work and possibly cause her to lose her yard. She stood looking at him and tried to think what should she do. The main thing she wanted to know was who had hired him.

As she looked closer at him she realized that he was seriously injured. His breathing was irregular, and it seemed that he was dying. She ran back to the house and got O'Rourke and Amy to come and help her get him to their house. She didn't want Captain Limon to find him as she was sure he would hang him summarily. They managed to get him into the house before the yard was awake, and she started trying to revive him. It was a chilly morning, and a lot of his distress was his low body temperature. She bundled him up and put him into her room. She didn't want anyone to know what had happened and assembled her family and told them what she wanted to do. She said, "I want to know who is behind this attempted sabotage. If Captain Limon hears about this, he will hang Luke, and with that we will never find out who instigated this. I propose we keep him here, and if he recovers, we may be able to get him to tell us who hired him."

Abby didn't think that this was a good idea. She said, "Luke is an incorrigible criminal. He will see your kindness as a stupid game, and he will play along. The minute he gets a chance he will run away and that will be the last you will hear or see him." Most of them agreed with Abby, but Geri persisted, and they finally agreed to her plan.

None of them knew that Luke had regained consciousness and had heard Geri try to protect him. He had been caught fair and square, and he should be in jail by now, but here he was in a warm bed and had that good looking Geri trying to help him. He wondered about this as it had never happened to him before. The only kindness he ever had came from his father and never from a stranger. His headache became so severe he moaned and lost consciousness. Geri heard his moan and hurried into the room. She put cold packs on his head, but had no idea if this was the right thing to do. She finally came out of the room and left Luke in God's hand and told Amy to take charge.

She went to work. No one noticed that anything had been done to the boat and work continued at a fast pace. They finished the work on the ship fifteen days early and slipped it back into the water. She received her bonus and made a healthy profit Culum wanted to stay longer, but the Captain was in a big hurry and told him they were leaving with the morning tide. Culum came to see Geri before they left and told her he wanted to marry her, and he would be back as soon as he could. Geri gave him one hundred pounds to buy back Amy's bond and told him that Mr. Brown had given Amy's father only fifty pounds so she was sure this was enough money to solve Amy's problem. She didn't say yes to his proposal, and they parted. Needless to say Culum was disappointed that Geri was not going to marry a seafaring man who would be at sea most of their married life.

CHAPTER 11

Over the next two weeks all of them took care of Luke. They had been able to keep his whereabouts a secret, and he had slowly recovered. During the first week he was planning to escape as soon as he could, but every time he tried to stand up he was so dizzy that all he could do was fall back in bed. Each night Geri would come in and feed him. He didn't know it, but he was falling in love with Geri.

The passing of the two weeks, the ship being launched, and no sabotage troubled Brian. What had happened to Luke. He sent out his spies to try to find out where Luke was. All he could find out was that a strange man was staying at the Wilbourne house. It was into the third week that he found out that the unknown man was Luke. He felt that he was a prisoner and that His scheme was in danger of being exposed. He knew he had to take drastic action and do it immediately. He had not hired a killer in a long time and was concerned, but that very day he was summoned to go to William Coles' home.

He didn't go and had no intention of going. He knew that the old man was still on house arrest, and he had no one to run the Coles Ship Yards. He was going to use this time to get rid of Luke and then he would handle Coles. He passed a message to the local bartender requesting a visit with Blackie. The bartender got a lot of money being a go between. All of this transaction was handled in code that only Blackie, a code name, and his clients knew this code.

The code for a killing was deer hunt. Luke was identified as the target, and the price was negotiated. Here Brian ran into a problem as Luke was one of their own. He had to have a strong reason before a contract could be made.

Brian lied and said Luke was squealing about his failed sabotage job at Wilbourne's. He said "Luke has made a bargain with Geri, and he is going to spill all of this to the authorities." He produced false documents that verified this, and the contract was made. Blackie hired an assassin to shoot Luke as soon as possible. This person established a position where he could have a clear shot only if Luke came to the window he was observing. He waited for three days and felt that he would have to get another position. It was that day that he noticed activity in Luke's room.

Luke was for the first time able to get up and not be dizzy. He could walk around the room, and he knew it was time to clear up this matter of his sabotage attempt. When Geri came home, he called and asked her to come into his room.

Geri had no feelings for Luke and was still angry by what he had intended to do. She came into the room and was talking to Luke. He had gotten up and had walked to the window talking about what he had done. As he was turning to look directly to Geri he stumbled and fell just as the bullet smashed into the place where his head had been. He knew instantly what had happened, and he pulled Geri to the floor as he expected another shot to be made.

O'Rourke ran into the room and seeing what had happened picked up his pistol and ran out of the house. He saw a man running away and fired a shot at him. He saw the man fall and ran towards him. He approached him very carefully as he didn't want to give him a chance to shoot him. The man was having hard time breathing and was in acute distress. When O'Rourke got closer, he could see that the man was shot in his chest, and he could see the blood bubbling out of the wound. He had seen these types of wounds before when he fought at Trafalgar, and he knew there was little he could do. The man motioned him to come closer, and when he did, he said, "I am done for. I want you to tell that son of a bitch Luke I didn't get him, but the organization will." When he said this, blood ran out of his mouth, and he strangled on his own blood. He gasped for breath and died.

O'Rourke slowly got up and went back into the house. Luke knew at once what all of his meant. He knew someone felt that he was or had squealed on the person who had hired him to sabotage the O'Dorcas Savage. He also knew that this person had manipulated his organization into believing that he had betrayed their code. With all of these thoughts in mind he turned to Geri and said, "I must leave here at once. If I stay, I will jeopardize all of you as I am a marked man." He didn't give them any time to respond and left. When he was gone, Geri said to O'Rourke to get our tracker and follow Luke. I want to know every place he goes and who he talks to.

Chapter 12

All during the time that Luke was with them, Geri and O'Rourke had talked about how they were going to get Luke to talk about who hired him. They tried to find out all they could concerning his past life. It seemed that Luke had been involved in criminal activity since his late teens. One person told them that Luke was always talking about his dad. Apparently his dad was in prison. They couldn't find out how or when he became so skillful working wood. This lack of information convinced them that Luke would not reveal who hired him. He was too secretive. They decided that they would let him leave and get their tracker to follow him and see if he would lead them to his employer. Now Geri was thinking that all they had to do was just wait and see how things evolved.

When Luke left, he hurried to find his only friend in the criminal organization of Bermuda. His friend told him that the only way he could help him was for him to appeal before their council and have a hearing regarding his behavior while he was a captive. The meeting was to be arranged the next night at their usual meeting place where Luke could confront his accuser. Geri's tracker had been successful in following Luke, and he reported that a big meeting of the important criminals of Bermuda was to take place that night. He had found the location of this meeting.

With this information, Geri went to the Governor's office and requested to speak with him on an important matter. When the Governor's Secretary told the Governor that a Geri Hogg wished to speak to him, he asked, "Is that the woman that helped me expose the Coles incident?" She replied, "Yes, she was a great help in our discovery of Mr. Robert Coles' activities. The Governor said, "Show her in immediately."

The wanderers

When Geri went into the office she said, "Your honor, I have no idea of how I am supposed to address you as I have had no contact with a person of your standing; so I ask you to forgive me if I do anything that is not appropriate." The Governor was pleased by this introduction and said, "Please sit down and tell me why you wanted to see me." Geri responded by saying, "Four weeks ago a Luke McGinty tried to sabotage my repairing of Captain Limon's ship. He injured himself in doing this, and I probably saved his life. I didn't tell Captain Limon of this incident as he would want to hang him. I wanted to find out who had hired Luke for this job. Anyway three days ago someone tried to kill Luke. I let Luke leave, and I had a tracker follow him. I have found out where all of the major criminals on the Island of Bermuda are meeting tonight. I felt that you needed to know this." Governor Archibald Richards was astounded by what he had heard. He called loudly to his secretary and said, "Get my prosecuting attorney, police superintendent, and the head of his Militia in my office immediately." He admonished her to say this was a highly secret meeting.

When all arrived, Geri gave them a comprehensive description of the meeting place. Plans were made for how they could capture all of these criminals. The Governor wanted Geri to stay in his house until this was over. He said "Geri, I don't know how much danger you might possibly be in, and I want to protect you until this event is over. I want you to be a guest in my home. I will send a message to your company saying you are attending a dinner at my house, and you will be back tomorrow." Things began to develop rapidly, and Geri was involved in all of it.

Luke agreed to accept the judgment of the council, and the death contract was temporarily suspended. That night he went to the meeting and found himself seated in the center of a large group of men. Off to the side was Brian Douglas. He knew then who had convinced the council to put out a contract on him. The meeting started, and evidence was presented by Brian. All of it were lies, but they were so cleverly presented that Luke was wondering how he was going to defend himself. This was not going to be a problem for him, for at that very moment there appeared a ring of militia around this group, and they were all quickly subdued.

The next day a summary Court was called by Governor Richards, and all of the men were put on trial. All received a quick sentence of guilty and were ordered to be hung that very day. After the trial, all of the people involved in this event met in the Governor office, and they all stood up when Geri arrived. The Governor walked around his desk and embraced Geri. He said, "Geri, you have made it possible for us to eradicate a major part of our criminal element. We are very grateful to you. Is there anything I can do to reward you for your service?"

Geri replied, "I spent a lot of time with Luke McGinty. I feel he is a good man who has had many unfortunate experiences. He did turn to crime, but I don't feel he is a criminal. I would like for him to receive a pardon. I will be responsible for him if you do pardon him." The Governor was taken aback by her request. Usually people wanted something for themselves. Here is this simple sincere woman pleading for the life of a man who intended to do harm to her. He found that he could not refuse and immediately issued orders that Luke McGinty was to receive a temporary pardon. He was to be bonded to Geri Hogg for a period of three years. If at that time he had maintained a clean record, then he would receive a permanent pardon. He issued this in a hurry because Luke was on the next list to be hanged.

Luke had a lot to adjust to. One minute he was before his peers and about to make his plea for his life, and the next minute he was handcuffed and taken to jail. He spent the rest of the night in jail contemplating his life. "How had he ended up in this situation?" he asked himself.

His thoughts went back to his mother. His earliest memories were of his mother. They were alone living in a small house. You might call it a shack. It was winter time, and they were so cold. He felt the same cold now as he sat in his cold damp cell. His mother was crying. She just lost her job, and they had nothing to live on. They just sat hugging each other trying to keep warm. Finally his mother got up and said, "We must go out and try to find some place that is warm and get some food." We weren't the only ones searching as many were in the same boat.

It was then that his mother decided to take him to the orphanage. He protested and cried for her not to leave him, but she did. All he could remember about the orphanage was it was warmer, and he had some food.

When he was older, he ran away. He never did rightly know what his age was, but he must have been two or three when his mother abandoned him. He was wandering the country sides and the streets of many villages and towns always trying to find food and shelter. He learned to steal and take advantage of any opportunity that came along.

One day he was wandering on a remote road and saw a man lying in a ditch. He had shackles on his legs and arms and was in distress. At first his inclination was to get away from him as quickly as possible. As he was hurrying away, the man moaned and said, "Please help me." He stopped and went back to the man. This man's pleading and his memory of his pleading to his mother not to leave him made it impossible for him to walk on by. He could see the man was starving and was very cold. He dragged him away from the road into the woods and built a fire. He had some food with him, and he gave it to the man. He knew that the man could not travel so he built a small shelter and began foraging for food. Over the next few days he was able to find a coat for the man, and enough food so that he became strong enough to travel.

His thoughts were interrupted by the jailer coming in to take him to his trial. All of the other criminals were sitting in a large group. Witnesses were giving their testimony and in came Geri. She testified against him. At the end of the trial they all were found guilty and sentenced to death by hanging. He had just gotten back in his cell when he was told he would be in the next group to be hanged. When the jailer came for him, he was surprised that he was not taken to the gallows but to the Governor's office. He was dragging his leg shackles and his arms were shackled when he walked slowly into the Governor's office. He saw Geri sitting in the corner. The jailer pushed him up in front of the Governor, and he was told to stand at attention.

The Governor said, "Luke McGinty, at the personal request of Geri Hogg I am issuing you a temporary pardon. You will be bonded to Ms. Hogg for a period of three years. If you have during that period of time been a good citizen, then you will receive a full unconditional pardon. If you violate these conditions, you will be immediately hung as was dictated by your original sentence. Do you agree to these terms?" Luke could hardly understand what was happening to him but hastily said, "I do." The Governor said, "Jailer, take the shackles off the prisoner." Turning to Luke he continued saying, "Luke McGinty, you are now in the custody of Ms. Hogg, and now, Geri, you may leave with your bonded servant." Geri and Luke left the Governor's office, and they were driven to the Wilbourne Yard. On the way to the yard very little was said. Luke was still amazed that he was alive and didn't understand how all his had happened. His questions would come later. Geri was wondering why she had done this. She had enough problems without having a bonded criminal. When they arrived to the Yard, she said, "Luke, you will sleep in a small room in the basement of my house. You will eat in the kitchen. You will work in the yard, and you will be under the supervision of Foreman O'Rourke. I do not like people to be bonded. Since this is the requirement for your release, I will follow the rules. I want you to understand one thing, I am not your jailer. If you decide to run away, it is your business. I will simply report your violation and heaven help you for the Governor really wants to hang you. Amy will show you to your room and dinner is served at 6:00 p.m. Work starts at seven in the morning." With that she left for her office.

Chapter 13

Since Geri had shown what she could do with repairing ships, she found that she had all of the business that she could handle. Brian, being hanged, left the Coles' Ship Yard without a supervisor. William Coles realized this and decided to talk to Geri. When he sent a messenger to Geri asking her to come to his house, she refused. She said to the messenger, "Tell your master that I do not want anything to do with the Coles family. Your son has already plotted against me and that is enough of the Coles family for me."

All this did was to make him angrier with his son. He sent a second messenger, and the message was to the effect that he did not know anything about his son's activities as the Governor was the first one to inform him about his activities. As a result of that he was under house arrest and could not come to Geri.

Geri grudgingly returned with the messenger.

William Coles greeted Geri with respect and some diffidence. He opened the conversation with a statement saying, "I am very sorry for all the trouble my son has caused you. I want to be open with you. I have allowed my son and Brian to try to destroy Abby Wilbourne and to plan to practically rob her. I regret this, but that is past, and I have a serious problem with my ship yard. I have no person to run it. I need to sell it or find someone to run it. Are you interested?"

Geri was not surprised by this as she had hired all of his best workers in order to keep up with her business. She replied, "What are you selling? I am sure you know that you no longer have a business." This shocked him as no one had told him about what had happened after Brian was hanged. Geri could see the dismay that came over his face. She almost felt sorry for him. She continued, "All I see that you have is an empty ship yard. Have you tried to sell it to anyone in the business?" He said, "Yes, and I have found no one who wants to buy it. They say they don't want to be next door to a very efficient ship yard as customers would see the difference in the quality of their repairs. Your repairs are well recognized by the island as the best the island can offer. I don't know if you know it, but the way you handled the O'Dorcas Savage has made a great impression on the ship yards in Bermuda. They know now for them to survive they will have to be better."

Geri had not heard any of this and felt that it was flattery, and she ignored it, and got to the point saying, "What do you want for the yard?" He gave her a figure, and she said, "That is ridiculous. I will not buy your yard for that price. I will go home and figure what I think it is worth and get in touch with you." She got up and left without any exchange of pleasantries. Geri did an intensive study of Coles' ship yard. She was amazed by how run down it was. There was vandalism, and much of the equipment was worthless. She wondered about this, and the best answer she had was that Brian Douglas and Robert Coles thought they were about to get Wilbourne's and didn't want to keep up the property. Since the buildings were of little value, she investigated the value of the land. She discovered that land prices were depressed, and this area was particularly depressed. Her suspicions of William Coles that he was flattering her became more evident. The best she could determine was that the top price for the ten acres would be fifty pounds per acre. She didn't rush back to William Coles. She decided to let him stew for a while.

William Coles was in deep trouble. His trial was coming up, and none of his businesses were functioning. His legal fees were high, and he was trying to sell assets without success. When a week passed, and he had not heard from Geri, he sent his servant to ask Geri if she would come to see him. Geri told the servant that she was too busy to come, but she might be able to come tomorrow.

Tomorrow came and in mid afternoon she went to William's house. William was obviously disturbed. He was near bankrupt, and he desperately needed to get some cash. Geri came quickly to the point. She said, "Mr. Coles, I have investigated your ship yard, and it is no longer a ship yard. There is nothing there that can be salvaged. The only value you have is the land. I have had your land evaluated, and I was told that clean land would sell for a maximum of 50 pounds per acre. I am emphasizing clean land to you because you have a lot of junk on the land that has to be disposed of. I have received estimates of the cost for this as being at least 20 pounds per acre. Mr. Coles, I know that you are in severe financial trouble, and I am not sure as to whether you have a clear title to this land. Here is my offer, and it is final. I will pay you 300 pounds for your land, and this is conditional on two things. You must have a clean title, and I must have a contract for a sale signed this very minute. What is your answer, Sir?"

Coles was surprised at the astuteness of Geri, and he had already evaluated his holding as being worth 300 pounds. He knew posturing would do him no good, so he signed the contract. She had O'Rourke with her, and she wanted him and one of Coles's staff to sign the contract as witnesses. She said, "I will pay you the 300 pounds when you present me a clear title." With that nothing else was said, and she left.

Culum Rafin had an empty feeling as their Brig filled its sails and pulled away from Wilbourne Yards. He was standing on the quarterdeck and kept the figure of Geri in sight as long as he could, and as they turned around the Northern corner of the St. George Island, he turned and looked to the north. He didn't linger looking at the disappearing islands. His thoughts were of Geri, and he wondered if or when he would see her again.

As time passed he became aware of the change in the way the Brig was handling. Before it was a sluggish responding ship. Now it was sailing like a schooner. It was fast and responded quickly to the wheel. This performance was so pronounced that Captain Limon came on deck to see what was happening. It didn't take them long to realize that Geri had given them a new Brig. Captain said, "My God, that woman can really repair a ship." He was going to repeat this all the way to Halifax.

CHAPTER 14

Halifax was about 650 miles away, and they made port in four days. This was a record for them. As they pulled into anchorage, they saw people gathering on the dock, and they were looking at their Brig. The people thought that a new ship that had come into the port. When they could read the name of the ship as O'Dorcas Savage, to say surprise would be an understatement. When Captain Limon and Culum went ashore, they were met with inquiring Captains. They were saying, "We heard that you were seriously damaged in the May storm, and here you are with a new ship." Captain Limon did the talking and said, "We just barely made it to St George's port of Bermuda. There were many damaged ships there. We couldn't get anyone to take us for repairs. Culum had met a good looking lady who had been a passenger on our ship, and when she got off the O'Dorcas Savage, he was determined to find her. He did, and much to our surprise, she had bought a bankrupt ship repair yard. She offered to repair our Brig at a favorable price, and she did what you see. What you don't see is that the Brig now handles like a schooner, and we made fast time to Halifax."

One of the Captains asked, "How much time was spent repairing the brig?". Culum replied, "Six weeks." They were in harbor for only a week. They sold their goods at a good profit, and the Brig was loaded with furs, salted cod and numerous trade items. They left Halifax and had a strong wind from the west.

The stay in Halifax had been hectic for Culum He had little time to think of his personal life. As the routines of the voyage developed, he began to think of his relationship with Geri. He realized that he was more interested in Geri than she was in him. They had talked about his becoming a Sea Captain. He could hear her words now, "Culum,

I know the kind of man you are. You think first of the sea, and second of the family you might have. I will have no part of that way of living. If I fall in love again, I will find a man that wants to be with me day and night. I want to experience a life together, and not a life where you will be gone for months, and you come home only to leave on the next tide. Culum, you are a very attractive man, but you like the sea too much to give it up for me." Hearing this he had said it was not true that he could not give up the sea, but being away from Geri made him realize that Geri was right. He did love the sea too much, and if they did marry, it wouldn't take long before he would want to go back to sea again. He felt a tug in his heart as he said this to himself. He realized that he could never have Geri. He was depressed for a few days and decided to talk to Captain Limon.

When he told his problem to Captain Limon, he said, "Culum, I had the same problem with my wife. When we were courting, she made the same request of me. I don't know how I overcame her demands because we did get married. I realize now how much I have missed not being with her day and night. My children do not know me. They see my father-in-law as their father. I am now retiring from the sea not from my desire to be home, but because my wife is very ill, and I want to have her last years with me if death should take her from me. I love the sea, but it has robbed me of a loving wife, and a chance to see my children grow up. If you have that same love of the sea, then I recommend you stay a bachelor. Culum, you can never know the despair I feel when I think my wife might already be dead. I would not have taken this last trip except for the need of my company to have a successful voyage. I just hope my wife is still alive." Culum was deeply affected by what his Captain had said. He knew that he wanted the sea first and Geri second, so there was no hope for them.

When they arrived to Belfast, Culum assumed the title of Captain and was busy the first few days getting ready for a return trip to Halifax. When he had gotten things under control, he went to see Mr. Reginald Brown. He found Mr. Brown in a local tavern. He approached him and said that he needed to talk to him about his bonded servant girl, Amy MacMoyre. He said, "Mr. Brown, I want to buy the bond you have for Amy MacMoyre. She has given me enough money to buy this bond."

Mr. Brown said, "Well, so she has enough money to buy her bond does she? I will have you know that I have no intention of selling it. I will find her one day, and I will teach her a lesson." This angered Culum and he said, "Amy told me about your request for sex as it being a part of her employment. This, Sir, is particularly repulsive to me. I took some time to look up some of your past that I don't think you will want to deal with. For example, I found out that you and your wife have an unusual agreement. As I read it, it indicates you can have another life as long as it does not become public. A strange request for a loving wife, but there are harsh penalties if you violate this. I think you know what those penalties are. So since you are refusing to release Amy, I am going to make public all of your affairs, and I am sure your wife won't like it."

Brown's face at first was red with anger and then it lost all of its color. He said meekly, "I think we can come to some agreement. There is no need for us to quarrel. Of course, I will release Amy from her bondage. What do you propose to pay?" Culum replied, "Amy had worked for a long time to earn the money she gave me. When I came to you with this request, I intended to pay the full amount that you gave to her father. Now I have no intention of doing so. I will give one pound for her bond, and if you try to bargain I will make your life unbearable." Mr. Brown hurriedly replied, "Sir, I had no intention of refusing your offer. I just happen to have Amy's papers with me, and I will immediately sign them over to you." Culum replied, "No, Mr. Brown, we will go in front of a magistrate and get this handled according to the law. I find you repulsive, and I want to see that this is done so that Amy will not have any further trouble from you. I know that you have reward signs out for Amy, and I demand that you remove them. If Amy has any trouble from these signs, you will hear from me."

Everything was settled to Culum's satisfaction, and they departed much to the relief of both. Culum wrote a letter to Geri and told her of what had transpired He enclosed **99** pounds and wrote that he would always love her, but she was right for he loved the sea first. He indicated if this ever changed, she would be the first to know. He hoped if that occurred that she would still be available. He gave a packet containing the bond papers and his letter to a friend Captain that was going to Bermuda. She would receive it in forty days.

Chapter 15

The first few days went fast for Luke. He liked O'Rourke, and he quickly adjusted to the work schedule. He had a lot of wood working skills, and it amazed O'Rourke. O'Rourke found himself placing more and more responsibility on Luke, and he seemed to enjoy it. After a week had passed, Geri wanted a report of how Luke was working out. O'Rourke said, "That guy is really amazing. He understands carpentry and has a great skill in working with wood. I think he is going to be your best worker." This report pleased Geri and she said, "We have this Coles property to rehabilitate. I want you to assign him and a helper to work on restoring the yard. I know that it is a mess, but tell him to do the best he can. Don't mention about destroying anything just say restore. I want to see what he can really do working by himself and directing another person."

After O'Rourke left, Geri started talking to Amy, Abby, and Robert. She said, "Amy, I don't want you to be kitchen help. I want to educate you, and I want you to become a sailor. I know you like sailing, and I intend to start a shipping company as soon as I can. I want you to be a part of that company. I will contact a teacher to come daily for two hours to instruct you. I hope this will give you a start in improving your reading, writing and arithmetic. When we have restored the Bermuda sloop, O'Rourke will start teaching you sailing." Amy was thrilled by this and went over to Geri and hugged her saying, "I could not have found a better sister."

Geri turned to Abby and said, "I feel that you have become a part of our family. How do you feel?"

Abby responded, "Before you came, I was lost. I had become a liar and cheat. You have given me a new start in life. I had always been a housewife, and I know that very well. Is it possible that I could become your housekeeper?" Geri responded, "As of now, we do not have money for any of us to be salaried. I am working without salary as is O'Rourke and Amy. Will you be willing to work without salary?" Abby replied, "Of course, you have given me a home and that is all I need."

Geri's thoughts now turned to her son. He was just three and a half years old. She could see that he was going to look just like his father. He was talking well and was a very active child. He seemed content to be with all of the people in his life. He was particularly attracted to Amy. Amy would play with him, and as long as Amy was around he was happy.

Geri wondered how she was going to cope with her work and be a good mother. She was thinking she should get a harness for Robert with a leash, and by doing this she could take him with her into the yard and keep some control over his movements. That way she could have some time with him. As she was planning this, she remembered the time when she lived in that little cottage outside of Dublin. Life then was so simple for her. She had a loving husband who supported her well, and she could be a contented housewife. Now she had a business with many responsibilities. She daydreamed about this for a while and said to herself, "The past is gone and the present is now. I must live in the now.

O'Rourke had two things to think about. He felt good about being the foreman of the yard and enjoyed working with the men, but this Luke guy puzzled him. He knew he had been a criminal for a long time, and he was concerned about what he might do. A week after he had assigned him to work on the Coles property, he decided to make a surprise visit to Luke's project. The ex Coles yard was a half a mile from Geri's yard. It was mid morning when he found Luke. He found that Luke had cleaned up all of the debris and had started working on the slides that were used to draw the ship out of the water. Luke was doing good work, and he told him so. He said, "Luke, I want to talk to you for a while. Assign your helper to do some work that doesn't need you and let's sit down and talk." Luke was immediately on guard as this was the way they talked to him when his father was taken away to jail. He remembered them taking him off the job and saying let's talk. Of course the let's talk was mainly to say he was fired because he had a convict father.

The wanderers

He walked stiffly with O'Rourke expecting the worst. He was expecting to be criticized, but since he was a bonded servant, he was sure he would not be fired. To his surprise, O'Rourke started off by saying, "I want you to know something about me, and I want to know something about you. I was ten years old when I went to sea. I started out as a cabin boy, and I worked up to boatswain mate. When I was 15, I returned to my home and found all of my family had died in an epidemic. I found Amy and Geri, and I decided to spend the rest of my life with them. They have given me a family that I have longed for."

There was a silence and finally Luke said, "My mother abandoned me when I was two or three. I don't know how old I am, but I guess I am about twenty five. I ran away from the orphanage when I was about six years old. I wandered around for about two years and found my father. He was lying in a ditch and was very weak. He had shackle bracelets on his wrists and his ankles. He had escaped from prison and had been without food for about a week. He was poorly clothed, and I stole a coat for him. I got us food until he could walk. We got out of Ireland and ultimately came to Boston, Massachusetts. He had been a skillful shipwright, and he got a job in a ship yard. I worked with him, and all I know is from his teachings. He was kind to me, and I told him he was my father. I never knew my natural father. We worked in the same yard until I was about eighteen. That is when my father was picked up by the local police as an escaped convict. A person from his home town had identified him, and he was returned to Ireland. When our boss found out about his situation, I was let go. I carried this stigma with me, so I could not get permanent work.

I soon found out that it was easier to steal than work, and my criminal career began. I was very skillful, and I would always leave just before the police found me. Several years ago I came to Bermuda. I joined the criminal group that was just hung and developed the skill of harming property or businesses of my clients' rivals. I was sought out because no one was able to identify me or my clients. If I hadn't fallen and knocked myself out, Geri would have never found me, and things would have been different for all of you. I am not a good person, but I don't think of myself as an evil person. I think of myself as an accidental criminal." O'Rourke was amazed by this story, and they just sat and looked at each other. Finally O'Rourke got up, and they both went back to work.

While O'Rourke was walking back to the Wilbourne's yard, the second thing he wanted to think about came to his mind. He was fifty five, and he had never had a woman. He had found himself looking at Abby and thinking about her as a possible wife. He had never approached her, and he wondered how he could start a different relationship with her. Before now she was just a discredited widow who did house work for them. He was going to have to talk to her like he did to Luke. He would talk about himself and get her to talk about herself. Maybe this could be the beginning of something.

The first person O'Rourke saw after leaving Luke was Geri. She asked how things were going with the Coles clean up. He replied, "Fine, I had a long talk with Luke. We exchanged life stories. He related what Luke had said about his life and emphasized the statement that he didn't really understand. It was to the effect that he had been a bad person but not an evil person."

Geri also was struck by that statement. As she considered it, she thought the word "bad' was a descriptive word, but the word evil had moral connotations. Was Luke saying he had a conscience? If this was the case then he really was an accidental criminal.

While she was pondering this, O'Rourke was talking about his beginning interest for Abby. He was asking Geri what she thought about this. Geri replied, "Joseph, (she always used his first name when they were talking about personal things) I can see why you are interested in Abby. She is an attractive woman. When I first met her, and she was pretending something she was not, I thought of her as a hard manipulating woman. When she gave up her husband's business, she became what I see now—a warm, attractive, middle aged woman. Why don't you talk to her and let her know that you are interested in her? That is how relationships begin."

This was all of the encouragement that O'Rourke needed. That night at supper time O'Rourke sat next to Abby. He talked to her all thru the meal, and when she went to the kitchen, he followed and insisted on helping her with the dishes. While they were washing the dishes, he told her about himself. He wasn't bragging he just wanted her to know all about who he was. Abby found his life's story interesting and asked had he ever had a girl friend, Joseph said, "I don't know why I never tried to be close to a woman. I visited many ports, but I never related with the girls on the wharf. I realize now that I missed out a lot by not pursuing and developing a woman that I could call my own. My fellow crewmen would think I was queer in both ways. Now I am in my mid fifties, and I realize how lonely I am."

He became silent as if he didn't want to go any further if Abby didn't talk about herself.

Thus both were silent for a long time. The dishes made a clattering noise, and both were in their own thoughts. Abby knew that Joseph was interested in her as a woman, but she was not sure she wanted to start another man-woman relationship. She hadn't been unhappy with her first marriage. They had no children, and in their later years her husband lost interest in her as a woman. They never had a passionate life together, and she did not know if she could handle that kind of intimacy. She felt that Joseph wanted a passionate lover, and this frightened her. O'Rourke was thinking, "How do I go further? I have told her who I am and indicated that I was interested in her. Maybe I moved too fast."

While these thoughts were going thru their minds, Abby started to talk and she said, "I am reluctant to talk about myself as it would seem to you that I was interested in pursuing the relationship I feel you are proposing. I was quite young to be married to a man that was twice my age. He was a mature adult, and I was a late teenager. We had no real passionate relationship, and we were, at best, companions. I wanted children, and he didn't. As he grew older, he lost interest in me sexually, and I lost those feelings also. When I lost those feelings, I felt free as I felt passion binds you to a person in a way that robs you of yourself. Yes, I am lonely, but I don't want the closeness that solves loneliness. As you can see, I am confused. Maybe we should be with each other and see if I can see a marriage in a different light." Joseph had wanted more, but at least she didn't close the door.

Charter 16

Amy was very excited about Geri's ideas of her future. The idea of being educated and learning to sail thrilled her. After supper she cornered Geri and asked when she could start her schooling. Geri said, "Amy, I am going into St. George tomorrow and see Mr. Burns. We have been getting a great increase of business, and I want to be assured that I can get adequate supplies. While I am there, I will inquire about a teacher for you."

The next day she went to St. George and met with Grady Burns. Their experience with the Coles family had been a bonding experience for both of them, and Grady greeted her warmly. She quickly got down to business. She said, "Grady, I am getting a large amount of business, and I need to be assured of adequate supplies. I want you to consider about locating either your store to my area or have a branch store close to me." Burns replied, "I have been thinking the same thing since you are my main customer. As you know the Coles Supply store is no longer functioning. I was wondering if you would like to partner with me, and we buy the Coles store. This store is in Hamilton, and I would be much closer to you."

Geri thought this would be a great idea and asked Grady when he could start this process. Grady responded, "I have already talked to William Coles about purchasing his store building, but as yet he has been too unreasonable." Geri replied, "I know Mr. Williams well. He is a trader. If you want to deal with him, you have to come from a power position, or he will dicker forever." Burns replied. "I think you are right. His trial is coming up, and it looks to me that he is in serious trouble both legally as well as financially."

Geri thought for a moment and said, "let's go to Hamilton and talk to him." As they were leaving the store, a man walked in, and Burns said, "We are closing. Can you come back later this afternoon?" The man replied, "I just want a minute of your time. I am looking for a Geri Hogg. I have a packet for her, and I have no idea where she is located." This startled Geri, and she said, "I am Geri Hogg." The man handed her a packet that was addressed to her and signed Culum Rafin. He said, "Captain Culum Rafin is a good friend of mine, and he asked me to deliver this to you as he didn't know how long it would be before he would be back to Bermuda." With that he saluted Geri and left.

Geri had to open the packet immediately, and told Grady to wait a few minutes while she found out what was in the packet. She read Culum's letter first. As she read it, she could hear his voice, and she found that she had feelings for Culum that she was unaware of. His saying that he loved the sea first and her second tugged at her heart strings, and she brushed away a tear. She quickly composed herself and opened the legal documents. There she read the official form for the termination of a bonded servant named Amy MacMoyre. It was signed by a magistrate and by Reginald Brown.

Her first thought was that Amy was free, and a big smile came over her face. She looked further and saw some money. She counted 99 pounds. She turned to Grady and told him the good news about Amy and said, "I almost forgot that I also came here to find a teacher for Amy." Grady was pleased about Amy and said, "I don't know of any teachers here who would give private lessons, but I will be on the lookout for them."

With that they left and went to William Coles' house. Grady was to do the talking, and Geri would enter when she felt she had something to contribute. William Coles was still under house arrest, and they were admitted into his study. He was cordial and inquired what brought them to his home. Grady told him that he was going to move to Hamilton and have his store there. He wondered if he was interested in selling his store building. William replied that he had not considered selling as he hoped someday soon he would be able to open it again.

At this point Geri interrupted and said, "Mr. William, we came here to talk business. This idea of yours about reopening you business is nonsense. You know as well as we do that it is very unlikely you will ever be able to open that business. If you are not interested in selling the building then we will be on our way, and I am sure that we can build or buy a building to our satisfaction."

Williams thought damn that woman. She is always on her toes. God, if only my son were like her, I would not be in this situation that I am in today. I had better make the best deal I can as I am sure she will do just as she says. He made them a price, and Geri told him they would investigate the building and get back to him that afternoon.

They went to the Coles supply store and found the building in good shape. There were some supplies there, and they would be hard to inventory. Grady said, "The way Robert Coles ran his business is quite surprising to me. He apparently had no control over his supplies, and I wonder if he was making any profit." They were discovering what William already knew. He had a failed business. He had been supplementing his son's business for years so that he would have something to do. Now he could no longer do this as he was fighting for his financial life as well as his freedom.

Grady and Geri spent two hours going over everything. Geri said, "Let's go talk to a banker about this property and also talk to someone who knows real estate values." They went to the largest bank in Hamilton and talked to its president. To their surprise, he was very interested about their inquiry concerning the Coles Supply business. He said, "You know, of course, Mr. Coles is under indictment for fraud and other charges. What you don't know, is that we have foreclosed on his building and its supplies. We are very upset by his not paying his obligations. We are not in the retail business; we are bankers. If you both would sign his note, I would turn over all of the Coles supply business to you.

Ms. Hogg I am aware of your success in the boat building business, and I would consider you as the prime person responsible for this loan. Mr. Burns, you have done only fairly well in your business, and as far as I can tell you have only one customer and that is Ms. Hogg. Ms. Hogg must have confidence in you, and I will take her judgment on that issue. I think you both should think about this proposition as you would be assuming a large indebtedness."

They could hardly control their excitement as they felt that the supplies in the Cole building would be more valuable than the loan.

The wanderers

The banker insisted that they found a company that would state that Geri was the owner as he felt more secure about Geri than he did Burns.

They left, and Geri said, "I am concerned about your feelings concerning his evaluation of you. Is this going to cause any problems between us?" Burns replied, "This is not the first time I have been aware of how bankers on this island have felt about me. I have operated on a shoe string for a long time, and now for the first time I have had some security especially since you started buying from me. Geri, I am a good manager of my store, but I am not a good business man. I know that you can manage business well, i.e. your ship yard. I need a partner that can help me in ways I am incompetent."

Geri was concerned about what Burns had said. She asked herself if she could extend herself in assuming this new opportunity. This was the first time she had ever questioned her ability. She thought about this questioning and came to the conclusion that in other issues she had a wealth of knowledge, but managing a supply store put her into an area where she had very little experience. She told Burns about her concerns and he responded, "Geri, I can sell, buy supplies well, and keep a good inventory control. What I have trouble doing is getting my customers to pay on time or at all. I tend to sell my product without awareness of the consequences of the sale. In other words can they pay or will they pay? I never had any trouble with you as you paid on delivery." Geri replied, "Why don't you just require your customers to pay on delivery?" He replied, "The customers I got were throwaways from Coles and other suppliers. They couldn't pay cash, and I had to take this risk in order to stay in business." Geri responded, "Coles is no longer in the business. Has this affected your business?" He replied the other suppliers had captured the Coles business.

Geri was beginning to see the problem. It was that Burns was not a good promoter of his business. He was selling the same products as others, but he was not out promoting them. She was beginning to see what her role would be. Did she want to do this along with her other activities. She said, "Burns, let me think about all of this, and I will get back to you in a week." They parted.

What had started as a supply problem for her business became the problems of a new business. She was going to talk to her family. When she got home she went to Amy and showed her the papers that relieved her from her bondage. Amy jumped up and down and kept hugging and kissing Geri. When things settled down, she told Amy she didn't find a teacher, but not to despair because she would soon. Amy replied, "Despair, not me, I am free, I am free!!"

Paul Winthrop was sitting at home in Boston, Massachusetts. He was exhausted. He had just finished his four year course at Harvard University. As far as he could tell, he was trained for nothing. All he had was a classical education and where did he go with that. He was despondent, and his family was concerned about him. His father said, "You need to get away from Boston and get your thinking in order." He wanted him to spend the summer with his sister who lived on the main island of Bermuda. Paul left on the next boat to Bermuda. He had spent one week at his aunt's house and was bored.

His aunt said to him, "Why don't you tutor people? You have a wonderful education, and you have a lot to give in the area of teaching. I know of a young girl who has been inquiring for a teacher. Why don't you check her out?"

At first a young girl didn't interest him, but when his Aunt said she was 16 and quite a beauty, he became immediately interested. He said, "Aunt Agatha, a good looking girl does interest me, and I would like to visit her this afternoon." His aunt said, "She lives eighteen miles away, and you would just get there and have to return." He went any away.

When he arrived to the Wilbourne Yards, he asked O'Rourke where he could find a Miss Amy MacMoyre. O'Rourke had not yet learned about Amy's freedom from her bond and was very cautious. He inquired what was his business with Miss Amy Hogg. Paul Winfield replied, "I understand that she is looking for a tutor, and I want to apply for the job." O'Rourke knew that this is what they had been looking for, and said, "You will have to talk to her sister, Geri Hogg." He led him to Geri's office and told him to wait, and he would get Geri. Geri had just returned, and when she heard who it was, she told Amy to come with her. When they arrived to Geri's office, Paul quickly arose and introduced himself. He couldn't believe that he had ever seen two such beautiful women.

Geri introduced Amy and herself. She said, "Would you please sit down and tell us of your qualifications." Paul was concerned about how they would receive his lack of teaching experience, and he knew that he desperately wanted this job. The idea of being with Amy was the best thing that had happened to him in a long time. Paul started saying, "I am visiting my Aunt in St. George, and she heard that Amy was looking for a tutor. I have just finished a four year course at Harvard University in Classical studies. I feel that I could teach Amy many things."

Geri said, "Amy and I have always been in places where there were no schools. Amy wants to be educated, and I want her to be skilled in Algebra, Geometry and Calculus. Amy is training to be a ship Captain as we are planning to trade in the West Indies. Are you qualified in these areas?"

Paul thanked his lucky star as part of his classical studies included all three of those math subjects. They talked until it was supper time. Geri asked him to stay for the night as he would have no way to get to St. George. When they all came in for supper, Geri introduced Paul Winfield to the group. There was very little interest in him by the group, but Amy was very interested in him as was he her.

After supper, they all sat together and Geri reported on her day's activities. She told them about the possibility of owning the Coles Supply company. She said, "What that company needs is a business manager. Grady Burns could manage the supplies and inventory, but he is a very poor business person. The banker told me he would only make a loan to me as he didn't think Grady Burns was strong enough financially to assume any of the Coles loan. Apparently they had foreclosed on William Coles as he was unable to pay off his note." The group was amazed by what Geri had learned, and they were silent for a while.

Abby started talking first and said, "When my husband was alive, I was his business manager. I handled his collections and tried to be sure that he didn't take on a job with a customer who was unable to pay for our services." Geri said, "That is exactly what the Coles Supply Store needs. Do you want to do this work for us?" Abby said, "I don't want to be separated from my family." Geri said, "It is just 2 miles from our yard to the Coles Supply building." Others talked about how helpful it would be to have control of our supplies. Geri said, "From a business stand point there are enough supplies in those buildings to pay off the loan. Let's think about this over the next two days and explore how we can arrange it so that Abby could be more at ease in working there if we decide to buy it."

Paul Winfield was impressed by how all of these people seemed to be so close and involved with each other. As they were going to their rooms, Geri told Paul he would sleep in the basement with Luke. Luke led Paul to the basement and said very little to him. As they were sitting on their beds, Paul started talking to Luke. He said, "I am amazed about how different people can be so close and concerned about each other. Have you been in with this group long?" Luke said, "About two weeks." It was obvious Luke was not interested in talking, but Paul continued asking questions. Every question asked was replied by Luke with few words. Finally Luke said, "Why are you asking so many questions?" Paul replied, "I come from a very formal family. We never discuss problems as openly as this group does. It fascinates me to been around these people. I just wondered how all of this came about."

Luke decided that he would shock Paul by telling how he came into the family, and maybe then he would go to sleep. Luke said, "I don't know exactly how all of these people came together, but I know how I got here. I was a criminal that was captured by the Governor's police and militia. Geri had a lot to do with my being captured. She testified against me, and I was supposed to be hanged The Governor owed Geri a favor, and she requested that I be pardoned. I was just ten steps from the gallows when I was taken before the Governor. He lectured me and told me he was giving me a temporary pardon. I was to be bonded to Geri, and if I did nothing that was against the law, I would get a permanent pardon in three years. If I tried to escape, I would be caught and immediately hanged." Paul was indeed shut up, and they both went to sleep.

The next morning Paul and Luke went to breakfast together. They said very little to each other. After breakfast Geri told Paul to come into her office. She liked Paul, but she wanted to be sure that he could really teach the math she wanted Amy to have. She said, "Paul, I know that Amy wants you as her teacher, but it is very important to me that I know if you are qualified to teach her in these areas. I am acquainted with Algebra, Geometry and some Trigonometry. Can you show me your abilities in these areas?" Paul responded, "I could respond better to your questions if I had a text book on these subjects." When Geri was studying Navigation under Captain Limon, he told her he was leaving the sea, and he would not need any of his books on navigation.

The wanderers

He had said to Geri, "I want you to have my library that I have used since I became a Captain." In this library were books on Algebra, Plane Geometry, Trigonometry, and Calculus. When Paul asked for books on these subjects, Geri brought out the books he requested.

Paul was surprised to say the least. He thought that he was among uneducated people, and here was Geri with advanced books of math, and she seemed to know something about them. He took the book of algebra and opened it and said, "Where should I begin?" Geri said, "Choose the easiest and the hardest part of Algebra for you to teach." Paul said, "Ms. Hogg, to answer that I must tell you first that it is dependent on the intellect of the student, but I can tell you what was the hardest for me to learn." He went thru each of her requests and was very convincing. She didn't know Calculus and didn't ask him to discuss that subject.

Geri realized that Paul was a scholar and would be an asset for both she and Amy. She asked, "Paul, how long do you plan to stay in Bermuda?" He told her he had at first intended to stay only that summer. He went on to tell her more about himself. He said, "I have just finished four years of study at Harvard University in Classical Studies. I have a lot of knowledge but no practical knowledge. I am only equipped to teach, but I want a profession that will enable me to make a living. My father is very wealthy, but I don't want to do busy work for him. I want to do a man's work." Geri was amused by what he had said. She didn't think he had the staying power to do a man's work. She decided to offer him an opportunity to see what he could do.

She said, "Paul, Amy and I have worked hard all of our lives and what we have is considerable, but we got it by hard work. I find it hard for me to believe that you really want to experience what Amy and I have and do it day after day. However, I have an opening in my ship building company where I could use you as an apprentice. There is no salary, but you will have room and board. Each day from eleven to one you will teach Amy, and I will pay you a pound a week. This money will come from Amy's earning, so I hope you will make it worth her while. Will you accept this proposal?" Paul was excited about what she had said because it meant he could be with Amy. He hastily said, "I want it."

Geri sent Paul to report to Luke, and Luke would instruct him in his work. She said, "At eleven a.m. daily Amy will be waiting in our dining room with the books I have shown you." With that she dismissed him, and he was off to where Luke was standing, and they both went to the old Coles boat yard that was now called the Hogg Ship Building Company.

Luke was not at all pleased with Paul being assigned to him. He knew all about these Winfields. This family had been responsible for his being fired when his father was caught and sent back to prison. He treated Paul coldly and expected more from him than he did from his other helper. Paul felt that Luke didn't want him working for him and was trying to get him to quit. Paul was out of condition for the type of work that he was doing, but he was determined that he would make it.

When eleven o'clock came, he was exhausted and staggered to his first lesson with Amy.

When he saw Amy all of his fatigue disappeared, and he began to grin like a Cheshire cat. They sat down and opened the book on algebra. The next two hours passed quickly, and he was surprised by how quickly Amy learned. When they ended their session, Amy said, "Paul, I want to concentrate on my reading. Will you assign me some books that I can read? I know that you have had a classical education, and I want to be familiar with classical readings. I come from the MacMoyre family, and my family is the keeper of the Book of Armagh. Geri adopted me, and I am now a Hogg, but I am very proud of my MacMoyre family."

Paul was surprised by what Amy had told him. He said, "I am going to write my aunt to see if she has any classical books." He was late getting back to his work, and Luke told him he would have to work late to make up for it. This didn't bother Paul as he was still glowing over being with Amy. Paul missed supper because he had not finished the work Luke had assigned him. When he did get to the house, Amy was waiting for him and had a hot meal on the table in the kitchen. Paul ate slowly so that he could have more time with Amy, and when he was finished, he went to the basement and went to sleep.

Chapter 17

Paul slept deeply, and only awakened when Luke rolled him out of the bed. This angered him, and he talked back to Luke. Luke slapped him hard, and he fell down to the floor. Luke said, "Stay down because if you get up I will beat the hell out of you." To Luke's surprise, Paul got up, and Luke knocked him down again. By this time the people upstairs could hear their words and the noise of their fighting. Geri sent O'Rourke down to see what was happening.

When he arrived, he found Paul was giving Luke as much as Luke was giving Paul. What neither Luke nor O'Rourke knew, Paul was on the Harvard boxing team and had won many bouts. It became obvious that neither one was going to give up, so O'Rourke broke them up and told them to wash up and come to breakfast. He said, "I will not tolerate any fighting in this house." They grudgingly quit, and both came to breakfast. Both showed signs of their fight.

After breakfast Geri told Luke and Paul to come to her office. When she asked what happened, Paul said, "I started it." Luke, at the same time said, "I did." Geri said, "Luke, you know your situation here. I will not tolerate fighting. You two must find some way to work together. Paul, I expected better of you. If you can't get along with Luke, I will have to find another tutor for Amy." She dismissed them, and they went to work.

Neither one said a word, and the rest of the day went in silence. That night Paul wrote a letter to his Aunt Agatha telling her of his change of plans and requesting a dictionary and any classical books she had. When she received the note, she packed up some books and a dictionary and drove to the Wilbourne Ship Yard which now had the name the Hogg Ship Building and Repairing Company. She went into Geri's office and requested to see Paul Winfield. Geri said, "He is working and cannot be disturbed. He will be giving a lesson to my sister at eleven. You can see him at that time." With this comment Mrs. Robert Downs thought that she, Agatha Downs, had never been treated this way and was nonplussed. She meekly sat down in an adjoining room and waited for Paul.

At fifteen to eleven Amy walked in. She said hello and asked if she could help. Agatha was pleased by her greeting and said that she was Paul Winfield's aunt, and she had brought some books he had asked for. Amy was excited to meet Paul's aunt and said that Paul would be there in a few minutes. She continued saying, "Paul is my instructor." Now Agatha knew why Paul was here. Amy in Agatha's eyes was a very beautiful young woman.

Amy had dressed especially for Paul, and she was strikingly beautiful. Her strawberry blond hair, her cute turned up nose, her full bodied feminine figure, and her big blue eyes created a striking appearance. They had been talking for a few minutes when Paul walked in. Paul looked different to Agatha. His depressed look was gone, and his eyes lit up when he saw Amy. After introductions Paul asked if she had brought any books. She said she had and inquired when he was coming home.

He said, "Aunt Agatha, I have a job here. I am tutoring Amy, and I work for Luke over at the Hogg Shipbuilding site. Right now I am supposed to be teaching Amy. Can you wait until five then I will have lots of time to talk to you?" Amy interrupted saying, "Paul, you can use my time to talk to your aunt. I have other things to do." As she was turning around to leave, Agatha said, "Thank you, Amy, but I must leave. Maybe Paul can bring you to my house this Sunday and have lunch with us. You do get off work on Sundays, don't you?" Amy said yes and plans were made for the coming Sunday.

When Agatha got home that evening, she was talking to Robert. She said, "Paul has gotten over his depression. He is working in a ship yard and tutoring an amazingly beautiful young lady. She has a cultured background. I think she is Irish." Up to this point Robert Downs was intensely interested in what his wife was saying. When she said Irish, he said, "Oh, one of those Irish emigrants. You know how I feel about them coming to Boston." Agatha said, "Get over it. I have invited her to this Sunday's lunch, and you had better be on your best behavior.

Sunday came quickly, and Paul and Amy arrived around noon. When Amy walked into their house, Robert Downs was stunned by the beauty of this young lady. She was well mannered and talked well. Robert could hardly stop talking to her. She told Robert that she was the adopted sister of Geri Hogg. When she mentioned Geri's name, Robert asked "Is she the one of whom the Governor is so proud?" Amy said, "Yes."

Eventually Agatha told Robert to give Amy a break and let her talk to her and Paul. Things went well, and when Amy and Paul left, Robert said, "What a wonderful girl Paul has found. If I were him, I wouldn't let that young lady get away. Agatha said, "I thought you said you didn't like Irish." Robert ignored that comment and said, "Did you know that her family is The MacMoyres, and they are the keepers of the Book of Armagh." Agatha smiled and thought that Robert was really stuck on Amy.

Two days passed, and Geri had a family session. All knew that Geri carried the financial burden of this transaction and were pleased that she considered them in her decisions. Geri said, "Abby and I have been going over the problems connected with her being the business manager of the Hogg Supply Company. Yes, we have decided to assume the loan of the company, and it will now be called the Hogg Supply Company. Abby's concerns of being isolated from us have been temporary solved. O'Rourke will be working with her."

Abby and O'Rourke had not progressed as much as O'Rourke had wanted, but Abby wanting him to be the connecting one, encouraged him. Abby continued keeping O'Rourke at a distance. She knew that he was a very desirable man, but she was afraid of the sexual demands that marriage promised. Finally one day she decided to talk with Geri about her sexual fears. She had just come home from work with O'Rourke, and he had kissed her. This move really confronted her with her problem. The problem was that she really liked his kiss, and for a minute relaxed in his embrace. Then suddenly she became fearful and pushed him away. She knew that she hurt him. She could see it in his face. He drew back and didn't say anything for the rest of the trip home. She tried to explain to him her fears, and tell him it had nothing to do with him, but he would not respond to her.

She started by saying, "Geri, I am having a problem with myself and Joseph. In my first marriage I had a husband that was not very interested in sex. He was thirty years older than I, and all he wanted was a companion. At first I was frustrated by his lack of interest in me sexually. As I grew older, I began to develop an aversion to anything sexual. As my husband grew older, he became unattractive physically and developed unclean habits that repulsed me. We lost any love for each other and just struggled along. His death brought relief to me. At his funeral I said to myself I would never be involved with a man. Now Joseph is falling in love with me, and I am becoming attracted to him, and all this does is make me more anxious." She paused and tears rolled down her cheeks.

Geri let Abby compose herself before she said, "Abby, you are describing to me what I would expect a virgin to say about sex as she was beginning her courtship experience. If, for example, Amy came to me with this problem, I would say relax and let your feelings direct you. Your feelings were telling you that you enjoyed his kiss. It was your bad memories that kept you from going on with your feelings. It seems to me you have a decision to make: do you want to be directed by bad memories or by the potential of a new experience. O'Rourke has a lot to offer you. He is dependable, strong and good looking, and this time he is your age. Why don't you give yourself a break and take a chance on life?"

Take a chance on life were the words that echoed in Abby's mind as she left Geri. She hurriedly started looking for Joseph. She found him in the study, and he was talking to Luke. She interrupted them and said, "Joseph, I want to talk to you alone." She started by saying, "Joseph, you have really messed up my life. Your courting had forced me to make a decision about me and you. After talking with Geri, I realize that I am living with bad memories, and they have been driving me and not letting my feelings have a say. I liked your kiss, and I now want to see where it might lead."

She had intended to say more but was interrupted by Joseph grabbing her and giving her a passionate kiss. It was her first passionate kiss, and she returned it. They stood close to each other and let their feelings take over. This time Abby did not turn away. They finally broke away and walked hand in hand to supper. They were now obviously a couple.

Luke and Paul continued being hostile toward each other. One day Paul said, "Luke, I admire your ability to do so many things well.

Whether you realize it or not, you have taught me many useful things. I spent all of my life studying, for I know not what. I am well versed in languages, literature, and math, but these do not pay bills and certainly do not prepare me to have a good job with a craft to back me up. You have all of this, and you got it all by yourself. Luke, you amaze me, and I would like to be your friend."

Luke was surprised by what he had heard. He didn't say anything for a while. He was reviewing in his mind about why he disliked Paul. It all went back to his being a Winfield Luke was never going to forgive what Paul's father had done to him. He had put a stigma on him when all he had done was to love his adoptive father. He decided he was going to have to talk to Paul about this.

He started off by saying "Paul, I have been angry with you because you carry the Winfield name. When I was just eighteen, I and my father were working in your father's ship yards in Boston. We were good workers, and I was happy and secure for the first time in my life. One day some police came into our yard and arrested my father. They claimed he was an escaped convict, and they had an extradition order to return him to Ireland to finish his sentence. He was my adoptive father. I met him just after he had escaped, and I helped him. I was about six years old at that time, and he took care of me and taught me all of the skills that I now possess. He taught me to read, write, and he introduced me to many fine books. He really saved me. My mother had abandoned me when I was about three, and I never knew my natural father. I, too, had escaped, but from an orphanage.

When they left with my father, your father came down to my foreman and ordered him to fire me. I remember it so clearly, and I can still hear his voice saying 'fire that son of a convict. I will have no criminals working on my job.' He must have black balled me, for I could not get a job in Boston. I could go on with my sad story, but now I must somehow separate you from your father if we are to be friends."

Paul knew that his father could at times be very cruel to his employees. He wondered if that was the reason he didn't want to go in business with his father. They just sat beside each other and nothing was said. When it came quitting time, they walked together back to their quarters. This was the first time they had done this. They never did talk about this conversation; they just became friends for life.

Amy and Paul were advancing rapidly with her tutoring. She studied hard and was surprisingly quick in comprehending all of her subjects. She was the kind of student that all teachers longed for. Much of Amy's effort was to please Paul, but as they progressed, she wanted to branch out and look at other ideas. In her simplistic way of thinking, she would ask questions that were very profound. She didn't let her mind get cluttered with details and showed Paul that she could do some very creative thinking. She shifted away from pleasing Paul and started challenging him intellectually. This excited him and made him very determined to have Amy for his wife. The summer passed fast, and Paul decided not to go back to Boston. He felt that his place was with Amy where ever she was. When he didn't come home his father decided to come to Bermuda and see what was going on.

CHAPTER 18

It was early September when James Winfield arrived on his yacht at the Hogg Ship Yard. Luke and Paul had gotten the old Coles yard back in shape, and they were building Bermuda Sloops. Geri had given them the authority to establish a separate division which would only build Bermuda sloops and schooners. James and Martha Winfield were rowed ashore and went directly to the headquarters of Hogg Ship Yards. When James Winfield was in a strange place, he tended to be overbearing and came into Geri's office demanding to see Paul Winfield.

His attitude irritated Geri, and she told him to leave her office as she did not tolerate any demanding people in her office. Winfield refused to leave so Geri gave two tugs to her bell. They lived in a tough neighborhood, and they had this signal that would alerted the yard men there was a problem in the office. Instantly two strong men appeared and took Mr. James Winfield and his wife back to their row boat and told them in no uncertain terms not come back because if they did they would regret it. So, for the first time, Mr. James Winfield was told off. They went back to their yacht and sailed to St. George.

They were rowed to his sister's house and arrived there with James being very angry and feeling that he had been insulted. Martha had different feelings. She started talking before James could and said, "James had his first comeuppance. He finally found someone who was not intimidated by him. In fact he was intimidated by her. Do you know anybody by the name of Hogg?" Agatha replied, "You must have run into Geri Hogg. She is one of our leading citizens and is the favorite of our Governor. She was responsible for helping the Governor rid a large segment of our criminal element. Don't mess with Geri. The government respects her, and she is a large employer of Bermuda." She turned to James and said, "You may be a big shot in Boston, but you will never have the influence in Boston that she has in Bermuda." With this being said James sank into his chair and said nothing.

He was in deep thought. This was the first time he had to consider his behavior. He had often wondered why his only son never wanted to work for him. He took courses that had nothing to do with his business. Was his son afraid of him or did he find the idea of working for him disagreeable? He had always assumed that the only way to get ahead was by being strong and demanding. If people were afraid of this behavior, it was their problem. Now, probably it was his problem. He wanted to talk to Robert and Agatha about himself.

That night he opened the conversation by relating this afternoon's experience. He said, "I have always bullied my way in my world and my business. Today I was bullied, and I didn't like it. Martha has put up with me all of these years, but my son has not. My behavior has driven him away from me. I had come here thinking that I could talk him into coming back and working with me. I apparently was going to use my typical bullying technique. I realize now that doesn't work with some people, particularly my son. He apparently chose not to confront me and thought distance would serve his purpose. I have been thinking many thoughts over these past few hours about my life.

My father was a gruff demanding man, and he built the company I now have. I worshipped my father, and I took his style of living as my own, and I feel that it has served me well as far as business goes. I am now looking at my family. We had two children. Our daughter married a nincompoop, and she has nothing to do with us. Now our son has drifted into another relationship, and I fear that I have lost him too." Martha came over and put her arm around him.

As they sat in silence, Robert Downs cleared his throat and said, 'James, when Paul came here he was depressed. He felt that he had no way to earn a living, and he didn't want to fall into a position that you created. He wanted to do something on his own. He didn't talk about not wanting to work for you as much as he wanted to decide his own future. It was Agatha saying he should tutor that led to where you see him now, and a beautiful young lady with whom he is now her tutor. They have visited us, Paul and Amy, and I am infatuated with her. I don't think that Paul has given up on you; I just think he wants to be his own boss. You need to realize that Paul is a quiet type person and will probably not ever use your style of management. I like my nephew, and I think that we should give him a chance to see what he can do. Right now, he and a fellow named Luke McGinty are running Geri's ship building company. You would be surprised about how skillful he has become. He has only been working there for a little over three months. He seems to have a natural talent to do what he is doing."

James Winfield listened quietly to Robert. There was no more conversation about what had happened. That night, when James and Martha were lying together and talking, James said, "Martha, I thank God that you have stood by me. I realize that I have alienated my children, and I am sure that I have not had a happy family. All of my struggles seem so worthless. I have a large company, but I buy loyalty. I don't know what I am going to do, but I am going to do something that will be different." They went to sleep holding each other.

CHAPTER 19

Geri had been busy the last three months acquiring business for her yard and starting two new enterprises. She told herself that she needed to stop and take an inventory of where she was and where she was going. Many things had happened that were different from her original plans. She had not made it to Halifax, and for now she had lost Culum. She wondered if she had really fallen in love with him. He was attractive and persistent in pursuing her. Was she flattered by this attention or something else? These thoughts were going nowhere, and she shut off these thoughts.

She went back to her wanting to establish a shipping-trading business. Was this a possibility? Bermuda was in a good location to trade with the United State and the West Indies. She had wanted Amy to become skillful in sailing with the idea that she would be one of her ship Captains, but she was noticing how interested she was in Paul Winfield. Paul was a surprise to her. He amazed her how rapidly he learned shipbuilding. She realized that Paul had a very good teacher, and Luke was a very capable ship builder.

Where did Luke get those skills? She remembered O'Rourke's conversation with him, but she didn't think this conversation explained all about Luke. She must engage him more. Abby and O'Rourke were engaged and were to marry at Christmas. She needed to build a small cottage for them. All of this was important, but she was avoiding considering her own life. She did not want to be a widow all her life. She wanted to remarry and give Robert a father. As it looked now there was no one available except Luke. Luke had come into her life when he was casing the yard for his client. She felt he was attracted to her, but since his injury and his sentencing, he had been distant and resentful concerning her. This relationship was going nowhere. She finally decided that her new direction was to build a fleet of Bermuda Sloops and maybe a few Schooners and start a trading company.

She may have thought that her relationship with Luke was not going anywhere, but Luke had other ideas. He was now in charge of the Hogg Ship Building Yard. He was in his own element, and he was going somewhere. His current situation with Geri was limited by his being bonded to her. For Luke this was a minor irritation. He and Paul were still basement people. He knew that this would have to change because of Geri's increased dependence on him. He knew that Geri was interested in having a trading company.

He decided to talk to O'Rourke about their breaking in the Bermuda sloop that he and Paul had just finished repairing. He had been studying about this boat and was concerned. The boat was very light and carried very little ballast. This was an advantage as it allowed the boat to carry more goods and have a bigger crew. What it gained in lightness, it lost in stability as it could capsize more easily. The deep hull was very stiff, and the red cedar made it light and strong. It was an open sea vessel, and the fore and aft rigs allowed it to sail upwind. He knew with a good crew he would have a fast boat, and a boat that would function well as a trading boat.

It was in Mid December when the Sloop was launched. He had long talks with O'Rourke about the sailing of this boat. He told O'Rourke that he had considerable experience in sailing, and the rigging of this boat had just what he was weaned on. The day of the launching came, and O'Rourke, Paul, and Luke were to sail it. O'Rourke had persuaded Geri to okay Luke to be Captain of the sloop.

There were strong winds from the west, and when they hoisted the sail, it grabbed the wind, and it was off with a surge. It sailed like a racing boat, and Luke handled it with ease. In just a few minutes the sloop was out of sight. Geri was worried as this wasn't the plan. They waited for two hours when it suddenly appeared from the south. It had sailed around the main island and had done it in that period of time.

Geri had mixed feelings; one of joy and one of concern that Luke had not followed the test plan. When they had moored the sloop, they came ashore, and they were exuberant about how the sloop had sailed. Their excitement overcame Geri's ill feelings, and she found herself saying that she and Amy wanted to sail with them as they wanted to feel the power of their new boat.

Off they went and sailed until it was dusk. As they were walking to their house, they were all shouting and having a great time. At supper that night O'Rourke got up and drank a toast to Luke ending by saying "our new Captain". This was further along than Geri wanted to go, but she drank a toast to him. That evening the talk was all about their new trading boat. Luke had a new position in the family now.

James Winfield had not gone back to the yard and after a week sailed back to Boston. He thought it was best not to interfere in his son's life, and he had hoped that they might someday have a better relationship. He did try to reconnect with his daughter. He quit calling her husband a nincompoop. He engaged him and started a relationship with him. He was surprised that he was an intelligent fellow and was successful in his field of writing. In time his daughter and her husband would have routine Sunday dinners with them. There was no direct contact with Paul, but Agatha kept them informed of his activities.

In December she wrote that the past Sunday Paul and Amy dropped in along with Luke McGinty and Geri. They had just launched a new Bermuda sloop. They stayed for two hours and left around 3 p.m. They said it would take them only 30 minutes to get to their yard. Luke McGinty was a name that James Winfield remembered. He had never forgotten that day when McGinty's father was arrested. He regretted what he had done that day. He should not have fired that young man. It seemed strange to him how of all of the people in the world, why did it happen that his son was now a close friend of Luke McGinty? Did Luke know of Paul's connection with him?

It was now 1835 and much was going to happen in that year. By midsummer they had two more Sloops, and Luke had made two trips to the Turk Islands and bought salt and taken it to Savannah, Georgia. They made a big profit. They were soon carrying grain, cocoa, brandy, and wine from the coastal United States to the West Indies. They were making so much money that all of the family was on salary and were to get yearly bonuses. One of the sloops was to be a fishing boat, and the other was to be a coastal vessel sailing mainly around the Bermuda Islands.

When O'Rourke and Abby moved into their cottage, Luke and Paul came out of the basement. After Luke's successful run to

Savannah, things began to change between him and Geri. Luke made it very clear that he was interested in Geri, but she was reluctant to even considerate him as a suitor. She admired him, but as long as he was bonded to her, she could not see a future with him. Luke was frustrated by this, and he went to the Governor and asked if he could do anything to lift his being bonded to Geri. The Governor gave Luke no real hope. He knew that he would have to do something to get the Governor to change his mind.

The trading was becoming so lucrative that piracy was beginning to reappear in the Caribbean. Luke felt that he was going to have to arm his sloop. He went to the British Naval yard in Bermuda and asked their advice on what to do in order to arm his sloop. He found that the English Navy had been using the Bermuda sloop as a war ship for nearly a century. In fact it was a Bermuda sloop that had warned Nelson of the French at Trafalgar and also brought news to England of Nelson's death. After arming it with three guns, he resumed his sailing to the West Indies. He had some trouble getting sailors that could aim and fire his guns. He got O'Rourke to check the docks to see if any men had these qualifications. He finally found three ex-naval men that fit his needs.

Luke realized that he had no experience in fighting with cannons. He tried to find books on gunnery and how to engage in naval warfare. This was a problem that books didn't solve. As he studied further and talked to British naval officers, he began to realize that the opportunities of battle determined many outcomes. In other words being alert and adaptive won naval encounters and won battles. He was uncomfortable with this fact, but this was all he could do. Before any voyage, he would have gun drills, and this included firing of his guns at a target.

The next voyage was without trouble, and Geri began insisting that she and Amy alternate on going on these trading missions. Geri had developed good managers in her yard, and she felt that she had more freedom. So on the next trip she went with Luke to the Turk Islands. On the way back to Savannah they were accosted by pirates. Luke could see that the pirate was rigged with sails that could not go upwind. Instead of fighting the pirate ship Luke put his sloop into the wind and sailed away from the pirates.

Geri was much impressed by Luke and was thinking more and more about Luke as a suitor. She found herself looking closely at his physical body and imagining her with it. It surprised her that she would have these thoughts. She realized they were sexual feelings for Luke but caring for him seemed to escape her.

Amy and Paul had advanced greatly in her studies, and they were beginning to study Calculus. They had already studied Newton's laws, and the astronomy connected with it. She understood the movements of the planets and with O'Rourke's help studied the stars that were used in navigation. Amy had a natural bent for Philosophy particularly argumentation. As this knowledge grew, she would like to test her ideas by using argumentation to forward her ideas. This helped her clarify her thinking. When Paul would take her to political meetings, she would impress people by the clarity of her thinking. In many ways Amy was becoming Paul's Pygmalion. Slowly Amy was becoming Paul's equal in knowledge and thinking ability. This pleased them, and their romance grew. Toward the end of 1835 Paul asked Amy to marry him. Amy was pleased, but her answer surprised Paul. She said, "Paul, I am too young to marry. I know that I love you, but I want be a mature bride. I am still a teenager, and I don't want to be raised by you. Geri has talked to me about marrying too young as she did. She said that she married the first man that came along that showed kindness and caring for her. He was more mature than she, and it limited her ability to handle his early death. I want to be full grown before I marry you." In Paul's eyes she was full grown and mature, but this was not Amy's feeling.

Chapter 20

Towards the end of 1835 Luke had just returned from Savannah, Georgia. As he stepped ashore on the dock, a shot was fired, and the bullet just missed his head. Luke instinctively ducked and ran for cover. There were two more shots and near misses. The security guard started firing back at the assailant, and the searching fire ceased. Luke ran to the safety of the closest building and caught his breath. He instantly knew what had happened. Someone had marked him for death. His mind went immediately to his criminal career and wondered who might want him dead and why.

The first thought was Robert Coles. This idea didn't make sense as to place a mark on someone required much money, and he knew the Coles family was nearly broke, and their trial was coming up in one week. At this point Geri ran into the building where Luke had taken refuge and rushed up to Luke and hugged him tightly. There were tears in her eyes, and she was saying, "Oh, Luke, I was afraid I had lost you. I had kept you out of my feelings and didn't know how much I loved you until I was told that someone was trying to kill you. I have been a fearful woman, and I have been reluctant to admit that I loved you." Her words stopped then because Luke was hungrily kissing her, and she was returning it.

When they pulled back from each other, they walked with arms around each other to the house. As they settled down Luke was telling Geri that someone had marked him for death. The assault on him was done by a professional killer, and it would take much money to hire such a person. I first thought that it was the Coles, but they don't have any money." Geri interrupted him saying this apparently was not so as William Coles was again able to hire an expensive lawyer who would manage his trial that was finally being held next week.

This started them wondering where and why he was getting so much money, and how could this be connected with Luke. Luke said, "When I was a criminal, I was sought out by many of the prominent business men of Bermuda to help them eliminate business competition. I was successful in this as I could do their wishes, and no one suspected me or the businessmen. I would be very threatening to these business men if I was called to testify at William Coles' trial." Geri inquired who these men were. Luke named six prominent business men who were very successful. Geri was very surprised and said that they should go immediately to the Governor and tell him what he had just told her. Luke said, "Geri, if I went to the Governor with this, I would be confessing to a series of crimes. I could be put in jail for the rest of my life." Geri replied, "Doesn't your pardon apply for this?" Luke said, "It was a temporary pardon subject to my not being connected with any other criminal behavior. The Governor could easily interpret this confession as a violation of my pardon."

Geri had always been pro active in her dealing with life's problems. She said to Luke, "Let me handle this problem. I will go to the Governor, and I will get you a permanent pardon. You just stay alive." She didn't wait for his reaction and was out the door. It took her only thirty minutes to get to the Governor's office, and she said to the secretary that she needed to talk to the Governor immediately, for she had very important information for him. The secretary knew from past experience that the Governor would be very interested in what Geri had to say and conveyed the message to the Governor.

At that very moment the Governor was talking to his prosecuting Attorney about the Coles' Trial. They were troubled by William Coles' recent ability to defend himself. He told his secretary to let Geri come in without delay. This time Geri was at ease in addressing the Governor and said, "I have come with some very important information that will help you with your trial of Mr. Coles, and also help you rid our community of some despicable prominent business men."

Both the Governor and the Prosecuting attorney were nonplused and asked quickly what information did she have that would do so much. She said, "Before I can proceed, I am going to need a permanent pardon in writing of Luke McGinty. It must pardon him from all of his previous criminal behavior. He has just been marked for assassination, and one attempt has been made on his life. He has made plans to leave Bermuda for good as he feels that if he leaves the death contract will be removed. I have been able to persuade him to stay until I could talk to you as I think it is important that his information should belong to you our government."

Both men were having a difficult time absorbing all of what Geri was saying. The first one to speak was the Prosecuting Attorney. He had some idea of what information that Luke might have, and he wanted it desperately. He said, "Governor, I think I know the information that Luke has, and if I am right, it would be a strong blow against criminal behavior in Bermuda. After all you were going to give him his permanent pardon in a year so why not now as I think you will be very pleased with what he can tell us."

The Governor thought for a while and said, "Geri, you have always been a comfort to me. You have done much to help our islands. I need to ask you why you are doing this; I mean, serving as advocate for a bonded criminal." She replied, "I have been in close contact with Luke for almost two years. I have learned to admire him for his honesty, loyalty, and his courage. When I saw people shooting at him and possibly killing him I knew that I had fallen in love with him, for the loss of him would devastate me." The Governor thought as usual Geri was completely honest about her motivations and smiled to himself and said, "I will do as you request, and you will have in your hand before I question Luke his complete unconditional pardon."

While the papers were being written up, Geri continued telling the Governor and the Prosecuting attorney that one of the people that Luke had information on was high up in his administration, and she feared about the secrecy of this meeting. She said, "When Luke comes forward with his information, these people will redouble their efforts to kill him. I want you to protect Luke during these next few days." High up in his administration upset the governor, and he could hardly wait for the pardon papers to be prepared for his signature so that he could have this information. While they waited, he ordered a military escorts to go to Hogg Yards, and bring Luke safely to his office.

The escort arrived to the Hogg Yards and insisted that Luke accompany them. They told him he was not under arrest that the Governor simply wanted to get him safely to his office. On the way to the office they were attacked two times at congested crossroads. All of the attacks were directed against Luke. When they arrived, the Captain of the guard reported the two attacks, and it confirmed the fact that there was a leak most likely in his own administration.

All sat down, and the Governor gave Luke his official unconditional pardon. With that the prosecuting Attorney started interviewing Luke about his experiences. Both men were shocked by what they learned. The exact reporting of what had happened, and how it was done, was amazing to both of them. They realized they were hearing the confessions of a master criminal. Both commented that they were glad he had given up his criminal activities. Geri and Luke were to stay at the Governor's house until the Coles trial was over and maybe longer. All of the people Luke reported were quickly rounded up and put in prison without bail. They all would have quick trials, but they still had influence outside jail and could harm Luke.

The Coles trial came, and all of the evidence was so compelling that the trial was almost over before it started. William and Robert were given twenty years of hard labor and the other men received like sentences. The high official was a high ranking Judge and was a shock to all. His sentence was the harshest of all. He was to be hanged as he was the one actively seeking the killing of Luke. This sentence seemed harsh to Geri and Luke, but when they confronted the Governor about it, he told them, "Many decisions this Judge made have been biased by his criminal activity and have been damaging to honest people. The others only damaged one person, and it was only their business, but this Judge damaged the lives of these people, and there is nothing I can do to correct it."

Chapter 21

After all of these legal proceedings had been done and things had settled down to where they could live their lives more normally, Geri insisted that they be married. Strange as it may seem, it was Luke that was hesitant. He still feared the mark that was put out for him was still in place as these influential people had enough money to continue this assignment from prison. For after all, he was the cause of their incarceration, and they should be full of feelings of vengeance. Geri said, "Luke, I am not going to let anybody kill you. You can count on that." They both laughed at this statement and Luke said, "Okay, you have been a widow once just be sure that it doesn't happen again."

So in late 1835 they were married. An interesting thing had happened to the Hogg family. Due to the two episodes where Geri and Luke had been instrumental in removing large criminal elements in the Bermuda population, they had become accepted by all of the prominent families of Bermuda.

The next five years were filled with consolidating efforts. Luke was spending much time with Robert who was six years old trying to establish a relationship and giving him a father that he had never had. Luke knew all about giving a father to an orphaned boy as that was his experience. As he would work with Robert, he would think of all of the times he had wished for a father to work with him when he was a boy. These thoughts brought about memories of his adoptive father. It had now been 7 years since his adoptive father had been returned to prison in Ireland. He wondered if he could get in touch with him.

One morning quite early, he was sitting drinking his coffee and in walked Amy. They started talking about their past, and Amy talked about how much she missed her family in Ireland. As they were talking, his previous thoughts came into focus again, and he asked Amy if her family had any influence in Ireland. Amy, with pride, said, "My father is the keeper of the Book of Armagh." Luke knew that sounded important, but he also knew that it was just a religious document and not a political document.

He continued with his concerns and discussed with Amy how he wanted to find out about his father who was in some prison in Ireland. Amy said, "What is his name?" Luke said, "I don't really know because we never really talked about names. You see, my name is McGinty, but I invented that because I had no name.

When my mother put me in front of the orphanage, I was only two or three years old, and she left no information about my background. My adoptive father did not want to discuss his real name because he was fearful of discovery, and he went by John Jones." Both of them were puzzled as to how he could further explore this. Amy said, "Didn't you tell us once that Paul's father fired you?" Luke said, "Yes, and it took me forever to forgive Paul for that." Amy continued, "His father had to read the extradition papers and probably knows the real name of your adoptive father." Luke was impressed by how smart Amy was and said, "Let's get in touch with Paul immediately."

Paul had just come in from a trip to the Turk Islands and was sleeping late. Amy said, "I will get Paul immediately." She always liked to be with him when he came back. When she went into his room and gently waked him, and he saw who was there, he reached up and pulled her down and gave her a big kiss. She protested, but obviously she was pleased. She said, "Paul, stop this. I have come to get you because Luke needs you. Hurry up and get dressed, and we will be in the kitchen having our breakfast." When Paul arrived, they explained to him the problem, and he knew exactly what to do. He said, "I think we need to discuss this with Geri as I know she has been planning to open a market in Boston."

As he was saying this, Geri walked in and Luke said, "We have been talking about my adoptive father whom I have always called John Jones. Amy has been suggesting to us that Paul's father might have records of the extradition of my adoptive father. When Amy awakened Paul, and he got involved in our discussion, he said that you had been talking to him about opening a market in Boston. I immediately started thinking that maybe we need to make a trip to Boston, all of us, you,

Amy and Paul. I want to explore this possibility of finding my father, and you starting a new market there."

As these ideas were expanding and all were getting excited about it, Amy suddenly said, "Paul, this is 1838, and I am now 20 years old. I am not going to mature much more than I am now. It is time we were married."

This was the kind of news Paul had dreamed of all of these years. He was overwhelmed with feelings and all he could do was kiss Amy in a long, tender kiss. Amy continued, "Paul, I want to meet your family. I don't want to be another cause that will separate you from your family. I want them to accept me before we are actually married." Paul said, "My father is a very rigid person, and I have long felt I could not reconcile myself with him. I have no objection of waiting until they meet you, but I have no intention of letting them separate me from you. Amy, you are my whole life. Without you, I would be lost. I have loved you from the first instance I saw you and looked into your bright blue Irish eyes. At first, I didn't realize how intelligent you were, but you rapidly told me. I love you dearly and will always love you." All were silent as they witnessed this expression of love, and it took a while for them to get back to the business of planning their trip to Boston.

Paul suggested that they contact his aunt and uncle in St. George and find out the situation with his father. It was Sunday afternoon when they all got into their Bermuda sloop and set sail for St. George. They rode their dingy ashore and walked up the hill to their house. Robert and Agatha Downs were surprised and pleased to see them, and more surprised when they told them the reason for their visit. They had learned to love Amy like they loved Paul. Robert and Agatha had seen Amy grow from a teenager into a beautiful young woman. They had long hoped for Amy to be their niece. When they told them, they wanted to go to Boston for Amy to meet Paul's parents and to explore opening new markets; they had some thoughts that they wanted to share with them.

Robert started off by saying, "In September of 1834, your father came and was going to convince you to return to Boston. He had an encounter with Geri and came back and stayed a week with us. He tried to bully Geri, and she bullied him back. The shock of being bullied changed your father. We have been in touch with him many times since that time.

He has written how he has reconciled with your sister, and tells us he is changing the way he is managing his company. When we told him that you, Paul, were friends with a person named Luke McGinty, he wrote back saying he knew that name well, and he was very sorry that he had fired that young man as he had no responsibility for his father being a criminal. He remarked to us that it seemed strange to him that the one person he had offended is now a friend of his son. I feel that he will be glad to see all of you, and you will have no trouble with him. I am delighted that you are going to Boston."

Paul had a hard time dealing with all this information, and he hoped it was true, but he still had serious doubts of his father's ability to change. Robert Downs said, "I am sending a letter to James on the next boat going to Boston, and I will include information about your coming visit." Paul said, "We don't know the exact time, but we would appreciate anything you can do to help us have a pleasant experience with my family."

It took three weeks to organize their enterprises so that they could be gone for a month. Geri put O'Rourke in charge of everything and felt comfortable with the maturity of her management. Abby was no longer a housewife, but a professional manager and had extended her influence with many of the projects of the family. They had to wait until the hurricane season was over before they considered going to Boston. Over the past five years they had experienced three hurricanes that had moved through Bermuda, and now were able to manage any damage that these hurricanes caused.

Paul said, "The winter is a very bad time to go to Boston. Northeasterners are very common, and it is very unpleasant sailing." They would wait until spring of 1839 to go to Boston. By then Geri and Luke had two children—a boy named Luke II born on February 19, 1837 and a baby boy Paul born on January 11, 1839. All children were to go with them.

They took their newest Bermuda sloop. It had been enlarged in length and had an extended bow sprite. This gave the ship a greater sail area so that they were able to move much faster. Most of the winds were coming from the west so for most of the trip the boat was heeled to the starboard side. It was about 500 miles to Boston, and it took them three days. When they sailed into Boston Harbor, they were surprised to see that people had lined the docks because this was a new ship for them to see.

After the boat had been moored, several ship Captains asked about the boat. The amount of sail that was available on the boat impressed them, and they asked where they were from. Paul said, "We came from Bermuda and got here in three days." That was very surprising to them, and they inquired where they had gotten such a boat. Paul proudly said, "We made it—the McGinty/Hogg Shipyard of Bermuda." One of the Captains said, "Oh, I know about that place. Culum Rafin is always talking about some woman down there who built wonderful boats."

Geri heard Culum's name, and asked the Captain where did he know Culum. He said, "Culum makes the trip between Halifax and Belfast and does that four to six times a year. Several months ago I was in a bar in Halifax and met Culum. It seems any time he gets a chance to talk about this woman, he does." This brought old memories back to Geri, but she had her man now, and Culum was history.

Paul hired a carriage to take them to his father's home. They arrived in the early afternoon, and his mother and sister were there. Everyone was so excited to be with Paul, and his new family. When they heard that Amy and Paul were to be married, there was nothing but joy.

The next few hours were spent with sharing information about what had happened with both families during the past five years. Paul's sister, Caroline, told Paul, "Our father has changed remarkably since he returned from Bermuda and was not able to talk to you. Mother knows how he felt as they were sailing back on their yacht, and she can tell you that he was deeply touched by his failure as a father. He felt that he had bullied you, and his family had not been shown love and understanding. He wanted to change, and I was the first one with whom he changed. He didn't tell me to come to see him; he came to me, and he asked me to forgive him for all of his bad behavior that had separated us. Father said, 'I have not accepted your husband as he is a writer, and I felt he was a non-contributing person to the economy. I know I am wrong to feel that way, and I want to change that. I am sure I have offended your husband in many ways. Will you help me reconnect with him, so I can try to find a better relationship with him? I know he is important to you, and therefore he is important to me, and I am going to see that it happens.'

Paul, you can guess how surprised I was to hear him talk like that—surprised and happy—and over the next few weeks, my father and my husband developed a warm relationship. You know dad was always a no-nonsense person who felt that reading literature was a waste of time. I will have you know that has all changed. He's read all of my husband's works and has sought him out to instruct him on reading classical literature. He said to my husband, 'I want to study classical literature because Paul was attracted to classical works, and I want to know about them so I can be knowledgeable of that part of Paul's life.' Paul, he has missed you terribly and I feel that you will have no trouble with dad when he comes home tonight."

The rest of the afternoon was pleasant, and when the carriage brought James Winfield to the house, all were waiting to greet him. He was greatly surprised, and the joy at seeing Paul again was only expressed by tears that rolled down his cheeks. He grabbed his son and hugged him tightly. They didn't say anything for a while, just holding each other and feeling all of the lost years.

Paul's father couldn't wait to find out why they were here. Paul said, "The most important reason is for you to meet my wife to be, Amy Hogg." Amy came over to her future father-in-law and hugged him and gave him a kiss on his cheek. That one gesture stole his heart away. He thought she was the most beautiful young lady he had ever seen. He soon found that it wasn't just her beauty that was attractive as she was a very intelligent young lady. It took a long time for all of them to settle down, and no business was discussed. This was just to be a family reunion, and business would come later.

The next morning Geri and Luke sat down with Paul's father and expressed a desire to find out what happened to his adoptive father. Before Luke could get started, Paul's father interrupted and said, "Oh, Luke, I was a terrible person in those days. I thought the only way to manage people was to overpower them and to sometimes be ruthless. I offended you then, and I had no reason to fire you. You were a competent worker. I should have helped you and not hurt you. I don't know what else to do except to say that I am sorry and being sorry does very little to comfort your pain. Can you ever forgive me?" Luke responded, "Mr. Winfield, for years I hated you beyond reason. It took a friend, your son, to get me past that hatred. I regret very much that my father was returned to prison, and I have wondered what has happened to him. You probably didn't know it, but I had no name, and my father never gave me his name as he was on the run. I invented my name, and he said his name was John Jones. I know it is not his real name, and I would like to find out what it is. I feel you can help me in that regard. Is it possible that you have the extradition papers that you had that day of his arrest as they would have his real name on them?"

Paul's father responded, "Luke, may I call you Luke?" Luke said, "Yes, please." "I was always a person who kept all of his records. I have a copy of the extradition papers in a file, and I know I have the real name of your father. All we have to do is go to my office and get my secretary to find the papers." That afternoon they went to Paul's father's office, and they opened the file, and there it said that his name was Jonathan McGinty. Luke was astounded and wondered now how he had gotten the name "McGinty". He thought he had invented it, but now he wasn't so sure.

The indictment of Jonathan McGinty stated that he had committed murder of his partner and was found guilty and sentenced to life in prison at Portlaoise Prison on Dublin Road, Portlaoise, Co. Laois. Luke did not believe this was the truth. He thought his father was too gentle to be a murderer. He told Geri, "I can't let this stand. We are going to have to go to Ireland." Both knew a lot had to be done before he could do this and put all of this on the back burner. For now they would enjoy being with Paul's family. During the next week Geri and Luke discussed with Paul's father about establishing a trading post in Boston. Geri explained how she was very actively managing a fleet of sailing vessels and traded all along the coast of the United States from Florida up to Virginia. She wanted now to extend up the coast to New York, Boston, and on to Halifax, Nova Scotia. Paul's father asked her what goods she traded. Geri responded, "It depends on the market that I am trading with, and I am here to find out what markets are available for me in Boston." She continued saying, "For example, the southern states have a great need for salt, and I buy salt in the Turk Islands and trade for their goods which range from cotton, grains, whiskeys, cocoa, wine and craft products. I am constantly growing in my inventory of trade items. Recently I have been trading sugar, and I was thinking maybe there might be a market for sugar in Boston. The sugar I have to trade is the refined sugar, and not the crude brown sugar that is placed on the market so many times." Paul's father was immediately interested in the fact that she traded in sugar, whiskey and wine. He asked her what kind of whiskey did she trade. She said, "Mostly I trade in rum." Business always excited Paul's father, and he immediately became aware of the opportunities this opened up for him and them. He said, "I have always been involved in building ships and other structures and have never gotten into the market of commodities, but I think that is something I should look into. Do you think you would want to partner with me?

My brother-in-law, Robert Downs, tells me that you both are very successful entrepreneurs and don't need any financing from me, so the only thing I could offer would be my connections in the Boston arena." Luke and Geri were pleasantly surprised and felt that they could let Paul and Amy stay in Boston, and in cooperation with Paul's father develop their trading post.

When they discussed this with Paul and Amy, Amy said, "I will only agree to it if Paul will marry me, and I want the marriage to be in Boston." When the family heard that Paul and Amy were going to be married in Boston, Paul's mother took over, and for the next two weeks there was hectic planning going on in the Winfield family.

Paul's parents wanted the marriage to be a grand affair, but Amy and Paul wanted it to be simple and in the family's traditional church. The only meaningful people to Amy and Paul were the people in Bermuda and Geri and Luke. Paul's family and Paul had many intimate friends, and it was hard to keep the number down, so in spite of Amy's wishes, it turned out to be a fairly large wedding. Amy and Paul were to live in his family's guest cottage, and Paul would stay there until the trading post was firmly established. They felt it would take approximately six months. So, by the end of the month, Luke and Geri sailed back to Bermuda.

Chapter 22

When they arrived back in Bermuda there was much to do to catch up on all the things that had happened in the past month. They had been designing and building a Bermuda schooner.

The schooner was a three-mast Bermuda sloop and was designed for long distance, open ocean travel. They planned to use this schooner as their means of going to Ireland. They found that the nearest port to the prison that held Luke's father was Dublin, so on June 1, 1840, they set sail with family for Dublin.

The latitude of Hamilton was 32 degrees and 18 minutes north and longitude was 64 degrees, 47 minutes west. Dublin had a latitude of 52 degrees, 21 minutes north and the longitude was 6 degrees and 16 minutes west. Their initial heading would be 44.9 degrees northeast, and they had 3,188 miles or 2,779 nautical miles to sail before they reached Dublin. It took them 19 days with their final heading being 87.2 degrees east. There were prevailing winds from the west, and they made a quick trip. Their schooner handled beautifully. It was much more stable than the sloops, and they felt a great deal of pride as they sailed into the Dublin Harbor. Needless to say, the boat was greatly admired.

As soon as they landed and went through customs, they went immediately to the prison that housed Luke's father. Jonathan McGinty had not received a single visitor in those ten years that he had been in prison. Luke was horrified to see how bad he was physically. He was unkempt and unclean. He was infuriated by the conditions in which his father was living. He could hardly stay there and talk to him because he was so upset. Geri helped him and engaged her father-in-law with questions they had both considered asking him.

The first question was did he kill the man? Luke's father said, "No, I was falsely accused, and I have thought about it for a number of years. Jim Bates was the man who was my partner, and we had a successful business which was doing well. One day when I went to work, I found him dead. He had been stabbed numerous times in the chest. I don't know why I was accused of this murder, but from some evidence I was not aware of, I was brought to trial and convicted of the murder of a man whom I deeply respected and loved.

I have been in this prison two times now, and this last time has been devastating to me. I see no hope for me, and I want to die." Geri said, "Jonathan, we are going to do two things. One, I am going to talk to the warden and find out if I can't buy a better situation for you. I understand that in the prisons that you are in that they allow members of the families to supplement their living conditions. The next thing I am going to do with your son, Luke, is to hire the best criminal lawyer that Dublin has, and we are going to research your murder charge. Luke and I don't want you to die, and we are going to do everything we can to clear you of this charge." With that, she got up and hugged that dirty old man and kissed his dirty old cheeks. This action had a profound effect on Jonathan. He thought, "Who could kiss me when I am so ugly and dirty. Luke surely found a wonderful person."

Luke and Geri left and went back to Dublin and hired the best criminal lawyer in town and told him the circumstances they wanted to explore. They told him they wanted him to research all of the court findings, and especially, the prosecutor's evidence that led to the conviction and the life sentence of Jonathan McGinty.

Callahan and Sons was a prominent law firm in Dublin, and Mr. Callahan had a long record of finding evidence on people who were falsely convicted. Since Luke had told him that they were able to finance their goal which was to free his father, they wanted no expense to be a hindrance in their search for his vindication. Luke said, "I expect you to use good judgment on this as I have opened my wallet to you on this, and I expect you to be an honest man." They didn't sign a contract; they just shook hands. Geri and Luke planned to stay in Dublin until Luke's father was liberated. They were prepared to stay six months or more.

The first thing that happened to Jonathan McGinty was that he was moved to a better cell and was allowed to bathe every day. He received better meals and had better treatment, so when they visited him a second time, he was a different man. He was clean shaven, his hair was cut, and they had given him clean prison garments. It was obvious that he now had hope for his future. Geri and Luke told him what they had done and who they had hired as his criminal lawyers. Progress went slowly at first, and Mr. Callahan found that for some reason, forces were operating that were hindering his finding information about the trial and the evidence against Jonathan McGinty. It was such an unusual structure that he was dealing with that he feared some stronger forces were at play.

He changed his direction of investigation and started trying to see who would benefit by Jonathan McGinty's incarceration. He started focusing on the nephew of his ex-partner, Mr. James Bates. He found that Bates and McGinty was a very prosperous business which in the original incorporation was owned by both partners equally. There were 15 employees in their business, and they were involved in trading commodities. The only person in the organization that caused some problems was Bates' nephew, Billy Murphy. He was an extravagant man and contributed very little to their company. Both James and Jonathan had talked frequently about what to do with Billy. James wanted to fire him and be rid of him, but Jonathan felt family was important, and he was encouraging James to try to find another way to resolve the problems they were having with Billy.

Billy was a hot-headed young man quick to temper, and when he would get angry, he had no judgment with his anger. His anger was impulsive and very destructive. When Callahan went to the offices of Bates and Company, he found that Billy Murphy was in charge of the organization. The firm had continued to be prosperous, and Billy had become very successful in involving himself in the political arena of Belfast, Ireland.

Callahan was immediately suspicious of this and began to immediately investigate more intensively Billy Murphy. The suspicions became more and more evident to him, and he began to believe that Billy Murphy was the one who had killed his uncle. He was very careful to not let Billy Murphy become aware that he was being investigated because he had a great influence in local politics. He had gone as far as he could in his investigation, but he still did not have the necessary data to convict Billy of murder, and he decided to have a conference with Luke and Geri and bring them up to date on what he had found.

Callahan started their interview with a statement that he was convinced that Luke's father was innocent and that James' nephew, Billy Murphy, was guilty of murder. He said, "I have no way to go further with this, and I wanted to consult with you to see if you have any ideas on how we could go further at this point."

Luke thought for a moment and looked at Geri as he said, "Mr. Callahan, I am a pardoned criminal. I know how the criminal mind works, and I know how to get in touch with people who know about this murder. When I was a criminal, we had our own code, and we would tell each other of crimes we committed because we knew we were safe. We told them because we were bragging or for various other reasons. Geri and I will go to Belfast, and I will connect up with the criminal element. I will find out exactly what happened to James Bates."

It took about a week for Luke to connect up with the criminal element, and he was able to find the person who had actually stabbed James Bates to death. He started following this man and hired some ruffians to waylay him. They took him to a remote area, and Luke persuaded him to talk. He had to rough him up pretty severely before he broke down and confessed what he had done. He told how a person named Billy Murphy had hired him to kill this man and paid him 100 pounds to do it.

He described the whole event of how it happened. He said, "I snuck into the building in the early morning hours and waited for James Bates to open the office door. When Bates turned to close the door, I stabbed him in the back and struggled to withdraw the knife. While I was struggling to get out the knife, Bates turned and started fighting me. It was then that I withdrew the knife and stabbed him many times in his chest trying to find his heart. Bates held on to me as he sunk to the floor and smeared blood all over me. I had to struggle to get passed him and out the building. I just missed running into the employees as I could hear them walking down the sidewalk."

Luke was horrified at this description and wondered how he was going to use it to trap Billy Murphy. He finally came to the idea that he was going to get this guy to try to blackmail Billy and hopefully in the process of blackmailing negotiations, he could have somebody to witness it and this information would stand up in court.

Before he went any further, he told his men to keep Blackie Smith, the murderer, in this building until he could contact another person to get some advice as to what to do. He promised them a bonus if they did well in this regard. He reiterated, "Do not kill this person."

He quickly drove the 100 miles to Dublin and went into Callahan's office. He described what he had done and what he had found out and asked him how he should proceed. Callahan knew that this evidence would not actually help them as the information had been gotten through duress and said they needed to find someone who was completely honest in the Belfast Police Department. It didn't take him long to discover that person who was by the name of Harry Kilkannon. Callahan and Luke went to see Mr. Kilkannon.

Callahan handled the interview. He started off by saying, "Mr. Kilkannon, we have been investigating the prosecuting office of Belfast and its police force, and we find there is considerable corruption there." They waited to see how he responded to this, but nothing was said. He just stared at them. So Callahan proceeded further. "We believe that a person in your community has been falsely accused and sent to prison for a murder he did not commit, and we have evidence of who really did the murder and why, but we fear to present this evidence as we feel the authorities would not accept it and would try to destroy it."

Kilkannon had been thinking about the situation in his police department, and he knew that it was corrupt, but up to this point, he could do nothing. He wondered if this would be an opportunity for him to deal with cleaning up the mess in his department.

He said to them, "Gentlemen, I am well aware of what you are talking about, not about this murder you are talking about, but the corruption in my department. If I pursue this with you, I jeopardize my position and maybe my life. I want to be sure that this person you're trying to save is worth it." When Luke told the name of the person and the events, he immediately remembered the case, and he knew deep down it was a put up job. He had always been ashamed of his department and their participation in that fraud. He saw this case as an opportunity to change that.

He asked them to go for a walk with him. He said, "I do not feel comfortable about discussing anything further about this in my office."

They left the building and were walking down one of the main streets of Belfast. Luke related to him what he had done and what he had discovered. He said, "I know this is illegal, but we had tried all legal means to get this information, and we were frustrated using legal means." Kilkannon knew exactly what he meant. He said, "Sometimes going beyond the law is the only way to get justice. I don't know how we are going to be able to use this man's information, but I want you to hold this man as long as you can because I am going to do some thinking about this. I don't want you and Mr. Callahan to ever come back into my office again. If we meet again, it will be at a remote place at my invitation."

It took about a week before they heard from Kilkannon, and they met in a small restaurant in a very remote area of Belfast. He said, "I want you to release the man that has made all of these confessions, and I have set him up to meet a very attractive prostitute. This man is known to have very aggressive sexual needs and has not been able to afford the better prostitutes. She works for us periodically getting information and is very good. I think when she connects up with him, we can set up a situation where legitimate people can hear his confession."

This was accomplished, and Kilkannon was able to present it, so it was not blocked by the criminal elements in his department. In fact, their efforts to block it, exposed the whole criminal elements of the department, and an investigation was started. Kilkannon was in charge of it. The investigation exposed the fraud in the prosecuting attorney's office and a number of cases were going to be retried.

Kilkannon was very grateful to Luke and saw to it that his father's problem would be the first that was attended to. When the real murderer was indicted and charged with murder, he began to confess about the involvement of Billy Murphy. Billy Murphy was arrested and charged with solicitation of murder and was convicted. Luke and Geri met Jonathan McGinty when he came out of the prison. He was much older than his years and had suffered much from his imprisonment, but these did not seem to bother him as he was so happy to be with his son and his son's wife.

CHAPTER 23

Jonathan did not want to reestablish himself in the Bates-McGinty business. He wanted to spend the rest of his life with his son and his son's family. It took more than a month to extract his interests in his business, and he left Belfast with his family a rich man. Jonathan had a different experience this time going across the Atlantic Ocean. He had the cabin of the First Mate and people treated him like a king. He thought about all of those years that he had been in that horrible prison and was thankful that he had a son and a daughter with whom to live the rest of his life.

They were going against a westward wind on their way back to Bermuda, and it took them 23 days to get to the McGinty-Hogg yards. It was in early August when they arrived, and the hurricane season was just beginning. They felt lucky to have escaped it as that was a concern all the way home to Bermuda.

Jonathan adapted well to the community of Bermuda and became well known. He was a scholarly man and well versed in many different things. He used to meditate in the evening and wondered what he should do with all his experiences. One day when he was talking to Geri about this, she said, "Why don't you write a book about your experiences?" He didn't know whether he wanted to do this as he had so many ugly memories, but then he happened to read The Count of Monte Crisco and decided that this would be a good model for him to write his own life's book.

The years rolled by and Geri and Luke had three children, two boys and one girl. The girl, Amy Geri, was born on May 5, 1841. Robert was obviously the leader of his brothers and sister and they had a very happy close family. Robert was a very adventurous boy and was always getting involved in things that were dangerous for him. He loved his mother, but he adored his father. He copied him in every way he could. He would go on the trips with his father to the West Indies and Boston. He visited Paul and Amy as they had set up a home in Boston. The Boston trading post produced much of the income that was produced by their company.

Paul had a new relationship with his father. They both learned to care for each other in a way they never expected to have. His father participated actively with Paul in his development of his new business. With his father's help the business progressed and developed into a large operation that spread from New York City to Halifax, Canada.

When Robert was 18 years old in 1848, he was spending a large amount of his time in Boston as his father wanted him to have a more involved education than was offered in Bermuda. He had special tutoring, and eventually was matriculated into Harvard University. He was a vigorous student and rapidly progressed in his courses and did not seem to have any handicap from his lack of early schooling. He graduated at the age of 22 and was having to make a decision about where he wanted to go. He loved his mother and father and longed to be with them, but there was something that kept driving him to consider Halifax.

Paul had a trading outlet in Halifax, and told Robert that he could run that business for him and see how much he wanted to stay in that area. So, here we find the family separated by many miles. Only Luke, Geri, their remaining children, Jonathon, O'Rourke, and Abby remain at the Bermuda yards. Jonathon, O'Rourke and Abby became grandparents to the children. Every two weeks Geri and Luke would get in their schooner and sail to the West Indies.

Robert had left in the fall of 1848 at the age of 18. He was 7 years old when the first child of Luke and Geri was born in 1837 and their second son was born in 1839. Their only daughter was born in 1841. So, when Robert left, Luke, Jr. was 11 years old, Paul was 9 and Amy was 7 years old. Robert felt the pain in his heart when he left because he felt he would not return for a number of years, but he also knew he must travel because it was in his blood, and he needed to experience the many different places that he had heard about from his mother and father.

Chapter 24

Robert Hogg McGinty was standing alone on the docks watching his parents and his siblings disappear from the Boston Harbor. He watched as they turned south and disappeared going around a curve in the harbor. He wondered why he was leaving the family that was so important to him. He had always been driven to go beyond the horizon and now he asked himself "Why". This stirred up many memories. He started hearing the roar of a violent storm. He was a small child, and his mother was gone. The ship was pitching and rolling, and he was so afraid. "Where is my mummy?" he wailed. He felt a deep despair. He shook his head and said, "I can't go on with this."

As he walked away from the dock, he felt strange and wondered why he did not want to think about that memory. His thoughts were too scattered to make any sense. He knew that he had awakened some emotional experiences that he didn't want to re-experience.

He started looking around at the area where he was walking, and he could smell the lilacs blooming, and the budding of the trees thrilled him, for it meant spring was nearly here. He started whistling a tune, and before he knew it, he was at his Uncle's office.

Paul Winfield was the manager of the Boston McGinty-Hogg Trading Company. His office covered all of New England and Canada. It had become the largest part of the McGinty-Hogg Trading Company. Robert walked directly into his Uncle's office not waiting for the secretary to announce him. This irritated Paul, and he told Robert that this was not the way to come into an executive's office. Paul had been training Robert to represent them in Halifax, Nova Scotia. Even though Robert had graduated from Harvard, little of its New Englandism had rubbed off. He still had the casual directness of his father. Some would consider it was bordering on rudeness. Paul Hoped that Halifax would be less sophisticated than Boston as it had only been incorporated in 1841.

Paul said, "Robert, you have understudied our procedures for the past six months. I feel that you know what needs to be done, but I don't feel that you will like the trading business. Are you sure you want to do this? I feel that you should sail more with your father and learn how to trade, but your insistence on going to Halifax puzzles me and your parents."

Robert didn't know how to answer this question. He only knew that he needed to be on his own, and he had heard his mother talking about Halifax all of his life. Besides, his natural father's sister lived in Halifax, and he wanted to know more about his Hogg family. He replied to Paul saying, "Uncle, I don't know why either. All I know is I need to get away and discover myself." Paul had those same feelings many years ago when he left his father's influence. He looked at Robert with a new interest. He said, "Robert, I think I understand what you are struggling with. In a way it sounds like me and where I was many years ago. I, too, had to get away from my father. Let me share with you some of my ideas of how I handled it, and how now, I think I should have handled it.

When I got out of Harvard, I was depressed. I had used my education to avoid dealing with my father's overbearing attitude. I was afraid that if I stayed in Boston, I would never be me but a copy of my father. Since I wasn't deciding for myself, my father directed me to go to Bermuda with the idea that I needed a vacation. You know the rest of that story. Now this is what I wished I had done. I wished that instead of running away, I had stayed and confronted my father and developed me where I grew up. I admit that by going away I found Amy and your adoptive father, for he taught me how to be a man. I wish I could have done it by myself."

Robert replied, "I have no problem with my father. He loves me, and he has spent many hours with me. He always insisted that I find myself and do what my feelings direct me to do. I have a different problem. For lack of better words, I have a wandering lust. I have to see what is beyond the horizon. It is a restlessness that drives me and keeps me impatient. I think that something is missing in me, and I can't seem to find it. It is like an itch, and it won't go away." Since neither had anything else to say, they parted, and Robert went to the docks and got a skiff and rowed to his ship. He bunked in the owner's cabin, and the Bridget B sailed at the high tide. It was a pleasant trip, and they arrived in two days.

Chapter 25

Robert was impressed by the very large harbor of Halifax. He arrived in June of 1852, and Nova Scotia had gotten the right to have a responsible government and was no longer just a British colony. He lingered on the ship and day dreamed. Was he afraid to start his new job, or did he realize that when he left the ship he was breaking his contacts with his past and maybe never see the ones he loved again? His conscious mind said, "Ridiculous, get off of the ship now!"

When he stepped off the ship onto the docks of Halifax, he didn't find it so strange. It was a British colony as was Bermuda. The only difference was that Nova Scotia had been given a responsible government. He made an early decision to house on the ship until he could find the trading post his Uncle Paul had said existed. As he searched for it, he found an empty building saying McGinty-Hogg Trading Company. To call it a building was stretching a description. He could see he was going to have to start from scratch. He thought that it would be wise to find his natural father's sister as she would know Halifax.

Finding Aunt Tabitha was not difficult, and he was received warmly by all. Tabitha Davis and her husband, Helmuth, had three children, Samuel, Harvey and Tabbie. The children were all older than Robert. When Robert arrived, Tabitha's family was in some financial difficulty. Helmuth had been injured on the job and could not work, and the two boys had been laid off. None of this was discussed initially as all wanted to get acquainted. Tabitha wanted to hear all about Geri.

Robert said, "My mother is a complex woman. Deep down she wants to be a simple housewife, but circumstances always seem to interfere with this desire. She has the ability to organize people and events in such a unique way that all benefit. I fear for her because of this ability, for people will impose on her. She is involved more in political life than is good for her. Many of her stands are good for the majority of the people but interfere with many powerful people. My father has already been targeted for assassination. My mother works too hard. I love her very much, and I feel that I did not have enough of her attention when I was growing up. I had too many people between me and my mother." As he was saying this, he teared up and that bad memory of the storm and his being without his mother came into his consciousness. He got up and turned away. He felt humiliated by crying before these people, particularly because he had no idea that he was about to cry. He knew now that he must be very careful when he talked about his mother as he had some very lonely memories connected with her. After he had wiped away his tears, he turned and said, "I am surprised by my behavior. I haven't cried in years. I must feel all alone here in Halifax. I think I had best go now and get about my business."

Tabitha would not let him leave. She knew that Geri's life had been hard, and she knew that it demanded much of her time. Robert must have had limited contact with his mother during critical periods of his life. She said, "Robert, you are not alone in Halifax. You don't know us now, but we are your relatives, your family. We Danes come from a small country, and we learn early in our lives that family is the only secure place for us. Will you let us take you into our family?" Robert was stunned. He found himself starting to cry again. Tabitha could see his distress and took him into her arms and comforted him. He relaxed and was further surprised by all of the family coming to him and hugging him.

This experience was too emotional for him, and he sat silently for a while. Tabitha and all realized he needed some time alone, and they went about their activities. After a few minutes Robert came into the room where they were and thanked them for their caring and said, "It is a warm feeling to be a part of your family." The afternoon passed slowly, and Robert stayed for supper. As he was leaving that night, he asked Sam and Harvey to come to his boat the next morning and have breakfast with him.

Both men came early to Robert's ship and they had coffee on the deck. After some casual talk Robert said. "I am starting a trading post for my mother's company. We trade commodities from and to our various trading stations. I am supposed to find what commodities that people here want to buy and what is available here that are valuable trading items."

Both of his cousins had worked on the docks and knew about shipping. They knew which products came into Halifax and which went out. They talked about this and about finding a warehouse with an office. As they were talking, Robert was trying to figure out how he could use his two cousins in his trading business. He sensed that Sam was more of a manager and Harvey was more physical in his thinking. Sam was talking about control and efficiency, and Harvey was talking about physical moving of items. By the time they finished their coffee and breakfast, Robert had hired them both.

They left the boat and went looking for a warehouse office structure. All of the prime locations were filled, and they had to look in less desirable areas. Since none of these were satisfactory, Robert decided that he would locate an office and later build a warehouse—office structure. Before they left the dock area, Robert was surprised to see a ship that had sails and a steam engine. He had heard of these ships but had never seen one. Sam said, "These ships are not uncommon." Robert wondered what they would do to ocean trade and travel.

His next great surprise was that Nova Scotia had an electric and telegraph company. The telegraph company really excited him. He went immediately to their offices and asked if they were connected to Boston. To his surprise he was told that Halifax, Nova Scotia had connected with the New Brunswick Electric in 1850 and that gave them a direct connection with Boston. Robert immediately sent a telegram to his Uncle Paul saying, "Arrived June 21 stop trying to find an office stop get Boston papers in three days stop. Robert." He felt a great relief as he no longer was isolated from the rest of the company. After this diversion they went to the local Hotel Caledonia. They had lunch and sought out a person that might handle rental properties. They found an office that was close to the dock and rented it and started their business.

The first thing of importance was to sell their goods. The ship Bridget B was loaded with salt and sugar. Robert had flyers printed, and Sam distributed them to all of the interested businesses. There was a rush for his cargo, and he felt the best way to sell it was by auction, either by the whole cargo or partials depending on the bidding. All bids were subject to his approval. Sam helped out with the bidding, and Harvey would distribute the goods as they were bought. Things went well, and the McGinty-Hogg Trading Company did very well.

While all of this was going on, Robert had hired Helmuth to search out products that they could ship out to their other locations. His main findings were salted cod, furs and lumber. The lumber was too bulky, but salted cod and furs fit well. He tried out Helmuth's skill in bargaining and was pleasantly surprised about his ability to bargain. So in three weeks he had started their new Trading Company and shipped out their first boat load of goods.

Paul telegraphed, "Goods arrived stop will ship regularly salt and sugar stop congratulations stop Paul." The whole trading exchange produced a large profit, and Robert deposited it in a local bank and established a relationship so that if he needed some rapid cash it would be available up to 5000 pounds. Sam was amazed by this amount of money, and all of the Davises were duly impressed.

Robert and Helmuth liked talking to each other, and on one occasion, Robert asked him if he knew anybody that was a good builder. Helmuth replied, "Robert, I was in the building business when I was injured. I helped build the Caledonia Hotel and other large projects." Robert asked, "What was your position in those projects?" Helmuth replied, "I was the construction superintendent when I was injured. I had started out as a carpenter's assistant and worked up to superintendent." Robert knew that a project like the Hotel Caledonia was complicated by the electrical, heating and plumbing and wondered how he performed in these areas. Helmuth said, "I knew enough about those projects so that I could tell good work and tell whether I was being over charged." Helmuth asked, "Why are you asking me all of these questions?" Robert smiled and said, "I am interviewing you for my building project. I was greatly impressed by your dealing with the purchase of the furs that we shipped out, and I wanted to find a way to hire you for my business. I need to build a warehouse with an office and an apartment with indoor plumbing. Can you do this?" Helmuth replied with a simple yes. With that, construction began on September 1, 1852. All construction was completed by February, 1853.

All of the problems of establishing his trading post were in place, and now he was going to focus on where his trading goods came from and where there was a potential for other trading goods. He quickly realized that most of the cod came from the Grand Banks located off the French islands of St. Pierre and Miquelon. The inhabitants of these islands spoke only French. This started him on a search for a French language teacher.

The only one in Halifax was Jeanette Levesque. When he found her, she informed him that she had a full schedule and could not accommodate him. She suggested that he use her daughter who had just arrived from Boston. She had been away for four years studying. He had some doubts about this but agreed to start with her on the next Monday.

At ten o'clock Monday Robert arrived at the Levesque studio and met Joanne Levesque, his French language teacher. She was a strikingly beautiful young lady. She had long curly reddish blond hair that hung down to her shoulders and beautiful blue eyes. She was about five feet, six inches tall and was a well formed young woman. He was so taken by her beauty that he handled his introduction very clumsily. She was very professional with him and gave no indication that she noticed his attraction for her. She inquired about his education and was not impressed by his attending Harvard. They began with how to pronounce the alphabet in French. She said. "The vowels are pronounced in the back of the mouth. The French language does not recognize the vowel shift of the English language. So, for example, the letter "A" in French is pronounced "Ah" not "A". "Ah" is in the back of the mouth and the English "A" is pronounced in the front of the mouth." The lesson lasted for an hour, and she assigned him a book on pronunciation of French words. She said, "We will concentrate on speaking French first and then grammar and reading."

When he left, he was quite taken with Joanne. He wanted to find out more about her. Joanne saw her mother later in the day, and she reported what an interesting student she had. She said, "He is about six feet tall, and he is very handsome. He looks very strong, but I like his large brown eyes. They appear sad, but as we studied together, his eyes began to sparkle. I think he is a complex man, but I instantly liked him." Joanne's mother replied, "I have met him, too, and I didn't see what you saw. To me he was just a young business man seeking how to get more business by speaking French." Joanne said, "Mother, you must be getting old not to see how attractive this Robert is." They both laughed and got busy fixing supper.

Robert had much to do. He needed to connect with the primary producers of the products he wanted to trade. He decided to see if Sam had any ability in this area. He said to Sam, "Do you have any knowledge where most of the cod are sold?" Sam responded, "Local fishermen fish off the Great Banks. They usually have their main purchasers and are under some kind of agreement with them." "Are you saying that they will only deal with those purchasers?" asked Robert. Sam replied, "Yes." Robert knew that he had to get some primary providers if he was going to maximize their profits. If all of the Grand Banks fishermen of Halifax were tied up to agreements, then he needed to seek other locations.

Chapter 26

He looked at his maps of this area and noted Sidney was on the north island of Nova Scotia. It seemed to be a fairly large place, and when he inquired of Sam if he knew of that location, Sam replied that he didn't know anything about Sidney. Robert knew then that he was going to have to get a personal knowledge of all of the surrounding geography. He knew that he was going to need a ship assigned to him so that he could find the trade items in Canada. As he explored his maps, he realized how many places spoke French only. This stirred him to get busy with learning French. His next lesson was that afternoon, and he decided that he wanted to have an immersion in French, and he will talk to Joanne about where he can do this.

He arrived early to his French lesson and had to wait. While he was waiting, Jeanette came in the waiting room. She stopped, and they began to talk. He said, "I am very interested in learning to speak French as soon as possible. Is there any place where I could stay where they only speak French so that I would be exposed to speaking French constantly? I learned Spanish that way when I went with my father to the West Indies. I am now very fluent in Spanish."

Jeanette was surprised that he could speak Spanish as it was very similar to French. She started talking to him in Spanish, and they had a good time testing each other's ability in speaking Spanish. The more they talked the more interested Jeanette became in Robert. She was beginning to see what Joanne had seen. She wondered if she should offer him a room and board in their house as a way of totally immersing him in French. She had been thinking of this idea of total immersion in French as a teaching tool, and maybe this would be the very person with whom to start.

They had been talking for about thirty minutes when in walked Joanne. Jeanette said, "Robert has said that he wants to be completely immersed with French speaking people as a way of hastening his learning of French. You know we have talked about offering this to students but have never organized ourselves in order to do it. It would mean that we would have to establish a room and board structure in our house and that would invade our privacy. What do you think?" While Joanne was thinking about this, she was surprised to hear her mother and Robert talking fluently in Spanish.

This so completely surprised her that she was speechless. She had devoted their first lesson to pronunciation, and here he was fluent in a romance language. She was a little angry about his not telling her that he could speak Spanish as she would have started differently with him. Finally, she interrupted them and said, "Robert, why didn't you tell me that you were fluent in Spanish? I feel foolish about my starting you with pronunciation when you already had learned a romance language." Robert replied, "Joanne, may I call you by your first name?" Joanne replied, "Of course, didn't I just address you as Robert?" Robert continued saying, "I didn't want to direct you in any way. I wanted to experience your teaching just as you would do any beginner. If I offended you, I apologize as I want you to be my teacher." Joanne's anger disappeared, and she told her mother that immersion was the best way to learn French, and if Robert was willing to accept what they had to offer in room and board, it was okay with her.

Over the next hour they worked out details, and Robert was to move in the following day. They would start the first immersion with that evening meal. Robert walked away with high spirits. He had been rooming with his aunt as a way for her family to get some income, but since all of the men were working for his company, there was no need for him to stay there. When he told Aunt Tabitha he was leaving, she was disappointed as she liked being around her nephew. When he told her why he was moving she was very interested as she had felt for a long time that she and her family should be able to speak French. She helped him to pack and told him he must always come to their house for Sunday dinner. He agreed and left saying he would spend that night at her house.

It was still late morning when he got to his office, and he found himself surrounded by people offering him items for sale. None had commodities he wanted to sell except for one Frenchman from Labrador. This person spoke poor English, and Robert asked Sam If he would go to the Levesque's studio and see if one of them could come and translate for him. Both women were not busy, but Joanne insisted on coming. This proved to be very profitable for both Robert and Pierre LaBlanc. This meeting would give Robert a direct supplier, and it gave Pierre a buyer that was fairer with him than the other buyers in Halifax. Most of the Halifax buyers were prejudiced about dealing with the French speaking people.

That afternoon Robert sent a telegram to Paul Winfield saying he wanted a ship assigned to him as there were many opportunities in dealing with the French speaking people, and they all were on the Saint Lawrence estuary. He needed to go to Labrador, Newfoundland, Prince Edward Island, and the Gaspe Peninsular.

Paul was impressed by Robert's progress and sent a letter to Geri about his success. He said that he was assigning a sloop for him to use. He told them about what Robert intended to do. He was going to set up small trading stations in Labrador and Saint Pierre Island. These were to be models for further expansion into the St Lawrence estuary and river. He told them he felt that Robert had very expansive ideas, and he felt that they were sound moves. "It is just possible that we will have an important business in Canada."

The business men of Halifax had up to now paid very little interest in the McGinty-Hogg firm. They had noted that they had brought in salt and sugar and apparently done well. The building of a large warehouse troubled them, but when they lost the Pierre LaBlanc account, they became very serious and wondered what they could do that would slow down or completely block this new upstart. They held a meeting to discuss this problem. All of the important members came. The discussion was around how much this new company would disrupt their accommodation for each other. In a way they had established a monopoly, and it was successful as long as all respected it. For a long time this monopoly had run into problems of interconnecting competitions. As their businesses grew, they were starting to compete with each other. The more successful businessmen accepted this as a natural development, but the firms that were not so successful were feeling oppressed and felt that they could become irrelevant. These two fractions debated, and the final decision was that they should take steps to try to put the new company out of business. Only one member objected and refused to go along. Peter MacCarty was that lone objector, and he was dropped from their organization.

After the meeting was over, the group left together except for MacCarty as he was told in no uncertain terms that he was no longer with them. As he was walking home, he wondered about the wisdom of his position. By his objection, he had put himself in the same position as McGinty, an outsider. He didn't like the feeling he had about this, but he knew he was right in making this decision. He said to himself, "I must talk to this McGinty fellow and see if he is worth all of this trouble." Having said this he lost his doubts and fears and began singing some Irish fighting tunes.

None of this meeting reached Robert's ears until a Mr. Peter MacCarty came calling. Peter waited a few days before he called on Robert as he wanted to be sure of his feelings. It was towards the end of that week that he went to Robert's office and asked to speak with him.

Robert had hired Tabbie Davis as his secretary, and she was trying to be professional and asked, "What is your business?" MacCarty was amused by Tabbie's attempts at professionalism and said, "I am a fellow businessman, and I want to make a friendly call welcoming him to our community." Tabbie said "Please have a seat, and I will tell Mr. McGinty of your desire. What name shall I give Mr. McGinty?" He said, "Peter MacCarty." She hastily got up and went into Robert's office and announced who wanted to see him. Robert could see that Tabbie was tense, and he said, "Relax, Tabbie, you are doing fine. Show the gentleman in." With that Tabbie went to the door and holding it open told Peter MacCarty to come in. Robert rose from his desk and went forward to welcome Peter. They shook hands and sat down on adjoining chairs.

Peter started off talking first. He said, "I am here because I am in disagreement with the majority of the businessmen of Halifax. Recently they had a meeting in which your company was discussed. They are afraid of your competition, and think that you are disrupting their business agreements. In other words they don't like competition. I personally like to compete as I think competition makes good business. When you compete, you give your customers the best buys, and if they are satisfied, you should be also, especially if you are making a profit. I came here today to warn you of their intent to harm your business and to let you know that I am not one of them."

Robert responded by saying, "Thank you for your courtesy to me. I would like to tell you a little about my company. My mother started this company in Bermuda in 1833. She had a sailing boat repair background and rapidly built up a boat yard. It wasn't until my adoptive father came along that she was able to start a Trading Company. My father was a very smart sailor and trader, and he quickly built up trading relations with the West Indies and eventually all of the east coast of the United States. We are now planning to expand into Canada. Canada is a big country. It is hard for me to understand why my company would be a threat to anybody as there is enough opportunity for all."

MacCarty replied, "They have business agreements that they feel stabilize their businesses. I call it a monopoly, and I feel that it destroys competition and in the long run that is a bad thing for our community." Robert was silent for a while. He didn't know how to proceed with their conservation.

Finally he said, "Is your position going to hurt your business?" Peter replied, "No, I really don't profit by being in that group, and I had been thinking of getting out of it. This position of theirs just stimulated me to take this action now." Both wanted to continue their conversation but neither knew enough about each other to continue.

Peter got up and said, "I must go, but in conclusion I want you to be aware that these people do not make idle threats. They will shortly do something to hinder you." Robert thanked him for his telling him about this meeting and said, "Our Company has had this kind of experience before, and I am sure that we will be able to handle it when it occurs. I have enjoyed meeting you. I have no friends in Halifax, and I would like for you to be my first friend." Peter replied, "One always needs friends, and I hope that we will be friends." Peter had other reasons for wanting to be a friend of Robert because he had taken a fancy for Tabbie.

Late afternoon came, and Robert moved into his room at the Levesque home. That night Joanne cooked their meal. It was a delightful French country meal that would have been served on any French farm. The bread, cheeses and the well seasoned vegetables were a new experience for Robert. The tastes were so pleasing that he found himself overeating. He said to Joanne that he would have to be very careful about how much he ate as he found her cooking very delightful. Jeannette replied in French that he must not talk in English. He must try using only French. She said the next sentence in Spanish that he must learn the French phrase "How do you say this" and if necessary pointing out the objects or using our French-English dictionary. Robert went to their dictionary and looked up 'Thank you for a good meal', and he said in French, "Merci pour grande le repas, Joanne." They both smiled and spoke back to him in French. He didn't understand what they said, but he tried to use his Spanish to try to understand their words, but this did not work. All he could do was to listen to their talk and try to figure out what they were saying. They would talk to him as if he understood, and when they spoke a word he could repeat, he would ask them in French what that word meant.

The first night was frustrating for him, and he went to bed early. He took the French-English dictionary with him, and he spent half of the night studying words. The next morning he did not try to talk and left early for work. Joanne was concerned that he would give up, but he left early because he wanted to find someone that could speak French to work for him. When he arrived, he said to Tabbie, "I want to hire someone that speaks French." Tabbie said, "I took French in school, and I can speak it some." He replied, "That will do for now, and I want you to help me to learn a French vocabulary. Talk to me in French first and then English any time you address me." She replied, "I am not sure if I can do that all of the time, but I will do the best I can, and I will talk to my French friend and see how I can improve."

That day he received a long letter from his mother and also one from his father. His mother was talking about his two brothers and sister. She was saying they were growing up fast and that Luke was going on most of the West Indies trips with his dad. She didn't talk much about business but seemed to be more content with writing about the family. His father's letter was all about sailing and business. He ended the letter saying, "Robert, I hope you won't have any problems like we have had and won't need the use of people I knew in my criminal life, but if you do, I want you to know that I have a dear friend that lives in Halifax. He is going straight now, but he can help if you need it. His name is Jacque LaMonte. He is French but speaks perfect English. Even if you don't need his criminal knowledge you will find him a good man and a loyal friend. He gives his friendship sparingly, and at first he will attend you as your being a son of mine. Good luck and I love you, Dad. P.S, I have written Jacque about you, and he will be in touch shortly."

It warmed his heart to hear from his parents. He could visualize them as he read their letters. After reading the letters twice he sat back and reminisced about his home in Bermuda. While he was doing this, Tabbie walked in and announced that a Mr. La Monte was there to see him. He went to the door expecting to see a well dressed man and found instead a sick man that could hardly stand up. He rushed over and caught him and lowered him into a chair. Jacque LaMonte could hardly talk, and said, "I am a friend of your father, and I am in desperate need of help. Can you help me? I have just gotten out of jail, and I have had horrible treatment. I was arrested on a trumped up charge and sent to prison for two years, but I have become so weak that they let me go, so I could die, and they would not have to fool with a dead body." With that he collapsed and could hardly breathe. Robert had Tabbie move La Monte into his newly built apartment in his warehouse. Tabbie and he went into the apartment and put Jacque on Robert's bed. Robert sent Tabbie to get some groceries and also to ask her mother to come to his apartment immediately.

Tabitha arrived, and Robert told her he wanted her to nurse Jacque back to health. She took over and started taking off his dirty clothes and gave him a sponge bath. She sent Tabbie home to get some of Helmuth's old clothes, and she dressed him in warm clothes. By then he had regained consciousness, and she started feeding him warm oatmeal with raisins. He wanted to eat fast, but she insisted that he eat slowly. She fed him every two hours, and he slept in between his feedings. By six o'clock he was much better, and Robert said he would stay with him that night.

When Robert realized that he would not be able to stay with the Levesques, he went to their house and explained his problem. He tried to say it in French, but he did poorly so he finally said it in English telling them what had happened and that he should be able to return to their agreement in a few days. In the meantime could he come every day to take French lessons from Joanne? It was agreed, and he left.

Chapter 27

The next few days were hectic. He was up all night with Jacque and in the day dealt with an increasing business. His treatment of LaBlanc came to the attention of the French speaking community, and several members of this group sought Robert to see if they could get the same consideration. Robert was very kind to them and even if they had no commodity that he could use they left feeling good about this new company. His French was improving rapidly, and he could speak crudely to Joanne. She would laugh at his attempts and say, "You talk just like a child." This pleased him, but he had no intentions of being a child talker for long.

By the end of two weeks Jacque was able to get along by himself, and Robert moved back into the Levesque house and was immersed in French. This time he could speak and understand most of what was said. In two months he spoke well enough so that he could communicate with his French speaking clients. It was then that he decided that he would take his newly arrived sloop and travel to the French island of St. Pierre. He wanted to establish a small trading post there.

When he told Joanne that he was leaving the next day to sail to Saint Pierre she said, "I have relatives there, and I have not visited them for a long time. Will you take me with you as it would be a great trip for me, and maybe my relatives can help you?" He needed very little encouragement from Joanne as he found himself strongly attracted to her. He had made subtle advances toward her, but as of yet, she had always treated him as a student and not a prospective lover. This frustrated Robert, and he felt that he was going to have to stop his lessons before he could get her attention. Maybe this trip to St

Pierre would change things. The distance from Halifax to Saint Pierre was about 350 nautical miles.

It was in late August when they set sail for St. Pierre. As he and Joanne were watching the disappearance of Halifax harbor, Robert said to Joanne, "Do you know why they call it St. Pierre?" She said, "St Pierre in English is Saint Peter, and Saint Peter is the Patron Saint of the fishermen of St. Pierre. You see St. Pierre has been intermittently inhabited since some Portuguese and Spanish came in the 16th century. It wasn't until the mid 1600's that my ancestors came to St Pierre. As you probably know the British and French fought over these islands and the rest of Canada. It wasn't until the treaty of 1763 that France gave up all of Canada except the group of islands now known as the St. Pierre and Miquelon group. Actually most of the people live on St. Pierre. Did you know that the British took back these islands when you had your revolution because France was on the side of the Americans? It wasn't until 1815 that France got these islands back. We St. Pierreans are survivors and are very proud of our heritage."

Robert was amazed by this history, and he was eager to meet the people of St. Pierre. The sailing in late August was with very calm seas. Joanne told Robert that the islands were very sunny and beautiful in late August all through the early fall. They found this to be true. As they approached to the south of St. Pierre, they came in sight of four small islands. Their chart showed them to be Aus Marins, Ile aux Pigeons, Ile aus Vainqueurs and Grand Columbier. These islands were stretched out along the southeastern part of the St Pierre Island and seemed to be an eastern extension of the southern peninsula of St. Pierre Island. The Captain had already talked to Robert about the dangers of approaching the strait between St. Pierre and Miquelon as the currents were very strong and difficult to traverse. The chart called them the "The Mouth of Hell".

When they landed, Robert was surprised by two things. One, the French words were different from any he had learned, and the accent was hard for him to understand. He said to Joanne, "They are not using French words I know." She said, "Robert, they are using words similar to the Norman language. Didn't you tell me that your mother taught you how to speak Danish?" Why don't you try to speak Danish to them?" When he did, they were very astonished and rapidly spoke back to him in a way that both understood what was being said. This made Robert a person of interest, and many strangers wanted to try to talk to him. Joanne was in a hurry and insisted that they go to her relatives. Here is where he had his second surprise. People gave directions not by streets and house numbers but by land marks and by structures that stood out. Fortunately Joanne had no trouble, and they got to her relatives fairly quickly.

There was much excitement as no one had expected to see Joanne. In the household were her Aunt, her husband, and her maternal Grandparents. At first no one noticed Robert, but as things settled down Joanne introduced Robert. They all greeted him with a hug and a kiss on both cheeks and immediately asked, "Are you serious about each other?" Joanne hastily said, "We are just friends. Robert is the manager of the McGinty-Hogg trading Company, and he is coming to St. Pierre to open a small trading post. I have been teaching him French, and since I had not seen you in a long time, I asked him to take me with him."

They only partially believed this account as they could see the interest of Robert in Joanne, and how much she seemed to be directing Robert. To them they felt that she was giving all the signs that Robert belonged to her.

While they were talking, the husband of Aunt Marie asked. "Robert, are you the one that speaks Danish? Just before you came a man was telling me that a Dane had just landed at St. Pierre?" Robert said, "Yes, I am the one talking Danish." This excited the family as they had a celebrity in their house.

When it became time for Robert to go back to the ship, the family insisted on his staying with them. Robert felt he was intruding and declined and was leaving when Joanne said, "Robert, you must stay. They really want you to stay, and it would be better for you as you would meet more people here as friends. Besides tonight is the last night of the Basque Festival, and you can see demonstrations of stone heaving (harrijasotdzaile), haitzkolari (lumberjack skills), and pelota (a game sort of like jai alai)." He knew very little about these activities, but he was sure that his mother did. He stayed, and it was a memorable night. All crowded up that night, and Robert and Joanne found themselves sleeping on the floor near the fire place. The nights were chilly, and they kept a low fire going all night long. Robert and Joanne talked till it was very late and had a hard time getting up the next morning.

The next day was filled with getting acquainted with St. Pierre. He didn't find a trading post, but he hired Joanne's Aunt and Uncle as his representatives. They were to keep him informed of the cod catches and notify him when the best time was for him to come back and make salt cod purchases.

On the way back to Halifax, it was obvious that Robert and Joanne were no longer just friends. They were sharing confidences about how they felt towards each other. Joanne was saying, "Robert, you keep telling me that I was too professional with you when I was teaching you. It amazes me to hear you say this. I was constantly giving you signs of my interest in you, and you never responded. You probably don't remember when I was teaching you some pronunciation I would always touch your cheek with my little finger. I can assure you I do not do that with my usual students, but you did not respond at all. If you were French you would have grabbed my hand and kissed it, and if I gave any other sign you would have kissed me. You didn't do anything. At first I thought you didn't want to flirt with me, but soon I realized you just did not get it. I was not going to be obvious even though I wondered how we were ever going to get past my being your French teacher." Robert reached over and gave Joanne their first passionate kiss, and it thrilled them both.

Robert talked about his difficulty in approaching Joanne. He said, "I was always afraid I might offend you if I started romancing you. I wanted so much to be with you, and I felt the only way I was getting to be with you was by your teaching me French. I needed to learn French, but soon I realized that I needed you more. I had just about given up when you said you wanted to go with me to St. Pierre Island." The rest of the trip was like a honeymoon for them except for the fact that they made no attempt to be intimate with each other. Joanne was a strong Catholic, and premarital sex was not on her agenda, but she indicated to Robert in actions, she was a very passionate woman.

Chapter 28

Robert stopped his French lessons when he hired Joanne as his interpreter. She went everywhere with him, and their romance bloomed. Over the next three months they travelled to many locations. Robert spent many hours teaching Joanne sailing, and by December, she could help him with all of his activities. One night they were working late, and an early winter blizzard came up just before quitting time. Robert usually took Joanne home, but the weather was so severe Joanne decided that she would stay that night with Robert in his apartment. When they closed the office, they went into Robert's apartment, and Joanne cooked a delightful meal. They sat together by his fireplace and talked about their future. They limited their kissing as they feared their passion for each other would overcome their commitment to wait for their wedding night. They became sleepy as they sat by the fire and decided to go to bed.

Robert was to sleep on a pallet by the fire, and Joanne was to sleep in his bed. They settled down, and both were having a hard time going to sleep. Finally, Robert got up and got in bed with Joanne with the idea they would do pillow talk and eventually go to sleep. This was their conscious intent, but they had no control of their bodies' intent. Soon they were kissing each other passionately and were beginning to explore each other's body. Joanne was seeking his firm penis, and he was exploring her breasts and her pelvic areas. When their emotional feelings became so intense, Robert rolled Joanne gently onto her back and raised up to look down on Joanne. They paused and looked at each other trying to see if either one wanted to stop. Joanne's answer was to pull Robert down to her, and Robert slowly inserted his penis. From then on their bodies took over, and the increasing intensity overwhelmed them only to be eased by a climactic contraction of their bodies. When they were able to talk again, they found themselves looking at each other with a joy they had never experienced. They went to sleep saying over and over how much they loved each other.

The next morning they hurriedly got up and prepared breakfast and were in the office before the rest of the office force arrived. As they were sitting together, Joanne was saying, "Robert, I am moving in with you today. I am not going to let my prohibitions keep me from you. You belong to me now, and I am going to claim you forever." This was their marital vows that to them were more important than the words of a priest saying you are now man and wife.

When Joanne didn't come home that night, Jeanette came to the office and found Joanne happily working with Robert. Jeanette was relieved that Joanne was okay but was concerned as to what had happened that night. Joanne quickly confirmed her worst fears by saying, "I am moving in with Robert tonight, and I want you to help me pack up my things." At first, Jeanette was speechless and could only ask what about their wedding. Joanne replied, "Mother, Robert and I have already said our vows before our God, and we are now husband and wife."

This did not satisfy Jeanette, and she insisted that they see a priest immediately and make arrangements for a quick wedding. Joanne said "Mother, you apparently didn't hear me when I said we are already married." Her mother threw up her arms and screamed, "Joanne, you must be married by a priest before you can live with Robert." Her mother was so upset that they decided that they would close the office and tend to her mother's demands. After long discussions with her priest, he finally agreed to marry them, and that night was one of the happiest nights of their lives.

Just as Peter MacCarty predicted, the McGinty-Hogg Trading Company started to have problems on their dock. The men that worked for them were threatened, and some quit. The ones that didn't quit were assaulted. Robert went to the police and reported his problem, but the police were of no help.

While he was pondering what to do next, Jacque LaMonte came into the office and told Robert he had contacted his old criminal friends, and they said that they had nothing to do with what was happening to his company. He told Robert that it was a tough group of ruffians attacking his men, and if he wanted, his friends could take care of them. Robert remembered what his Father had said that sometimes legal means didn't work, and then you must do what is necessary. He told Jacque to take care of it and to thank his friends for their help.

That night when the ruffians returned to harass Robert's business, they were met with some opposition. In fact, the opposition was so severe that all of the ruffians ended up in the hospital. When the police questioned them they said," We were just having fun, and things got out of hand." When they got out of the hospital, they went to collect their money and told the association it was too dangerous to deal with that McGinty firm.

The leaders of the association assigned one of their members to contact the criminal element with the request that they set the McGinty warehouse on fire. Jacque told Robert about the plan, and he went to the police with his information. The person who was to set the fire was a policeman and the plan was for him to go to collect the money for the job. The fire was set and immediately put out without any damage. The policeman went to report that the fire was not successful, and he was commissioned to build a bigger fire. With that and the exchange of money, the businessman was arrested. It didn't take much to get him to talk, and all involved were charged with attempted mayhem and arson. They were convicted and some went to jail.

Peter MacCarty witnessed all of this and was impressed by the way Robert handled it. Ever since he had first come over to introduce himself, he had always found ways to visit with Tabbie. Eventually, he was seriously dating Tabbie, and when Robert and Joanne got married, he proposed to Tabbie. They did not have a long engagement and were married in the spring of 1856. It was that spring that Robert and Joanne went to Bermuda to visit with his parents.

They had their own Bermuda Sloop and with the help of Tabbie and Peter sailed to Bermuda. They spent two months and left just before the hurricane season began. Tabbie got a chance to meet her Aunt Geri, and Robert made two trips with his dad to the West Indies. Joanne stayed with Geri while they were gone, and they both developed a strong relationship. In fact Joanne fell in love with all of Robert's family and was delighted to be a part of it. Geri's two boys were now 19 and 17. Luke looked just like his dad and was deeply involved in everything his dad did. Paul had more of his mother's management and organizational skills, and he was already deeply involved with the company's activities and could give a detailed report of how Robert was doing in their Canadian business.

To the surprise of Robert he had some suggestions about what Robert could do that would increase profits. Robert was very pleased with this and invited Paul to go back with them and enter McGill University as he and Joanne were going to move their headquarters to Montreal. All thought this was a good idea, and when they sailed back, they would stop only for a day in Halifax and then sail onto Montreal.

Helmuth was put in charge of the office at Halifax, and Sam was to travel to their various trade stations. Harvey was the dock manager along with Jacque.

Chapter 29

The plans to leave in a day were delayed by an unexpected event. While Joanne and Robert were in his office, Tabbie came and said a man named Culum Rafin wished to speak with him. Without waiting to have Tabbie bring him in, Robert rushed out into the waiting room and greeted Culum with a big hug. They were both laughing with joy on being together again. There was much to talk about. Culum had left Robert and Geri when Robert was just four, and twenty-three years had passed. Culum was in his late forties, and he was ready to consider doing other things. The sea was still in his blood, but he could see that sailing was not to be the main way of traveling the seas.

He had been to the Glasgow shipping yards and had seen them making steel hull steamships with sails, and he knew that his life on the seas was about to change in a way that was not pleasing to him. The bottom line to all of this was that Culum was looking for a different job.

Robert, Luke, and Geri had talked about the changing of sailboats to steel hulled steam-sailing boats. They realized that their boat yard would have to be radically changed if they were to stay in the boat building-repair business. They felt that it would take ten years to make this change, and they were already planning what they would do.

Geri was saying they would eventually have to move to Canada to compete in boat building, and she wanted to get into that challenge as soon as possible. She said Canada because she felt that such a large country would have resources that would make it possible to build steel boats without the large expense of importing steel to Bermuda. Besides Bermuda would never have the people that were skilled in that type of ship building. Their long range plan was to stay in Bermuda, and use the ship repair facilities as long as it was profitable. At the same time they would start building a ship yard in Halifax that could build these new boats.

One of the reasons for Robert to go to Montreal was because it was becoming the financial center of Canada, and they wanted Paul to study so that he could run their own bank. All of these thoughts ran thru Robert's mind while he was listening to Culum. He didn't see how Culum could fit into what they were planning.

Culum had continued talking as Robert had been thinking, and Robert suddenly heard Culum say that his boss was looking for a partner to build a ship yard in Halifax which would build the state of the art steamships with steel hulls. His bosses were investors and would not be a part of the management of the business. Culum finished by saying, "Would Geri be interested in this proposition?" Robert's plans changed, and he sent Sam with Paul to Montreal so Paul could matriculate into McGill. He and Joanne, along with Culum, sailed back to Bermuda.

It was a great surprise when Robert came back so soon. Culum, being with them, was a surprise for Geri since she had not seen or heard of Culum for over twenty plus years. Luke had heard about Culum and wasn't too happy to have him in Bermuda. He didn't need to worry, for Geri made it very clear that whatever had been between Culum and her was over. Culum quickly got into his presentation of what his bosses had proposed, and the more they talked, it was obvious that this was an opportunity that Luke and Geri could not afford to miss.

Geri was a hardnosed bargainer, and she knew the only way that she could ever come to any deal was for her and Luke to go to London and talk to these investors. She asked how quickly could Culum be able to go with them to London. He said, "Today." It would take a week to get their schooner in port, and Geri needed some time to line up some advisors that worked in London. She used the advice of her friend, the Governor, and when they left, she felt that she had not left any stone unturned. It took 23 days to sail to London, and they hit the ground running.

They contacted the people they were going to use in their discussions, and things went well. The investors did their homework well, and they were interested only in the bottom line. This is where the hard bargaining began. The investment group wanted to have 60%

ownership of the new company, and Geri wanted 70% ownership. Her argument was that all they were investing was money, but she was not only investing money, but also the expertise that would make this investment work. They finally agreed the investors would have 35% ownership, and McGinty-Hogg would have 65%. In their final meeting with their advisors, one of the principles said, "Geri, you are one hell of a bargainer. We could not have done as well as you did. Any time you want to do this type of work, we would be glad to hire you as our consultant." Geri smiled and left.

The next three months were involved with moving their main operation to Halifax. Luke and Geri moved into Robert's apartment, and Luke, Jr. stayed and was to run their business in Bermuda. Amy Geri, their daughter, came with her parents as she was just 15. There was much to do. The location of the new ship yard was the first problem. It was important to keep their intentions unknown until they acquired the necessary land.

Culum was appointed by the investors as their representative. This puzzled Geri as she knew that Culum knew very little about ship building. She wrote her investors that if they wanted Culum to be their representative, she wanted him to go to the best ship yard that was making steel hulled boats and to spend at least six months studying their techniques. She wrote that Luke, her husband, was going. The investors liked Geri's suggestion and felt that they had a partner that was looking out for their interests as well as her own.

All of this shifting around changed the direction of Robert. He and Joanne were to center their efforts in Montreal. When they left Halifax in 1857, they had a baby boy, Pierre, and Jeanette, his mother-in-law. Joanne's family was the only family Jeanette had. She was insistent that they take her with them. She said, "Joanne, you and Robert are my family, and besides, the people of Montreal are mostly French speaking, and I can be of help." They took their Sloop with them, but it would return to Halifax as it would continue the company's work in trading.

On arrival to Montreal, the first effort was to find lodging for the family. At this time most of Montreal was on the Island of Montreal which was originally called Ville Maria. They found a house close to the industrial port which was close to the entrance of the Lachine Canal. Robert knew the canal had been built in 1824 and was surprised at how many changes had occurred in river traffic. Even though he was interested in river traffic, his task now was to find and establish a bank for the trading company. He was surprised to find that the banking industry was thriving at that time. He wondered how he would begin the process of establishing a bank when there was already so much competition.

He strolled down St. James Street (Rue Saint Jacques). He knew he was going to have to study the banking structure before he started establishing a bank for the trading company. Wondering if there was someone who could advise him on this, he went to the established banks and observed the people as they worked. It became obvious to him that the person who seemed to be the manager of all the activities sat at a front desk where he could greet all of the customers. He decided to talk to one of these people, and it was the manager of the Bank of Montreal.

Robert did not have the skill of conversation, but he did have the skill of being straight forward. He opened the conversation by saying, "I am a representative of the McGinty-Hogg Trading Company. We have been very active in trading out of Halifax and have recently extended our operations to Montreal. We have no information about banks in Montreal, and I was hoping you could give me some insight as to how the banks in Montreal work."

Mr. Henri Poincare responded saying, "We are always interested in new industries coming to our town. Are you interested in opening an account with us?" Robert responded by saying, "Yes, we will open an account here, but that is not the reason I am talking to you. We have always been a trading company, and we have a lot of cash flow. We are searching for a way to invest it and at the same time give us access to money for future projects. We have been considering for a long time starting a new bank. I have been wondering where to locate a bank in this area. Our president, Geri McGinty, assigned me the task of investigating Montreal as a place for our bank to be established. Mr. Poincare, I am a trader, and I know nothing about banks or bank management so I am seeking out a person who would be involved with us in developing and managing a new bank. Can you give me any information in regard to this?" Mr. Poincare responded, "I am surprised that you came to us making this kind of inquiry as what you are proposing is a formation of a competitor. Do you have any idea of how much capital you would need to start a bank, or what conditions our city has for chartering a bank?" Robert said, "I am completely ignorant of this. That's why I need an expert to deal with this problem. As far as the capitalization of the bank, we are prepared to infuse the new bank with twice the capital demand that the city of Montreal might request." Mr. Poincare said, "Do you realize what this sum is?" Robert responded, "No, I have no idea." Mr. Poincare said, "It would take at least a hundred thousand pounds to begin a start up." Robert said, "We had intended to have the capitalization at five hundred thousand pounds." This really got the manager's attention. He started thinking about his position in his bank.

His bank was owned by a group of investors who had been very resistant in increasing his salary and seemed to take him for granted. Over the past ten years, he had increased capitalization of his bank by two times, and he felt that he should have received some reward for this. He realized his thinking was putting his position in jeopardy with his own bank, but he felt he should continue to explore the opportunity that this man was presenting him. He finally said, "I think I need to know more about your company before we proceed with this discussion. Would you be willing to give me more information about the financial security of your company?"

Geri had realized that Robert would have difficulty opening a bank without a complete accounting of her present holdings, and she had a legal document drawn up describing the resources of the McGinty-Hogg Trading Company. It was broken down into profits connected with the ship building and their trading company. It was over a million pounds in value with a net yearly income of over two hundred thousand pounds.

These figures were startling to the bank manager as very few of the businesses in Montreal at that time was that successful. He said to Robert, "I think we need to go out and have lunch together." They left the bank and went to a local restaurant, and there Poincare told Robert that he was dissatisfied with his position. He had worked for ten years for this bank, and he had increased the capitalization two times, but he was never rewarded for this. "I need to make a change, and maybe you have the opportunity I have been looking for." Robert was surprised at how the conversation was going and said, "I have given you a full accounting of my company, but I know nothing about you. Can you give me any supporting evidence about your qualifications?"

Poincare replied, "I can give you the statements of my bank over the past ten years that I have been president, and I can give you some recommendations from people who are prominent in the banking industry. You can investigate these, and we can get back together as I will also investigate your company."

After lunch was over, they parted, and Robert returned to their little house to consult with Joanne. They both agreed that he had to do research on this man because it sounded too good to be true. As they were sitting around talking, Jeanette walked in and added to the conversation. She said, "Robert, one of my students, Mr. Samuel Bowman is a leading banker in Halifax. We became close friends after I finished teaching him French. We have communicated by letters since that time. Has the sloop left for Halifax?" she inquired. Robert said, "No, it's leaving tomorrow morning." Jeanette replied, "I want to write a letter and have it delivered to this banker in Halifax because I feel he will know considerable information about Mr. Poincare." Robert liked this idea and immediately wrote a letter to Mr. Bowman and included Jeanette's letter. He took it to the Captain of the sloop with instructions that it be hand delivered to a Mr. Samuel Bowman of the First Canadian Bank of Halifax. He asked in his letter to Mr. Bowman for him to give a reply to the Captain that delivered it as it was important that he get this information as soon as possible. Jeanette in her letter said she always enjoyed being in touch with him and that Robert was her son-in-law.

In one week's time, Robert received his answer. Mr. Bowman knew of Mr. Poincare and knew that he had done an excellent job in the start up and running of the Bank of Montreal. He said, "I would recommend him highly to help Robert start and manage his new bank."

When they met on the Friday a week later, both had favorable reports of each other and were ready to negotiate what rewards would be for the manager of the new bank. Robert said, "My Company is always straight forward in its negotiations with new employees. We have researched what a bank manager should receive. What do you expect for your services?" Mr. Poincare replied, "The salary is important but not as important as rewards for good service. I want a structure that will reward me for making your bank successful. It can come in the form of money or part ownership of the bank or both."

Robert replied, "Our president, Geri McGinty, does not allow partnerships of any businesses she is involved in, but she does pay well for good services. She is willing to give you a good salary plus bonuses at the end of the year if you perform well, but I am sure she will not allow any part ownership." Mr. Poincare was disappointed by this and told Robert he was. Robert got up from the table and said, "Well, Mr. Poincare, I am afraid we have gone as far as we can go with this problem. Why don't you give yourself some time to think about your conditions and our conditions and see if there is any kind of reconciliation that can be accomplished?" They parted with Robert feeling that was the last time he would see Mr. Poincare.

Chapter 30

Paul McGinty had matriculated into McGill University and was housed in the local dormitory. As soon as Robert and Joanne arrived in Montreal, he was notified of their being located at #12 Rue Saint Marie with the request that he come to them as soon as he was free from his classes. Paul was delighted to hear from his brother, Robert, and rushed through his courses so he could get there in time for supper. He was familiar with Joanne's ability to cook and was eagerly looking for a good meal. All were very happy to be re-united with each other, and Paul was delighted to have his relatives in the same town as he.

While Robert was talking about his experiences with the bank manager, Joanne was talking about the family. She was relating about the fact that Paul's father had left for Glasgow, Scotland, and would be separated from his mother for six months. His mother was actively buying land for their proposed ship yards, and all of the family had been moved to Halifax except Abby, Joseph O'Rourke, and Luke, Jr. Jonathan McGinty insisted on going with Luke to Glasgow as he felt his connections with his old company would be of service to Luke in his efforts to learn about making iron hulled sailing ships. She ended by saying, "Our family is relocating and scattering." Paul asked about his baby sister and was told that she had entered a secondary school in Halifax and was very happy with her new location.

A few days passed, and to Robert's surprise, Mr. Poincare came to his home and wanted to talk to him. They sat down in the living room and started talking about what Poincare had been considering. Mr. Poincare said, "Robert, I have given it considerable thought (he was using his first name now) about conditions of your employing a bank manager. I realize now how unhappy I have been at the bank

The wanderers

where I am working. Even though I am disappointed about not having any ownership, I think we can develop a relationship that will benefit us both." Robert said, "Henri, I am glad that you decided to talk to me further about this as my banker friend in Halifax was very complimentary of you, so let's discuss how best we can start this new bank." They agreed on his salary with bonuses.

They decided the first thing was to acquire a good location, and the Rue Saint Jacques was the best location for a new bank. When that decision was made, Henri told him about a small building that was two blocks down from the Bank of Montreal on the Rue Saint Jacques that was available for purchase. He suggested that they go down to the location and see if it would fit as a location for a new bank.

They found a small building that really was not large enough to accommodate what they needed for a bank. They would need to expand it. The first question they asked was whether there was any adjacent land that was available for them to expand the building on. It seemed that there was, but the owner of the adjacent land wanted a larger sum for his land than the cost of the old building. This would take several weeks of negotiation before they could come to terms, and the building of the new bank began in January of 1857.

Over the next three years many things happened to the McGinty family. The bank was established and functioning well. Luke and Jonathan had returned along with Culum Rafin, and they had started building a yard and had almost completed it. It seemed like everything was working out fine for the family. By 1860 Robert and Joanne had a new boy and girl. Robert was 30 years old and Joanne was 28, and they felt their family was complete.

Paul Winfield started writing to Geri about conditions that were evolving in the United States. He was reporting that the country seemed to be dividing itself, and he was deeply concerned about whether they would be able to resolve their differences. He said to Geri, "I do not approve of slavery, but I realize that slaves are the primary labor structure of the plantation systems of the South. Even with cotton gins, they are still very dependent on slave labor. I fear that compromise is not going to be possible. As you probably have heard, a very liberal candidate from the Republican Party has come forth. His name is Abraham Lincoln. Many in the North are very pleased with him, but there is an uproar in the South as they feel if he is elected

President, drastic changes would occur, and these would be imposed upon them, i.e. abolishing slavery.

Now I am thinking about my family," Paul Winfield said. "I will not allow my sons, Paul and Luke, to be in any kind of war. I am thinking seriously of leaving Boston, and either going to Bermuda or Halifax and turning over the management of our facilities here to my father and our current manager. This will be a big move for Amy and me, and I have not come to this decision easily. I want to get your ideas on what I am thinking."

Luke and Geri McGinty were very surprised to read this letter and had no idea of the dangers that were approaching. Both of them had no experience with war, but they knew it was something that was going to change the whole structure of their company. They wrote back to Paul Winfield saying they would make all the adjustments that were necessary for he and his family to come to Halifax as they wanted to protect them in every way they could.

This wasn't the main concern that they had, for they knew that Bermuda had been a significant location in the War of 1812, and they felt that again it would become an important station for both sides of the conflict. Both sides would be seeking their facilities in Bermuda, and they were wondering how they could anticipate these needs and prepare for them. They felt surely battles would not be fought in wooden hulled sailing ships but would be fought with steam driven, iron clad ships. This meant that they should be thinking about how their new facility in Halifax would fit into this demand.

Chapter 31

Paul McGinty finished his courses in banking at McGill University in the spring of 1860. He was immediately placed under Henri Poincare and was in training to become an assistant manager of the bank. The bank was progressing rapidly, and in its third year, they had doubled capitalization, and Mr. Poincare was satisfied with the bonus he had received in regards to this success.

On November 6, 1860, Abraham Lincoln was elected President of the United States. Paul Winfield immediately started planning the moving of his family to Halifax. His father asked him to wait as long as he could as he hoped that some compromise could be accomplished. Paul Winfield followed events closely, and the first move that was very disturbing was the secession of South Carolina on December 20, 1860. For a while it seemed to Paul that this might be all that would happen to the Union, but on February 1, 1861, Florida, Mississippi, Alabama, Georgia, Louisiana, and Texas seceded. On February 11, 1861, he followed Lincoln's entourage of family and friends leaving Springfield, Illinois, and going to Indianapolis, Indiana; Columbus, Ohio; Pittsburgh, Pennsylvania; and Buffalo, Albany, and New York City. They finally turned south to Philadelphia, and there stayed at the Continental Hotel. What impressed Paul were the large crowds Lincoln received along his journey.

The assassination attempt of Lincoln in Baltimore convinced Paul that he must act now. He realized that no Southern state had Lincoln on its ballots, and that Lincoln was strictly a Northern President. He was boarding a Bermuda Sloop on April 12, 1861, when South Carolina fired on Ft. Sumter, and he was approaching Halifax when Lincoln issued an order for the Northern states to send 75,000 troops to Washington D.C. for its defense. When Lincoln ordered Federal troops to Washington, it was announced that Virginia, Tennessee and Arkansas seceded, and the Civil War had begun.

Paul and his family rapidly settled down in Halifax. Amy and Geri were together again and were planning to be working with each other as they had in Bermuda. Their two boys were grown, and only their daughters were at home and were the same age of 16. Geri was born in 1811, and Amy was born in 1818 so they were respectively fifty and forty-three years in age. They felt that their world was wide open for them, and they were going to enjoy it to its fullest. Luke Sr. and Paul Sr. were going to work together as they had in Bermuda, and Paul W, Jr. was to go to Montreal to work with Robert. Luke Winfield was to work in the ship yards, and he was to be trained to manage that facility.

Paul Winfield left In May, 1861, for Montreal. He was to live with Paul McGinty. Since they both had the same first name they decided that they would be identified as Paul M and Paul W. Paul M's first job was to introduce Paul W to the business community. Paul W was not to be in banking but was to be in charge of the trading post that Robert had established. Robert would stay in Montreal only as long as it was necessary to train Paul W. When this was accomplished, he was to go to Toronto and there establish a trading facility for their company. Joanne and Jeanette regretted leaving Montreal as they enjoyed the French culture that was dominant there.

It didn't take long for Paul W to be accepted in the social structure of Montreal. When his father's firm moved into Halifax all of the original owners and their families were required to learn French and Paul W was fluent in speaking French. Paul W was very aggressive in his business and personal life and was soon dating all of the attractive young ladies in Montreal. The business men of Montreal realized early on that they had a new strong competitor in their midst, and they respected him and admired him for his honest dealings.

As time passed, Paul W became attracted to one young lady by the name of Beatrice. Her father was a very successful businessman, and he liked the way Paul W did business. At first he promoted the relationship only to realize that it turned off both of them. They had to find themselves without parental help. In a very short time, they were going out together quite often. As their relationship became more intense, Paul started putting sexual pressure on Beatrice. He felt that they were more and more committed to each other, and that sex was a part of that commitment. Beatrice didn't see it that way, and they had a difficult time with each other.

Beatrice's main argument was that they were not engaged, and even though they liked each other very much, she didn't see that as a firm enough commitment. Paul W finally agreed and formally requested of her father that he be allowed to marry Beatrice. Both families were pleased, and the engagement was announced to all of Montreal. Paul W thought they would start their sexual experience, but this did not happen. He tried to be understanding, but slowly he was withdrawing from Beatrice.

In early 1862, the work load at their Bermuda ship yard and trading post was overwhelming Luke, Jr. and Joseph O'Rourke. The war was presenting repair work for the Union and the Confederacy. Geri and Luke, Sr. decided that one of the children must go to Bermuda. Paul W was the only one that they could pull away. When Paul W heard of their decision, he was delighted as it would get him away from Beatrice, and maybe he could find another love. He told Beatrice that he was leaving, and it was best for them because they disagreed on basic issues, of which sex was one. He didn't give her a chance to say anything and left.

Beatrice's father was furious, but Beatrice would only tell her mother what the problem was. Her mother didn't know what to tell her, and it was obvious to Beatrice that she was about to lose Paul. Beatrice was a proud person and was used to having people give into her. When Paul W's ship left Montreal, she realized her position with Paul W was very destructive to their relationship, but for now it was too late. She remembered Paul W telling her that his request of sex from her was based on his need, and she would have to trust him and not be afraid that he would misuse that intimacy.

She realized that Paul W was right. She had never really trusted Paul W, and now he was gone. For two months, Beatrice moped around the house and seemed to have no interest in anything. Finally, her father confronted her about her behavior and said, "If your behavior is related to Paul W, I will be glad to send you to Bermuda."

The idea at first frightened her, and she began to realize that her refusing to have sex with Paul was not related to her moral feelings but to her fear of commitment. She struggled with this and finally decided to go to Bermuda and see if she could recapture Paul.

When Paul W left Montreal, he had no feelings of loss. He realized he never really had Beatrice. One of the first things he did when he came to Bermuda was to tell Luke, Jr. about his lost love affair and said, "Luke, I want to meet a woman that isn't afraid of sex. I have spent almost a year pursuing a woman that was unable to consider sex with me, and I don't want to have that experience again." Luke said, "The Governor's daughter and I are having an affair, and we plan to marry soon. Elizabeth and I felt that sex was an important part of a marriage, and we wanted to be sure that we really liked being sexual with each other. We are looking forward to our marriage." Paul didn't need Luke's help in finding women, and he was starting to seriously date a young woman by the name of Malinda Jones.

Beatrice's father knew the Governor of Bermuda as they had gone to Oxford together. He gave Beatrice a letter explaining who she was and asking if he, the Governor, would look after her while she was in Bermuda. Beatrice was upset by the letter and did not give it to the Governor. She felt she could take care of herself, and she didn't want anything between her and Paul W.

Her ship landed in the harbor of St. George, and she had some trouble getting to the McGinty-Hogg Shipyards. She found the family home first and introduced herself as the fiancé of Paul Winfield, Jr. Abby and Joseph were home at that time and immediately led her to their guest room. Beatrice was told that Paul W would be in for supper in about an hour. They were pleased to have that hour so they could get acquainted with Beatrice, and she told them all about she and Paul W having had a falling out, and she was here now to reclaim Paul. Both were very impressed with Beatrice. What they didn't know was Beatrice had changed from a demanding child-woman that Paul knew to a very mature and determined young lady. She knew now what she wanted, and she was going to fight for it.

When Paul W came home that night, he and Luke were laughing about their day and were looking forward to their going out on a date with Luke's fiancé and Malinda. Paul entered the living room and was surprised by Beatrice running up to him and giving him a passionate kiss and not letting him get away from her.

This infuriated Paul W, and it was all he could do to keep from saying angry words. Instead, he took Beatrice into the next room and said, "Beatrice, we are thru. I am dating another woman, and I have no intention of being involved with you ever again." Beatrice had expected this response and didn't challenge him. She said, "You were too mature for me in Montreal, and I know now that I should have been with you. The past is gone, and I want to start again with you as I realize that I am in love with you, and I don't intend to give you up." Paul W said, "Beatrice, I am happy here, and I enjoy dating my new girl friend. I have no desire to start over again with you." With that he went to his room and dressed for supper.

Paul W was very silent at supper, and he resented it when Beatrice sat next to him. Here he was mad as hell, and there she was talking as if nothing had happened between them. Luke, Jr. knew all about Beatrice, and he was amused by how easily she handled what was to Paul W a disaster. Abby and Joseph really enjoyed Beatrice as she brought a light hearted feeling to their group.

At 8:00 o'clock Luke Jr. and Paul W left for their date, and Beatrice spent the night enjoying Abby and Joseph. They went to bed at about 10:00 o'clock, and when Abby and Joseph were asleep, Beatrice slipped into Paul's room and got in his bed. When Paul arrived home at midnight, he found Beatrice sound asleep in his bed. He looked at Beatrice and was aware of her beauty. He decided the best way to get rid of Beatrice was to start having sex with her. He undressed himself, and when he pulled back the sheets there lay Beatrice completely naked. He was so shocked that he could hardly hear Beatrice saying, "Come to bed." He responded by getting his clothes and leaving the room. He didn't want to get involved with Beatrice ever again, and he realized if he had sex with her, he would get in a relationship he did not want.

When Paul W left Beatrice, she knew that she had won the first round as he could not ever say she was afraid of sex with him. Paul W didn't sleep well that night. The next day Paul W did everything he could to avoid Beatrice. Beatrice did just the opposite. She would follow Paul W around and did it in such a skillful way that it didn't interfere with his work in the yard. Luke, Jr. liked Beatrice and tried to teach her about the work that they were doing. In fact Beatrice was determined to make herself indispensable. She was becoming a gopher for the whole staff. Her activities and her interest in Paul W amazed the men, and they wondered why he paid so little attention to her, particularly since she was such a good looking woman.

All during those days Paul W was fuming inside and wondering what he was going to do about Beatrice. He decided that he would talk to Abby and Joseph. He managed to get away from Beatrice and went home early. Abby had just come home from Hamilton and was resting in the living room. Paul W had run to the house and rushed into the living room and sat down panting next to Abby. Abby had known Paul W since he was a little boy, and she considered him her grandson.

After he got his breath, Paul W said, "Nana, (all of the children called Abby, Nana) I was engaged to Beatrice for over six months. We thought we were in love. I put sexual pressure on Beatrice as I felt that if she was interested in me in a real sense and trusted me she would respond to me sexually without the security of a marriage contract, and we could go forward with our life together. She put conditions on me for us to proceed with this request. Mainly we were to announce our engagement to all of Montreal, and then we would consummate our relationship. This didn't happen. Instead she insisted on a long engagement, and after waiting for several months, I told her I was not going to wait any longer, and I was leaving the next morning to come to Bermuda. She didn't say anything, and I left thinking that our relationship was over. Here I have started a new life for me, and I am dating a new young lady. I feel that my life is over concerning Beatrice. Now here she comes, and thrusts herself on me and tells me she made a mistake, and she realizes that my request for a sexual life was reasonable, and she is ready to proceed. She is now able to accept the fact that if it doesn't work out, she will be okay. My problem now is that I don't trust her, and she no longer has that control over me of the promise of sex. For too long it dominated me and made me unhappy. I don't want to ever be so needful of sex that I will postpone my life."

They were silent for a while as Abby was trying to figure out what to say. She said, "Paul W, I can only talk to you from how I feel about this problem. I grew up under different circumstances than the ones that you and Beatrice have grown up under. You both have come from very influential families. You both are well educated and have been exposed to many ideas that were not in my life. You have been exposed to the idea of love as an important part of a man and woman's life, and you had to be sure that you were in love, and you had a deep trust of each other. These are difficult tasks when you are in love and sex is a large part of your attraction to each other. It is a confusing task for young people to understand and be comfortable with each other. I can see that you were dealing with your growing sexual needs and wanting to know if Beatrice really trusted you. I don't know what Beatrice was dealing with, but whatever it was, she obviously feels different now as she doesn't put sex in the path of separating you. She seems to see you in a different light. If I were you, I would start over with her and see where it goes." Paul W. replied, "I have thought these same things, but I just don't want to start over with Beatrice." Abby continued by saying, "Well it lies in Beatrice's court as to what follows as you now can take yourself out of the picture."

With that they both just sat and got deep in their own thoughts. Paul W was wondering how he would feel if he did really take himself out of Beatrice's life, and he was surprised by a feeling of loneliness. He knew that he still had to explore more with Beatrice and see why he still felt lonely when he thought of losing her. Abby was thinking how lucky she was to have a husband like Joseph and to have such wonderful grandchildren like Paul W and Luke, Jr.

That evening Beatrice sat next to Paul, and he talked to her. It was light chatter, and Beatrice had no idea what was going on. At the end of the meal, Paul asked Beatrice if she would come into his room as he wanted to talk with her. In Paul's room there were two lounge chairs that Paul used to read in. One held his feet, and the other he sat in.

He started off by saying, "I never expected to see you again. When I first saw you here, I was surprised, and then I was angry because you had been a pain in my ass. You were at one time the only person in the world I wanted to be with, but as we got to know each other, things changed. I don't think that either one of us was willing to be real with each other. I have often wondered why I was so insistent on having sex with you. I know I was very aroused by you, but now this doesn't seem so important. I have changed in these past few months, and I am not the person that you knew. The only reason I am talking with you now is because when I had a long talk with my Nana (Abby), I realized that when I thought of losing what I thought I had with you, I felt an intense lonely feeling. I don't know if it belongs to you or to my loss of an idealized you. The bottom line to all of this is that I am willing to find out if it is the real you that I fear losing."

There was silence. Beatrice was surprised and impressed by what Paul W had said. She never suspected that he was such a deep thinker. It was a little intimidating to her at first, but as she absorbed what he had said, she saw real hope for them. She knew now more than ever that Paul W would be the only man she would ever want. She didn't know how it was all going to turn out, but she was determined to fight for him. She said, "Paul W, I love you in a way I never knew existed. When you left, I was in a ho hum position with you. I had felt that you were too pushy for my taste, and I was glad when you said our engagement was over. I didn't know at that time how much you had entered into me and my feelings.

You probably know by now that I was a self centered brat at that time. My whole world was around me and my importance which the engagement brought to young girls in the Montreal society. I lost myself, and you in all of that hula bah lu. What happened to me in those two months you were gone was a lot of self searching. I decided I wanted to grow up, and when I did that, I began feeling a great loss. That loss was you. For over a month all I did was feel sorry for me. That got me nowhere. I would mope around the house, and finally my father said to me, 'Beatrice, if that young man, Paul W, is the cause for all of your depressing behavior, then I am willing to buy you a ticket to Bermuda and see if you really should be depressed over the loss of him.' So here I am even more convinced that you are the only man I want to have in my life. I want you and your children to be with me all the days of my life. I know that you do not feel as I, but I am very patient and hopeful that somehow you will change in your feeling for me." She stopped talking, and they both just sat quietly together. All had been said that needed to be said and both were going to just let it happen as it would.

Chapter 32

When Paul Winfield, Jr. left for Bermuda, Robert and Joanne had to delay leaving Montreal until they received replacements. Many changes in management were being made in the Halifax Headquarters of McGinty-Hogg Trading Company. Geri wanted Amy to be involved with her at the Headquarters. Luke, Sr. was becoming interested in the iron steam ships and was building them for the company and intended to have a fleet of these ships replacing their sailing fleet. He had recalled Luke, Jr. to Halifax for a six months course in the use of these vessels as he wanted to get into trading with Britain and other European nations.

The U.S. Civil War opened many trade opportunities. He knew that the southern ports would be blockaded and that the South's main crop for export was cotton. Knowing that Texas had a long border with Mexico, he knew there would be a lucrative trade in cotton, with the return shipment of arms and other needs that the Confederacy did not produce. He wanted Luke, Jr. to take the lead on the Mexican trade and leave Paul W in charge of the Bermuda station.

Luke, Sr. felt that Bermuda would evolve into a haven for the Confederacy, and they would depend on the McGinty shipyard for repairs as well as trade to both fighting nations. During all of this shuffling about, an event occurred that alerted them to the dangers of this conflict. In November, 1861, an American warship stopped a British Mail Ship and took off two Confederate diplomats. London demanded an apology and the return of the two Diplomats. To reinforce this demand, Britain dispatched a force of 14,000 combat troops to Canada and mobilized 40,000 militia. Lincoln finally released the Diplomats and that crisis was resolved, but it made Britain determined to change its relationship with Canada so that she would not have to defend her.

In 1862 the United States government started demanding the return of their citizens that went to Canada to avoid the war. This would and did directly involve Paul and his two sons. Canada refused to deport Paul and his sons, but it convinced Paul that he must become a Canadian-British subject. This was no problem for Amy as she was still a British citizen, but her children and Paul did have a decision to make. All of her children loved Bermuda and Canada and wanted to live in Canada the rest of their lives so all became Canadians.

By the middle of 1862, Robert finally left for Toronto. This time he was in what was called Upper Canada. It was predominately English, and the French speaking people were in the minority. Robert's first interest was the Great Lakes. He knew that it was a huge basin with five large lakes. He had visited Lake Ontario many times, but he was surprised at the growth that had occurred on both sides of Lake Erie. It seemed to him that the United States had made the greatest effort to exploit Lake Erie.

He found that there was a regular passenger service between Chicago and all of the growing cities in Wisconsin. Although furs and timber were still great commodities, he saw large shipments of grain coming in from Lake Superior as well as around Lake Erie. He quickly realized that there would be a boom for the agriculture and manufacturing goods from Canada mainly going to the United States. He wanted to get some ships on Lake Erie as soon as possible.

The closest shipyards for steam vessels were in Buffalo, New York. He tried to negotiate buying from those shipyards, but they were dedicated to supplying the Union's need for ships. He wrote Geri that he felt that they should build a ship building yard on Lake Erie as close as they could to Toronto. This was going to stretch their resources even though they had increased their resources considerably in response to the war. Geri felt that the better chance for them was to concentrate on Lake Superior as it had not been developed as much as the other lakes.

She wrote a long letter to Robert saying, "I want you to hire a geologist to go with you; and I want you to spend all of your time locating iron and coal deposits. I want you to buy either the land or the mineral rights of any iron or coal deposits that you find along the western shores of Lake Superior. I want us to position ourselves to benefit from all the grains that will be produced in the prairies of west Canada, and if possible own producing coal and iron mines. We will be more like producers than traders."

This meant that during the summer months Robert was gone from his family. When the winter came, the lakes were frozen over and all shipping ceased. This separation caused problems for Robert and his family. By the end of the War, he and Joanne returned to Montreal and would live the rest of their lives located there.

When Amy and Geri were reunited, they were determined to work together as they had in the beginning of their lives together. Both had sixteen year old daughters, and it was no problem for them to be actively involved in the McGinty business.

Geri decided that they would shorten the company name to McGinty Trading Company. Paul, Sr. was made general Manager of McGinty Trading Company. Geri became the C.E.O. of her company and Amy was Vice President. Luke, Sr. was in charge of their steamship fleet and all of the trading with the Union and the Confederacy. Things seemed to settle down as they progressed with their company.

In December 1863, they were directly involved with the Chesapeake affair. The Confederates captured the ship, Chesapeake, and took it to Halifax. McGinty Trading Company helped restock it, and it was traveling around Nova Scotia when the Union recaptured it in the waters of Nova Scotia.

Chapter 33

Within six months Paul W and Beatrice found themselves with just Abby and Joseph. They had the total responsibility of the Bermuda operation. Paul W began to realize how capable Beatrice was, but he was still reluctant to reengage romantically with her. Beatrice didn't mind because she knew something that Paul W didn't recognize. She could sense his excitement when he was around her and his increased concern for her as he wanted to be sure that she wasn't hurt while working around the yard.

Paul W convinced himself that he was just being a good manager in protecting his employees of which Beatrice was one. One thing Paul W was aware of was that he liked to talk to Beatrice. He wondered why he was so resistant to her as he was convinced that she really did love him. One day he said to Beatrice, "Beatrice, I know now that you really love me, but I don't know why I am so resistant to being involved with you. I know I am attracted to you sexually, but when I realize this, I withdraw from any consideration of being with you." Beatrice replied, "I think I understand your reluctance in loving me. I did try in our beginning to control you by using the promise of sex as a controlling weapon. You will never know how much I regret doing that, and I regret that I hurt you in such a way that it is hard for you to want me again. All I can say is, I am different now, and I will never use sex to control you. I will never use sex as a demand for marriage. I will accept you as you want to present yourself to me. I don't need marriage to be your lover and a devoted wife."

That night they decided that they would sleep together. It was difficult for Paul W, but Beatrice was at peace as she was with her man. Late in the night in a half awake state, Paul started making love to Beatrice. He tentatively reached over and touched her breasts. His hands lingered as he slowly ran his fingers onto her stomach until he reached her pubic hair. He paused and gently rubbed her pelvis. He could feel Beatrice breathing rapidly, and she started exploring Paul W. She found and gently caressed his erect penis. She rose up slowly and gently kissed his penis. When she did this, all of Paul W's resistance vanished. He pulled her into his arms and kissed her passionately, and his lips and tongue searched for hers. By this time they were fully awake and were frantically rubbing their bodies together demanding that he penetrate her body with all of the force that he could give as she raised her hips to meet his thrusts. The intensity of their bodies was almost unbearable, and they exploded into each other. Slowly they awakened from this ecstasy and were telling each other of their love. They went to sleep shortly, and when they awoke, they were united. They knew it would be forever.

By the end of the American Civil War, Luke, Sr. had established the McGinty Company as an international shipping company. He and Luke, Jr. were involved with trade between the North American continent and Europe.

Geri and Amy were very active in the management of all the diverse structures of their company. When their two girls were eighteen in 1859, they were sent to Mount Holyoke College for Women in South Hadley, Massachusetts, and they graduated in 1863. The two young women had similar names, and they were as bonded to each other as were their mothers. They would advance the company into the twentieth century.

Culum Rafin was forty-nine in 1861. He was still a bachelor and was beginning to wonder if he would ever find any woman that was like Geri. His job with the investors in Geri's company had ended, and he now worked for the McGinty firm. He no longer wanted to go to sea, and he worked mainly with Paul Winfield, Sr. One day he walked into Geri's office and was surprised to find a new secretary. Helen McHenry had been recently hired by Geri.

A few days before, Helen had come to see Geri. She had a letter from Effie McKay. Geri could not believe that Effie was still alive. Effie was always close to Geri's heart because she was there when Geri was in the lowest point of her life. Effie helped her when her first husband was killed and made it possible for her to survive and move on with her life. She was Geri's life saver. Geri eagerly opened the letter, and it was a letter of introduction of Helen McHenry. She wrote to Geri about Helen. She said in her letter, "Geri, when Helen came into my life, it was like being with you again. She was forty years old and childless. Her husband of twenty years had abandoned her, and she was half starved. It seems that he had found a young woman and had gotten her pregnant and decided that he was thru with Helen. Helen was trying to make a living, but no one wanted a middle aged woman.

She had wandered all over Dublin and in desperation decided to go to Belfast. I don't know why, but she only got as far as our little village. I was lonely, and I took her in and nursed her back to health. As you know there are very few opportunities for women in Ireland, so I suggested that she go to Nova Scotia and find you as I knew you would be willing to help her. When I told her of what you had done with your life, all she could think of was getting to you. Somehow we got enough money to get her passage to Halifax, and off she went. I hope that you can help her. She is a good woman, and life has not been kind to her. I think of you every day, and thank God you came into my Life. I love you, Geri. My deepest Love, Effie." There were tears in Geri's eyes as she closed the letter.

She brushed them aside and said, "Hello, Helen. Thank you for delivering this letter to me. I owe much to Effie, and I see that she did for you what she did for me." With that she sat and talked with Helen. She soon realized that Helen had few qualifications except that she was a very attractive middle aged woman. Her blond hair was just slightly graying, and her deep blue eyes were attractively sad. She was trim and neatly dressed and generally made a good impression.

Geri said, "Helen, I run a complex company. The only way I see that I could hire you is as my receptionist. The lady out front handles all of my outer office and keeps people from disturbing me. She is pregnant and wants to retire and be a housewife so her position will be open. Are you interested? She can teach you her job, and I think you can be of much help to me."

Helen burst out crying. She couldn't believe that any one would think she was worth anything. Geri came around her desk and hugged her until she stopped crying and told her she had a small apartment for her, and she would start work this very minute.

The wanderers

Geri asked Helen to go to the woman who led her into her office and have her come back into Geri's office. When they returned, Geri said "Helen, this is Betty Hart, and, Betty, this is Helen McHenry. She is going to replace you when you leave, and I want you to instruct her in all of your duties. You are also to advance her a month's salary which will be the same as yours. This evening at quitting time I want you to take her to our guest quarters and see that she is settled and tell the cook that for the time being she will be taking her meals there." With that she dismissed them, and all went back to their work.

Culum was not only surprised but also taken by this new woman. He could see that she was about his age, and he really liked her looks. After he and Geri discussed their problems, he asked who the new lady was at the reception desk. Geri said, "Culum, she is none of your business. She is a good person, and I don't want her to be one of your play toys." Culum said, "Geri, I know I have been loose in my sexual behavior, but now I want to find me a wife. I made a big mistake when I chose the sea and not you, and I do not intend to do it again. I don't know if this Helen is the one I am searching for, but I want you to know I am going to find me a woman that I can love." Geri was surprised and said, "Culum, I want that for you, also, and I hope you really mean what you have said."

Chapter 34

Paul McGinty was twenty seven in 1865. He was Geri and Luke's second child. He was always a quiet child and was inclined to be less out going than his brother and sister. He worked just as hard as the rest of them, and everyone knew that they could always depend on him. His baby sister adored him, and he her. It was obvious very early that he was the smartest one in the family, and Geri saw that he got the best education that one could have.

He chose McGill because he wanted to be a Canadian. Geri chose banking and finance for him, and he found that he liked it. He flourished under the guidance of Mr. Poincare, and at the age of twenty-nine in 1867 he was made president of the second largest bank in Montreal. Mr. Poincare had retired, and Paul M was in complete charge of the bank.

You would think his position would attract a lot of the Montreal's young women, but to the contrary. Paul had a hard time getting women to be interested in him. He was a handsome man, but he had difficulty in making small talk. He had limited social skills so the women he did date wouldn't date him long enough to find out what a great guy he was. He had decided he would probably be a bachelor all of his life.

Because of his skill as a banker, he was given a Professorship at McGill University and was considered one of the best teachers in the school of Banking and Finance. Students loved the way he taught. He had the ability to make difficult subjects of finance easy to understand, and he had received many awards for his teaching skills.

One day he was giving a graduating address for the class of 1867. It wasn't on finance or banking but on how he felt that his students should find their way in the real world. He was telling them that in the very near future Canada would be a nation and not a colony of Britain. They would be the leaders of a great nation. He said, "We are a nation that has a great wealth in natural resources, and I know we will be one of the leaders of the modern world." He ended his speech with saying, "Grab your future and live it with confidence and joy. God bless Canada." There was a thunderous applause.

In the audience was a thirty year old woman who had gone to Mount Holyoke College for Women. She was a native of Montreal and had wanted to go to McGill, but they would not matriculate her. She had established herself in Montreal as a painter and was seen by many knowledgeable people as a brilliant painter. Her name was Ann Galt.

As Ann was walking away from the campus, she was thinking that she wanted to meet this man, Paul McGinty. He had a sensitivity that appealed to her. When Ann was in deep thought, she rarely would be aware of what was going on around her. She was carrying books and didn't see a crack in the sidewalk and stumbled and nearly fell. She felt an arm grab her and steady her. She looked up and saw that it was Paul McGinty who had helped her.

She was dumbfounded and could hardly say anything. She heard Paul M say, "I have stumbled on that crack many times, and I have tried to get them to fix it for a long time. Now I am glad I was unsuccessful for it has given me a chance to meet such a beautiful woman. Are you okay?" She replied, "I was walking and not looking where I was going. Yes, I am fine. Aren't you Paul McGinty who just gave the Commencement Speech?" Paul M replied that he was and asked what her name was. She said, "My name is Ann Galt. I come to the McGill campus often as I am trying to get them to let me take some classes here. You know they don't allow women to come to McGill."

Paul replied, "Yes, I do know this, and my mother and I have been advocating that the University change this policy. My baby sister had to go to Mount Holyoke in order to get her a college experience, and we both felt that it was outrageous that she had to leave Canada to get a college experience." Ann asked, "When did she go to Mount Holyoke." Paul replied, "Let's see. She was eighteen when she matriculated. She was born in 1841, so it was 1859 when she went to Mount Holyoke. She graduated in 1863." Ann replied, "I graduated in 1859, so I just missed her.

This conservation was going so well that Paul M wanted to get to know Ann better and suggested that they go to the nearest cafe and have a cup of coffee. Ann said, "Yes," and they spent the rest of the day together. This was the start of many dates.

When Ann wanted to display her paintings, Paul M set up a display in the main floor of his bank. Her paintings were a great success, and all of Montreal was talking about their budding painter. She had many people asking for portraits, but she was very selective. Paul M wanted her to paint his mother and father together. This really excited her as she knew that she was in love with Paul M.

Paul M wrote his mother and father asking if they would come to Montreal and let Ann, the woman he loved, paint their portrait. It was the statement "he loved" that brought them to Montreal. They had thought that Paul M would always be a bachelor, and the possibility that he might marry thrilled them. When they arrived, they were delighted to discover that Paul had found a beautiful young woman, and that she was such a talented person. They sat four weeks for their painting and felt that it was the best four weeks of their lives. The painting was magnificently displayed in the bank building and crowds of people came to see it. The painting clearly revealed the tender care of the artist. The entire McGinty family was awe struck. Luke, Sr. took Paul M aside and said, "Paul, don't let that young lady get away." Ann heard him say that and said, "Don't worry, Mr. McGinty, I won't let Paul get away." This was the first time all knew that they were engaged.

Paul and Ann's relationship was entirely different than Paul W and Beatrice's relationship. Neither one made demands on the other. They were so grateful that they had found someone whom they could love and be loved by that any needs that developed by their growing attachment were easily met by both. They had the ability to talk out their needs and resolve them with the joy of sharing. Sexual needs were no problem for them as they knew they would at some time become important in their expanding relationship. They put no barriers on their sexual desires. When sex became a need, they simply made it a part of their growing life together. Their marriage was a simple affair, and only meaningful people were there. Neither Paul M nor Ann had any real close friends, so Paul wanted his father to be his best man, and Ann wanted her sister to be her maid of honor. It was a family affair and very satisfying for all.

CHAPTER 35

Helen McHenry rapidly mastered her job and became very important to Geri. She worked hard to understand how the company worked and was able to institute changes that increased the efficiency of the office. She became more than a receptionist, and was considered by Geri as her office manager. This change brought about a hugh increase in her salary and Helen's reevaluation of herself.

She started thinking about who she was. Helen came from a desperately poor family. They were poor tenant farmers and lived on potatoes for their main staple. Her mother and father had many children and could hardly feed them. Very early the boys were apprenticed out, and the girls were to marry as soon as they reached puberty. Many of her sisters were married at fourteen. Helen was sold as a maid to a prominent banker. Helen called it sold as her father got 15 pounds in the transaction.

The sum effect in all of this was that Helen realized that she never developed any self esteem. She was just an object to be sold to anyone who might come along. This is what happened in her marriage. To her husband she was a good looking package that would satisfy him sexually and take care of his other needs and produce children for him as he would need laborers for his expanding farm. When no children came, he became disinterested in her and eventually threw her out of the house.

As she really looked at herself, she felt the pain of all the abuse she had experienced, and anger boiled up in her body. Her face became red, and there was a pressure in her chest. She screamed out her rage. As she calmed down, she stared at herself in the mirror. She saw a pretty middle-aged woman. Her reddish blond hair was turning to an attractive gray. She had a trim figure, and she felt that she could compete with any woman of her age. She was beginning to build her self-esteem.

All of this change had taken place before Culum started trying to get to know Helen. At first he had no idea what kind of person he was trying to date. When she didn't show any interest to his first approaches, he was puzzled as he had found that his techniques had always worked with other women. He finally got the message. Helen was not like any of his other women. In fact she treated him just like Geri had when he had approached her on the O'Dorcas Savage.

This thought set him back, and he wondered what he must do to interest Helen. On the O'Dorcas Savage Geri could not escape him, but in this world he was in now, Helen had a lot of authority. He was at a loss, and he decided that he would just talk frankly to Helen.

One day he happened to be having coffee in the company's break room. He was thinking about Helen when she walked in. Culum got up from his chair and offered a seat for Helen. This small gesture pleased Helen, and she found herself talking to Culum. Culum was not his forward self and was having a hard time talking.

This surprised Helen as she expected that he would be his typical self assured man who felt that he was God's gift to women. Instead he was saying in a hesitant voice, "Helen, I have been trying to date you for over three months, and you have completely ignored me. What is it about me that irritates you and makes you not want to have anything to do with me?" Helen was not impressed by this as she thought that it was just another ploy of Culum's. Even though she had this idea, she thought she might as well tell him her objections of him so he would finally leave her alone.

Helen said, "Culum, you are an egotistical bastard. You think that all you have to do is snap your fingers, and women will fall all over you. I am fed up with men like you, and as far as I am concerned, I wish you would pursue the women that are so foolish as to let you take advantage of them. I came into this break room, and now all you have done is spoil my rest period." She got up and went to the other side of the room.

To say Culum was shocked would be an understatement. All he did was just sit there and think about what she had said. Was it true of him? Did he think he was God's gift to women? He needed to talk to

Geri because she would tell him the truth. He did nothing until Geri asked him to come to her office for a conference on a subject dealing with their business.

When the discussion was over he said, "Geri, I want to ask your advice on something that is bothering me." Geri said, "Yes?" She said this hesitantly, fearing what he might say. Culum said, "Geri, I have been trying for at least three months to get Helen to have a date with me, and she refuses every time. Last week she was sitting with me in the break room, and when I asked her why she didn't want to date me, she told me. It was a shock to me what she said, and I have been asking myself if what she said is true. I am thinking there is some truth in it, but I want your ideas about what she said. So here goes. She said that I am an egotistical bastard who thinks he is God's gift to women and that I should leave her alone and go to those foolish women who believe my crap. I am paraphrasing her words, but that is what she meant." He stopped and waited for Geri's reply.

What he got was Geri bursting out laughing and saying, "And to think that I was worried about Helen. I should have been worried about you, for I can see you have got a tiger by the tail. Culum, Helen is not for you because you would have to change a lot before she would be interested in you. Helen has been thru the ropes with men, and now she knows she is a worthwhile woman, and that she deserves a man who loves her for what she is and not for how she looks. It is apparent that you have shown Helen your worst side—your egotistical side. When you were in Bermuda, and you were considering me as a person you might quit the sea for, you were kind to me and to Robert. That kindness was very appealing to me. You have changed, Culum. You have become a very cynical man, and you express it with that egotistical debonair air that you promote when you are trying to impress a woman. You have developed this facade very well, but to a woman who wants a giving loving man, it turns her off. My advice to you, Culum, is go find another woman." It took a long time for Culum to understand what Geri had said.

Over the next few weeks Culum was sulking around and was finding that it got him nowhere. Did he want to change? For a number of years he had never found a woman he wanted to marry. Was this related to the way he attracted women? Was he attracting only women that were like him? They were in life just for the day and not the long haul with all its ups and downs that produced lasting relationships where caring and loving grow and bring comfort and tenderness that salve the troubled soul. Caring and love were the things he had missed, and he was never finding them in the women he was able to attract. He was becoming more and more convinced that his only hope for finding a loving woman would only come about if he somehow changed. How was he going to change?

The first thing he did was to stop this front he had. He stopped being debonair and cynical and became a quiet and attentive man. He started trying to see how other people felt and was not so interested in his own feelings. When he learned to listen to other people he was surprised by how much he enjoyed people. The more he was interested in them the more they wanted to be around him and wanted to know him.

These inquires of who he was troubled him. He was finding that he didn't feel comfortable being that open about himself. He began asking himself, "Who am I? Why do I seem to fear revealing myself?" Past memories began echoing in his mind. He was hearing his father criticizing him. As a child he soon learned that what he was did not please his father. To avoid this he stopped revealing who he was. Why did his father not like him? His mother had died birthing him. He was not raised by his father until he was six or seven, and then it was because his care taker died, and there was no one to take care of him. Did his father not love him because he caused his mother's death? He had wondered this many times when his father would rage about him and his behavior. Did his father hate him because he felt he lived, and his mother didn't? These thoughts upset him, and he felt tears in his eyes. He lay back on the bed and wept deep sobbing moans. Why didn't you live, Mother? Why didn't you live?

That night he had a troubled sleep, and the next morning he said to himself that it was time to be himself, and the only way to discover it was to be completely honest with his feelings. He felt his feelings were what he really was, and if he was afraid to express them, he was repeating what he had done when he stopped being himself with his father.

When he said this, he felt anger towards his father and sat down and wrote him a long letter. He expressed what he felt his father had done to him, and he was very angry with him. His answer came with his father coming from Denmark to Halifax.

One day his father suddenly appeared and was sitting in his apartment when he came home from work. At first he didn't know what to expect and simply went into the room and sat down and waited for his father to speak. His father said, "I got your letter, and I thought that I should come and talk to you." Culum interrupted and said, "If you are about to criticize me, you can just leave as I am a grown man now, and I will not tolerate that behavior ever again." His father replied, "If I came for that, I would have stayed home and ignored your letter. I came to tell you I was a terrible father. I was a bitter man who had lost the only person in the world that I had ever loved, and I hated you because every time I looked at you, I was reminded of what I had lost.

As I grew older, and after you left saying you would never come back, I realized that I had destroyed your mother's last gift to me—you. She wanted me to have a son, and I destroyed you in my bitterness, and I lost her dying gift to me. I never loved you and not having you loving me and me loving you was the worst thing I could have done to you and me. The past is gone; is there any hope for us in the present?"

Culum responded, "I don't want the past, and if I say no hope, I am just extending the past. I don't know if I can love you. I think you are saying that you are willing to try to love me. Is that what you are saying?" His father said, "I don't know if that is it or not. All I know is that I don't want things to be as they have been since your mother died. I am lonely and without any one to love or be loved by. That is all I know." They sat in silence, and Culum finally said, "Let's go and get something to eat and then why don't you stay for a while and let's see what will happen."

His father did stay, and they slowly began to feel more comfortable with each other. His father began cooking breakfast and dinner for them, and they started sharing the days with each other. One day Culum started talking about this woman he wanted to date. He said, "I have had many women in my life, but I never was able to want a permanent relation. I would engage, and after a while I would just drift away. There was one woman that I really loved, and I felt that she was considering me for her husband. I had to leave with my Captain, and I was going to come back and be with her. When I got away from her, I got into that same position as I did with all women. I wrote her a letter that I loved the sea first and that I would only come back when I got that out of my blood. That was a lie. I was afraid of commitment. I lost that woman to another man who was not afraid of loving and committing his life to her. Now I have found a woman that is similar to the first woman, and she will have nothing to do with me. She is a very smart woman. She knew that I was not a sincere man when it comes to dealing with women. She thinks I am an egotistical debonair fool that only foolish women would have anything to do with. You know, Dad, she is right." This was the first time he had called his father by any name. They both looked at each other and wondered what this meant.

His father said, "Son, I am happy that I am your Dad. I don't deserve it, but I know that I love you, and for the first time, I realize what a wonderful gift your mother gave me when she birthed you. You never received any love in your life with me, and it seems that you are reluctant to receive love from people that are able to give it to you. Do you think that this new woman is capable of loving?" Culum replied, "I don't know, but I do know she will have nothing to do with my pretend self. I know now that I was playing a role of being a sharp devil may care kind of guy in order that I wouldn't be hurt. You know, Dad, you were the only person that I ever was close to, and you hurt me bad. So I must associate being close to a person with being hurt bad." His father with great distress in his voice said, "Oh, God, I knew that I had hurt you, but to realize that I have made you fearful of having closeness and love is the worst thing I could have ever done to you." They both wept, and it seemed they would never stop.

This emotional catharsis exhausted both of them, and they went to bed early. Interestingly, both slept soundly that night, and the next morning there was something different in the way they acted toward each other. It was hard to describe, but they both felt a caring for each other. When Culum left for work, he hugged his father good bye.

Culum stopped pursuing Helen and avoided her. He was ashamed of his behavior toward her and felt it was better to not be with her. He didn't try to date, and the women in the office began to take notice of him. He didn't try to engage them and that surprised them. Geri noticed his change, and one time after a meeting, she asked him to stay as she wanted to talk with him.

Geri said, "Culum, I have noticed that you are more serious about your work and have increased your contribution to the company markedly. Luke tells me you are now the best person working for him, and he thinks I should give you a raise and a promotion to a higher position. What has happened to you?" Culum said, "I am living with my father now, and I am very happy to have found him." This statement surprised Geri because she thought that he hated his father. She said, "Didn't you tell me that you hated your father?" Culum said, "Yes I did, but we have worked out our difficulties, and we now love each other, and I am happy for the first time in my life." Geri wanted to pursue this, but Culum said, "I don't want to talk about it as all of it is still too painful for me." She ended the conservation by saying she wanted him to report to her office the next morning as she now needed an assistant to help integrate all of their diverse holdings.

Culum left not too happy about this move as it would put him into too much contact with Helen. He was still smarting from the memory of her verbal attack and feared that he would experience it again. When he got home, he told his father about the promotion and expressed his fear of working next to Helen. His father said, "Culum, you are different now, and if she is as perceptive as you think she is, she will not attack you. Anyway if she does say nasty things to you brush it off, for she is not as sensitive as you thought. Walk on away, and do your work." Culum was surprised how these simple words made him feel strong and whole again.

The next day he went to work, and his desk was next to Helen's. He said nothing to her and did his work efficiently. She had suspected that he would harass her about dating, but this didn't happen. She was pleasantly surprised. Weeks passed, and nothing was happening as far as their relating to each other. Helen was confused because she found herself being attracted to him.

She decided to talk to Geri about Culum. She said, "Geri, when you brought Culum to the office, I was concerned about him pestering me, but he doesn't, and in fact he tries to avoid me. His whole personality has changed, and I find that I am attracted to him. Am I losing my mind?" Geri replied, "Helen, you don't realize how many women in this office have come to me with the same story. They say they try to flirt with him, but he doesn't pay them any mind. I don't know what has happened to Culum, but whatever it is I am grateful, for he has made my work so much easier. In fact, I am going to promote him to the board."

Helen was stunned and walked out of the office wondering. She started trying to engage Culum, but he ignored her. Finally, one day she stopped him and asked him to go to the break room with her and have a cup of coffee. He thanked her for the invitation, but he was too busy to go. She couldn't believe it; he had turned her down. She withdrew from him for the next few days, but found that her attraction to him was only increasing. She felt she was going to have to find some way to get his attention. She knew talking was not going to work. She decided to bring some of her best cookies to work and, casually, offer him one. She waited until mid afternoon and pulled several cookies out of her desk and offered him one. Surprisingly, he accepted. They talked a little bit but that was all that happened.

The next day mid morning Culum brought out some Mexican sweet bread and offered her a slice. She was so surprised by this and asked where he got such delicious bread. He said, "I made it." They ate it in silence and continued their work. Helen realized that there was much more to Culum than she had realized and decided somehow she was going to get to know him better. Try as she may nothing happened.

One day she didn't come to work, and Geri was concerned about her and asked Culum to go to her apartment and find out if anything was wrong. He had no difficulty finding her apartment and knocked on the door, and no one answered. It disturbed him, and he went to the manager and asked if she would check on apartment 212 and see if the tenant was okay as she had not come to work, and he could not get a response from her. The manager was a middle aged motherly woman who had been concerned about Helen as she never had a friend or visitor. She rushed upstairs and knocked vigorously on the door. With no response she opened the door, and they found Helen unconscious on her bed. Culum carried her downstairs and got her into his carriage and rushed her to the hospital. In the emergency room the doctor told him that she had congested lungs, and they feared she had pneumonia. When they asked if she had any family, Culum said he was the only one and that he was a distant cousin. He signed all of the papers and said he was responsible for all expenses. He left the hospital only to tell Geri what had happened and said he would stay with her until she was better. He told Geri that the prognosis was bad, but he was hopeful for her.

It was a week before she had a crisis. In other words her fever broke, and she started to recover rapidly. When this happened, he stopped coming, and she started asking the nurses what had happened to her. The nurse told her that her cousin brought her to the hospital in a coma, and he had been with her until she had gotten better. Helen was confused as she had no cousin and asked to see the admissions papers. When she read them, she saw they were signed by Culum Rafin. Culum had taken care of her.

One week later she was back at work, and Culum said nothing. She could not help herself. She had to talk to him and she said, "Culum, I read my admission papers, and you signed them. I am confused how that happened." Culum replied, "Geri asked me to go to your apartment and see if anything was wrong. I found you unconscious, and I took you to the hospital and that was all." Helen replied, "Culum that was not all. You apparently stayed with me for all the time I was so sick that they thought I was going to die and only left when I was conscious and almost well. I just don't understand you." Culum said, "Look, Helen, I did what I did because you needed someone to help you. That was all there was to it." Helen said, "Culum, why are you avoiding me? I have been trying for a long time to get to know you, and you avoid me." Culum said, "Helen, you told me a long time ago you wanted nothing to do with me, and I decided to never bother you again."

Helen thought for few minutes and recalled what she had said to him. She had called him an egotistical fool. She said to herself I must have hurt him more than I realized. She looked at him tenderly and said, "Culum, that statement doesn't apply to you now. Will you forgive me if I hurt you when I said those words?" Culum replied, "Of course, I forgive you, but you were only telling the truth. I was then just as you stated." Helen said, "Culum, I want to know you better. Do you think you could have a date with me?" He laughed and said, "How about dinner tonight at my house, and I will cook."

When Helen arrived at Culum's apartment, she was greeted by his father. As they were walking to the living room, his father, Frederick, was talking about how delighted he was to meet her. He said, "You know, of course, Culum talks about you all the time." Helen was not aware of this but was pleased. He continued, "When I first came to Halifax to be with Culum, one of the first things he was talking about was how was he going to change so that Helen would be interested in him, and here you are." Helen was amazed that Culum had thought that much of her that he wanted to change his way of living and his way of presenting himself to others. She knew that he had been very successful in what he was doing and was impressed that he put that much value upon her. About this time Culum came into the room, and they started talking about different things. He stated, "Dinner is ready, and we can eat when you all are ready." It was a success, and all enjoyed themselves.

She knew now that she must capture Culum because he represented all the things she wanted in a man. With this mutuality, they soon were intensely involved with each other. Soon they were living together. Helen made a point of the fact that she did not want to have a marriage. Her previous marriage had bound her to a very difficult man and had made it very difficult for her to separate from him. She felt that a marriage contract was a document of enslavement, and she would have none of it. Culum didn't like this idea because he wanted to have a contract with Helen. He felt that it would give him the security that she would never leave him. This condition was not a problem for them; they just simply had different ideas.

It was six months into this relationship that Helen missed her period. She wasn't concerned about it because she was 40 and Culum was 50, so she knew the chances of being pregnant were very slim. However, she missed a second one, and she began having strange feelings in her pelvic area. Then the third month, her clothes were beginning to get tight, and she knew she was pregnant. When she told Culum that she thought she was pregnant, he was excited, and her father-in-law was ecstatic. Both men became very concerned about Helen. They were remembering that Culum's mother had died during the birthing of him, and they were fearful for Helen. Helen told them that was nonsense. She was a different person, and it was a different time.

Culum investigated the best obstetricians in Halifax and found a doctor who had trained in Austria under Semmelwiss. Dr. Semmelwiss had taught him that it was very important to be aware of the dangers of infection in the birthing of a child, and he was the first obstetrician to insist on sterile conditions during the birthing of a child. This was somewhat reassuring to the two men, but they still were concerned, and when the time came for the delivery, they were extremely anxious.

Helen handled the delivery easily, and an 8 pound 6 ounce boy was now in the family. When Helen realized that she was pregnant, she insisted on being married. She didn't want her baby to be considered a bastard. They named the baby boy Frederick Culum after his father and his grandfather. Both Helen and Culum felt that they would have no other children, but they were wrong. When Frederick was two years old, she gave birth to a baby girl whom they named Helen Geri, and two years after that, another baby girl was born whom they named after Culum's mother, Inger Karen. Having these three children did not stop Helen from continuing with her job as their grandfather loved being with his grandchildren.

Chapter 36

Paul W and Beatrice found themselves alone with Abby and Joseph managing the McGinty Trading Company in Bermuda. Their relationship was very warm and caring and within a year's time a baby boy was born. He was named James Paul after his father and grandfather. When Beatrice's father, Johannes Daniel Radisson, heard of her pregnancy and the birth of the baby boy, he wrote a long letter to both of them saying it was important to him that they come and visit him and her mother and let them have at least some contact with their only grandchild.

It was quite difficult for them to leave Bermuda at that time as the Civil War was very actively creating business from both the Union and the Confederacy. Even though iron clad vessels were doing the main Naval battles, there were still a lot of wood sailing ships to be repaired. They did, however, return to Montreal, and Johannes sat down with Paul W and talked about the future.

He asked, "Paul W, what are your plans for the future? Are you going to stay in Bermuda or come back to Montreal?" Interestingly enough Paul and Beatrice had been discussing that very same thing. Both had decided that if it were possible, they would stay in Bermuda for the rest of their lives. They both had been hurt by the society of Montreal and wanted nothing to do with it. Johannes understood this feeling and said, "Paul W, you and Beatrice are my only family, and I have a large business that if I should die first, my wife would be unable to manage it. Since I realize that you no longer want to be in Montreal, I am not going to encumber you with this inheritance and its obligations. I have been thinking that I would sell my company here and move to Bermuda to be near our family.

The wanderers

As you know, my business is in two areas, one being furs and merchandising and the other being hotels. I feel that Bermuda will not maintain its position in boat repairing because wooden sail boats are of the past. The climate in Bermuda is very mild and inviting to people who want to have a warm vacation, so, Paul, I think that you and I should start a tourist business in Bermuda and build lush hotels that would attract people from the United States and Europe and, hopefully, Canada."

This idea intrigued Paul W and Beatrice, and they were extremely happy about it. She had missed her parents, and the idea that they would be living close to her comforted her. Johannes had other ideas about who should buy his company in Montreal. He said, "Paul W, I want you to approach McGinty Trading Company and see if they would be interested in acquiring my fur business. I have an idea they will be delighted."

This was exactly what McGinty Trading Post needed, and they started negotiating the price. Paul Winfield, Paul W's father, became interested in the negotiations and asked young Paul McGinty to investigate the hotels that Johannes owned. Paul M, as you recall, was a careful banker, and he diligently pursued studying the physical structure of the property, its location, and the economic return. He reported to his mother, Geri, that he felt it would be a good idea to purchase the entire business structure of Johannes Daniel Radisson.

After much discussion a fair price was arrived at by both parties, and Frederick Daniel and Gjerta Karon, his wife, moved to Bermuda. It was in 1864 when they did this. At that time there was too much conflict going on so that materials were not available for building hotels. They had to wait until after the Civil War was over before they could begin to develop their tourist business. By this time Beatrice had birthed another baby boy and baby girl, and they felt their family was complete.

After the war the sailing repair business overnight disappeared, and by 1869 Geri decided to close the ship yards in Bermuda and offer them for sale. Paul W and his father-in-law bought the land and developed it. They called it South Hampton. Their first hotel was completed in 1871.

In 1872 Robert Hogg McGinty was 42 years old and Joanne, his wife, was 40 years old. Their children were in their late teens and early 20's, and they felt they would have no other family. However, in June of 1872, Joanne birthed a baby girl named Maria Louisa Hogg McGinty. This was a surprise baby and was nurtured and adored by the whole family. Geri couldn't get over the fact that at the age of 60 she was again a grandmother of Robert's child.

Robert had been the company's advance man for a number of years. He had traveled all over Upper Canada and into the Northwest territories. He had experienced many different encounters with the native people and business people along all of the Great Lakes. At 42 he was tired of traveling and being away from his family and told his mother that he needed for her to position him in an area where he could be with his family every day. So, Maria Louisa would have her father in her life.

CHAPTER 37

Maria was 18 in 1890. For the last ten years she had lived with her grandparents, Geri and Luke. In her early years she had not been able to get along with her mother. Maria was always confused about why she and her mother were always at odds. One thing she knew was that she was not like the rest of her family. Her two sisters were tall, blond haired and blue eyed and her brother was five feet, ten inches tall and also blond haired and blue eyed. Maria Louisa was five feet tall, brown haired with hazel eyes. She had always felt she didn't belong in this family. Her parent family was calm and directed with their feelings, but Maria was impulsive and demanding with her feelings. Her mother could not cope with her behavior, and they were constantly fighting. Finally, her mother threw up her hands and insisted Robert do something as she could no longer tolerate her daughter.

Robert talked to his parents, and they agreed to raise Maria. Maria Louisa loved her grandparents, and they had no problems with her behavior. When she was impulsive and demanding, they would ignore her and waited until she was calmer and then address the issues. Maria soon learned that her behavior was exhausting to her and getting her nowhere so she gradually changed. She adored her Grandmother Geri and started copying her mannerisms, and the way she handled her problems. The more she became like her Grandmother the more she and her Grandfather got along. In fact, they became inseparable.

Maria was not a student; she was more of a doer than a thinker. She liked to explore and not study, so she found it hard to stay in school. When she completed secondary school, she told her Grandparents that she didn't want to go further with her formal education. She said, "Mom and Pop, (as she called her Grandparents), I want to learn the world by exploring it and not by reading about it. I have been with Pop to the West Indies, Bermuda and the British Isles. I loved it, especially being with Pop. Now I feel that I am a grown woman, and I want to explore by myself. I want to explore Canada. I want to see the Great Lakes and all points west. I want to fly away and see the world."

Geri was concerned by these requests and resisted. It was Luke that understood what she was saying and how she felt. They all talked together and decided that it was a good idea that she explore, but Luke and Geri wanted her to do it in the framework of their trading stations. They had trading stations all the way to Alberta, and they felt that if she stayed close to these places they would feel safe about her wandering.

So in the summer of the year 1890 Maria Louisa left Halifax and went up the St. Lawrence River. She passed through the Lachine Canal and didn't stop to see her parents. She got to Lake Ontario and was fascinated by its size and the beauty surrounding it. The little villages around it intrigued her, and she almost wanted to stay and visit for a while. Niagara Falls stunned her with its grandeur. She would get as close to the bottom of the falls as she could and just stand bathing herself in the spray that rose all around her. Her crossing of Lake Erie was very disturbing as she was caught in a storm, and the waves frightened her. She had no desire to ever be on that lake again. Finding the Detroit River that emptied into Lake Erie fascinated her, and she visited the United States for the first time.

She went through Lake Huron and Lake Superior, and by the end of the summer she was in Winnipeg, Manitoba. She felt the winter in Winnipeg was too cold for her and planned to go the next summer to as far as Alberta and see the Canadian Rockies. She wrote many letters to her Mom and Pop describing the land and telling of the people she met. She said, "I am going to New Orleans for the winter as I want to have a southern winter.

By using the Canadian Pacific Railroad as a way to travel, I will go to Calgary, Alberta and see the Canadian Rockies. In midsummer I will go back to Winnipeg and take the Northern Pacific out of Winnipeg and travel to Minneapolis. I hope I can get a steamboat to go all the way to New Orleans, but on this part of the trip I will have to respond to what is available. I expect to be in New Orleans by November, 1891. I love you, Maria."

The wanderers

She was able to get as far as Memphis by late November. She checked into the Peabody Hotel and planned to stay there until spring. The Christmas holidays brought many wealthy families from Mississippi and Arkansas to Memphis. Maria was a good dancer, and she attended all of the Christmas and New Year balls that were at the Peabody Hotel. It was there that she met a handsome young man named Richard Godwin. He owned a large plantation near Jonesboro, Arkansas, and traded in cotton futures. His office was located near the Peabody Hotel. They struck up a romance and became engaged. Maria's grandparents insisted they come to Halifax, and they did.

The trip to Halifax was long and difficult. It took almost five days. Maria was excited about her fiancé' and showed him off. Luke had some reservations about Richard, but he couldn't say why so he caused no difficulty. Geri had no opinion but was pleased about Maria's happiness. The visit was a success for all, and when they left, Maria and Richard were very happy. Richard was pleased that Maria came from such a prominent family. One incident occurred that puzzled him as he had never heard of it.

On the day they were leaving, Luke asked Richard to come to his office because he wanted to talk to him about Maria's inheritance. Luke opened the conversation saying, "Richard, all of Maria's inheritance is in a trust. It is a trust that specifically states that when she marries, the husband will have no control over the trust. The interest of the trust is to be given to Maria and her family, but she will have no access to the principal. The trust lasts into the generation past Maria and when that generation dies, it is to be distributed to the survivors. As you know, no one can predict the future, and all I want to do is to give Maria some security if things go badly for her."

Richard was somewhat taken aback by this and said, "Sir, am I being told that you do not think that our relationship might survive, and I might take advantage of my wife? Sir, you may not know it, but I am a very wealthy man. I own a very successful cotton trading business that last year made $500,000 profit. I also own a 2500 acre cotton plantation, and I see no reason for you to fear for Maria's security." Luke could see that Richard was upset, but Luke felt that his financial structure was in jeopardy.

He responded, "Richard, Geri and I have been in your type of business for many years, and we know the risks you have to take to earn the money you do. I am just saying that I have arranged for you and Maria to have a safety net. If you perceive this as an insult of your ability, then so be it." As Richard calmed down, he thanked Luke for his concern and in a half hearted way apologized. Luke noted this, and his concern for the success of their relationship increased.

The trip back to Memphis was uneventful. Richard did discuss with Maria his conversation with Luke. He said, "I think your Grandfather has some reservations about me. He seems to think that I take too many risks, and I think he wants me to reevaluate how I do my business." Maria asked, "Why do you think this? Did he specifically say that he was concerned about your business?" Richard replied, "No, but he said my business was risky." Maria asked, "Is it?" Richard replied, "Yes, it is, but I have been doing it for ten years and have not lost money." With that statement they let it drop and talked of their coming wedding.

Chapter 38

Alsey Thornberry was in his law office meditating. Today, June 21, 1890, was his 56th birthday. Oh, how the years had passed. His thoughts drifted to his first marriage. Elizabeth was 21, and he was 22. In fact, it was this very day in June, 1856, that they were married. "To me it was my only passionate marriage. That marriage night was filled with so much passion. God, I loved Ollie so much. The next six months were the most joyous months of my life. Ollie had an easy pregnancy, and we were hopeful about our new family. Her delivery was easy, and we had a lovely little girl. We named her after my mother and were so happy. The next day Ollie developed a high fever, and she started to draining pus from her birth canal. Oh, God, how frightened we were. Things got worse quickly, and we knew she had puerperal fever. Ollie and I had seen it in so many women in our community and feared the worst and the worst happened. In five days, Ollie, the love of my life was gone. As she was dying, I held her in my arms and just before she died she said, "Alsey, I love you, and I will be waiting for you in Heaven. Take care of baby Francis. Goodbye, dearest." I couldn't believe she was gone, and I wept bitterly. The day of her death was, let's see, December 15, 1856.

Oh, those were bitter days. I had to find a wet nurse for Francis, and I was so lonely. I had always thought that I would be a farmer like my father, but I began thinking that I was interested in the law. It would take me a long while to find a lawyer who would let me read with him.

The next three years were hard years. I had started a general merchandise store in Mark Tree, Arkansas, and it was marginally successful. I was buying farm land and renting it out. Francis was three and I needed a mother for her.

There was a farm family that lived near Mark Tree, Arkansas, and they were having a hard time making it. They had mostly girls, and it was necessary for the girls to leave their home as soon as they could. I will never forget the day that Mr. Bradsher came into the store and asked to speak to me privately. I thought that he wanted to get an extension on his bill, but instead he wanted to talk about his daughter, Nancy. He said, 'You need a mother for your little girl, and Nancy needs a home. She is twenty one and a strong woman. She is a good girl, and she would make a good wife. Would you consider her as a wife?' I had not considered Nancy in that regard and was surprised by his statements. I didn't say anything for a while, and Bradsher became restless. I hurried up my thoughts and said I would come to his house that evening and talk to Nancy Bradsher. All thru that day I considered the idea of marrying Nancy. Nancy was a plain looking young woman. She was about five foot four inches tall, and had a good figure. Her hair was black and drawn back into a knot behind her head, and she had the kindest blue eyes I had ever seen. We talked, and we both knew that we were not in love. She said, 'Mr. Thornberry, the only thing I can offer you are my loyalty, and that I will willingly take care of your needs. I won't expect you to love me, and I will be willing to bear you children and take care of Francis. I will consider her as my child.'

I was pleased with her straightforwardness. I told her I was not a cruel man, and that I would be kind to her. If she did as she said then I would be satisfied to marry her. In three weeks we were married. We didn't engage in sex for several weeks as I felt that we needed to get acquainted with each other. Our first child was stillborn, and Nancy was very upset. Our marriage was mainly during the time of the Civil War.

I had gotten my lawyer license and was doing well when war broke out. I was opposed to succeeding from the Union, and I went to the Capital to try to stop the vote to succeed from the Union. I was unsuccessful and returned to Jonesboro. Many people in the area were upset with me, but my brothers who were for secession kept any trouble from me. The next five years were hard for Nancy and me. She was true to her word and was very loyal to me. We developed a strange kind of caring for each other. We had no children until the war was over. On November 26, 1865, Ida was born. She was a plain baby girl, but we loved her. When the baby, Ida, came, we finally developed a loving relationship. It is strange to me that every time I develop a loving relationship tragedy struck. It was when Ida was almost one year old, October 7, 1866, that Nancy became ill. She awoke one night with severe pains in her stomach. They became worse, and finally she developed a high fever. When the doctor saw her, she was very ill. Her stomach was distended, and she had a very high fever. The doctor thought that she had either a bowel obstruction, or she had appendicitis. He told me that there was little he could do, and Nancy died that night (October 11, 1866). My first thought was how could this happen to me twice. Just when we had found each other, she was gone, and here I was again me with a baby girl and no mother.

I don't know how I got thru the next few months. I told myself that I would never marry again. I found a wet nurse for Ida, and thank God, Francis was ten years old, and she could help with her baby sister. Nancy was the only mother that Francis had known, and she took Nancy's death hard.

It was about this time I started to get into politics. I met a John Price Mardis. He was a lawyer, and his son, W.B. would eventually marry Francis. Those years were reconstruction years, and the people that were unionist were in favor with the government. Most of my family was Confederates, and they protected me and my family during the war. After the war I protected their families from the government.

Any way John P. wanted me to run for an office. I didn't run, but I did meet his widowed sister. She had three children, and I had two children. Her youngest child was the same age as Francis. Many Sundays we would meet at our church and have a picnic lunch together. We got to liking each other and talked about joining our families. It was October 30, 1867, when we married. Both of us had experienced losses, and I think we both had been chronically depressed all of our lives. We didn't want to have any children together, at least not until we got our mixed family grown. When Francis was sixteen, she married W. B. Mardis and that year we had our first child together. Eugene was a puny boy and was always sick. He died on October 14, 1878. It was hard for us to take. At that time we had two girls, Amanda Ruth born on November 1, 1874, and Beatrice was born on January 21, 1877. Amanda Ruth was just like me, and Beatrice was the spitting image of her mother and had her personality. Now Amanda is sixteen and Beatrice is thirteen, and I expect to hear Amanda Ruth soon coming down the hall to my office to get me to go home. Why have I been thinking about all of this? Things are going well, and the children and my wife are well. Do I fear good luck?" His thoughts were interrupted by Amanda Ruth shouting, "Dad, I am here. Let's go home."

Chapter 39

Maria and Richard were married three weeks later, and the wedding was simple with mainly Richard's friends attending. Maria's father, Robert, came from Montreal and gave his daughter in marriage. Geri and Luke were sick and too old to travel that far. Maria and Richard settled in Memphis, and things went well. By the end of 1892 Maria was six months pregnant and doing well. They were very happy and felt that only good things would happen to them

The country at that time was experiencing a marked rise in inflation, and the Presidential campaign was filled with a debate on what to do with the inflation. In November, 1892, Grover Cleveland was reelected President, and he promised that he would curb inflation. On March 3, 1893, he was reinaugurated and immediately got Congress to repeal The Sherman Silver purchasing bill of 1890.

The country was overbuilt with railroads, and when the Philadelphia-Reading RR went bankrupt, the financial bubble burst. The United Kingdom had a banking failure and a run on all of their banks. Many railroads were over burdened with debt as they had overbuilt and went bankrupt, i.e. the Union Pacific, Atchison Topeka and Santa Fe, and the Northern Pacific.

There were many silver mines with their own railroads, and silver prices rapidly depressed. When the United States Government was no longer buying silver there was no way to sell silver at a profit. People rushed to exchange silver notes for gold notes and soon the statutory limit for gold in the treasury was reached, and people could no longer exchange silver for gold. There was a credit crunch, and people could not get loans.

This was disastrous for Maria's husband. His cotton futures business collapsed, and his speculation in silver notes ruined his business in Memphis. He was able to hang onto his plantation near Jonesboro, Arkansas, and they had to leave Memphis and live on their plantation. Their baby boy was born during this time, and this created an added burden on their marriage. Richard was fighting for his financial life, and Maria needed him to help with their family. They were able to struggle with this, and Richard felt that all he needed to have happen was to have a good crop in the summer of 1893, and they would be able to weather the storm. This was not to be as Richard had to borrow money to put in a crop and that summer was a scorcher. There was no rain from May to September, and his crop was completely burned up. He could not repay his loan, and the bank foreclosed on his plantation.

Richard began trying to find anything that would help him recover, and he asked Maria if she would ask Luke to lend him money against her trust so that he could get a new start. Luke refused saying, "Maria's trust would furnish them a good living, and he would not finance any speculation." Richard was at first very depressed and then became very angry. He tried to find someone to blame for his misfortunes and ended up attacking Maria. At first it was just being critical of everything she did, and then when he was drunk, he became physically abusive. It was following one such attack that Maria decided to get a divorce.

She first went to their Memphis friends and tried to get them to take her case. She indicated that she was independently wealthy, and she could pay for their services, but none was interested. They all said that it was too difficult to get a divorce, and they didn't have the time to spend on such cases.

Alsey Thornberry was not hurt by the depression of 1893. His pain came on July 8, 1893, when his adorable Beatrice died suddenly. She had been in perfect health and was just sixteen years old. One week before her death she became sick with what the doctor felt was influenza. She had some fever and cough, but otherwise it seemed that she would recover without any trouble. The night before she died she became seriously ill. Her fever spiked, and she became comatose. She died in the early morning hours and never regained consciousness. Her mother, Amanda Jane, was devastated. She had been in poor health for several years and seemed to give up. She quit eating and became bedridden. By February 1, 1894, she was dying. She called Alsey to her bed and said, "Alsey, you have been a good and faithful husband. You gave me a home when I was widowed, and you loved the children I brought with me. I have loved you all these years that we have been together. I know that you have suffered many losses as I have, but you are stronger than I am. The loss of my first husband, Eugene, our boy, and now Beatrice is more that I can bear. When Beatrice died, I felt that I could no longer live and in fact I wanted to die. I know that that is unfair to you, but I have been powerless to stop my despair. Will you forgive me for failing you when you must have needed me in your grieving as much as I desired to die from it?" With that she kissed him goodbye and went to sleep and died on the night of February 13, 1894.

Chapter 40

When Amanda Jane died Alsey was unable to continue his law practice. He would just sit and brood and Amanda Ruth took over the management of the household. She was twenty years old at that time and there had been a remarked change in her personality.

When she was a young girl, she was a tom boy. She loved to run, ride horseback, and spend most of her time on her father's plantation. Alsey was deeply concerned about her boyishness, and when she was eighteen year old, he sent her to a girls' finishing school. She was there for two years, and when she returned, she was a different person. In many ways this change caused much regret in Alsey. Before she had been an open and gay person, but now she was controlling and manipulative. It seemed that she saw herself as a southern belle who was to be indulged with every wish she desired. She handled the help in a superior sense and caused problems with keeping people working for them. Alsey didn't know what to do about this, but to some extent this change in personality was helping him deal with his grief. She would block people from seeing him, and this gave him a certain amount of comfort.

One day when he was sitting in his office trying to work with Amanda Ruth managing the outer office, he heard a loud exchange of voices. Apparently, a person was talking to Amanda Ruth in a very disturbed way. There was silence, and Amanda Ruth came into his office. She said, "Father, (she no longer called him dad) there is a young lady outside demanding to see you. I told her that you weren't seeing anybody, but she insisted. As I was trying to show her to the door, she took off her sunglasses and showed me two blacken eyes. I was shocked by the abuse she had received, and I felt I should interrupt you. Would you be willing to see her?"

Alsey thought for a while and wondered if he wanted to become involved with a case that might be connected with marital abuse. As he thought about this, he realized that he had to make a break sometime from his isolation and grief and maybe this was his chance. He said, "Amanda Ruth, show this lady in, and I will see what I can do."

Maria had been trying for several weeks to get a lawyer to accept her case. When her husband became aware that she was seeking a divorce, his physical abuse of her increased. She moved out of their home and had moved into an apartment. This morning he had broken into her apartment and knocked her around in front of their baby. When he left, she had gotten a neighbor to take care of her baby boy, William, and she began searching again for a lawyer. Alsey Thornberry was the second person she had tried to see. She opened the conversation with Alsey by saying, "Mr. Thornberry, thank you for seeing me. I am desperate to get help in dealing with my marriage. My husband has been a very successful man in the past and maybe you have heard of him. We owned the Godwin Plantation which has recently been repossessed by the bank." She paused and waited to see if there was any acknowledgement of this. Alsey said, "Yes, I am familiar with the Godwin family, and I am aware of his loss. Richard was a very successful cotton broker in Memphis, and I was surprised to hear that he was bankrupt." With this response, Maria continued. "As you know the depression of '93 has affected many farmers in this area, and it has been devastating to Richard. His bitterness towards me started when he tried to use my trust as a means of trying to recover his fortune. My Grandfather's refusal to let him use the trust as a security for a loan enraged him. He, at first, was simply depressed and then he became very angry.

He constantly was looking for someone to be angry with, but there was no one except me. He first started being very critical of me, and then it changed to being physically abusive. The physical abuse started mainly when he was drinking, but now it occurs at any time. It became so severe that I left my home, and now I live in an apartment. This morning when I got up, I heard a noise at the front door, and with a chain lock on the door, I cautiously cracked the door, and it was Richard. He was drunk and demanded to come in. I refused, and he broke the door down." At this point she took off her sunglasses and showed her blackened eyes. She said, "Mr. Thornberry, I cannot tolerate this any longer. I need an injunction to stop him from seeing me, and I need a divorce."

Alsey was shocked by the injury to her face. He wondered if there was also bodily injury that he could not see. He said to her, "Did he injure you in any other place on your body?" Maria replied, "Yes, there are bruises all over my back, and he severely bruised both of my breasts."

Alsey could not tolerate any abuse of a woman, and he felt an anger that he rarely experienced. He thought for a minute as he was experiencing this and wondered if he could be professional with this person as he was so angry over her being abused. He said, "Ms. Godwin, you're telling me of this abuse angers me, and I don't think I can be professional with you in trying to deal with this problem. You see I feel for a lawyer to be effective he must not have any emotional feelings about the problems his client is presenting. I would recommend that you seek somebody else who would be more professional than I could be."

Maria responded, "Mr. Thornberry, I have looked many different places for a lawyer to take my case. Most of them say that they are not interested in divorce cases. They say that getting a divorce in Arkansas is very difficult and resolving property issues is almost interminable. None have been willing to take my case. I am desperate. You are my last hope. It pleases me that my husband's abuse makes you angry because I feel strongly that if I don't have a person emotionally committed to this problem, I will not be able to get a divorce. Would you please try to overcome your feelings and take my case? I am a wealthy woman, and I can afford any expenses that you might incur."

Alsey was silent for a long period of time. He had been thinking in his grieving about all of his losses and how despaired he was, but he began to realize that his tragedy wasn't nearly as severe as what this young woman was experiencing. He said to himself, "I need to get into a good fight in order to escape all of my despair. I think this case could offer that to me."

Finally, he started talking to Maria. He said, "Ms. Godwin, I have reconsidered what you have said, and I will take your case. The first thing we need to do is get an injunction against your husband forbidding him to be within, let's say, 300 feet of you and your child. Then I will file a Motion for Divorce with the Chancery Clerk, and we will start the process."

This started an 18 month experience between Alsey Thornberry and Maria Louisa Hogg McGinty Godwin. During that period of time they became friends on a first name basis. In fact, both of them became very fond of each other. There were many instances of Alsey having to put Richard in jail as he continued to try to abuse Maria. Finally, one Friday afternoon in late December, 1895, Alsey received a call from the Chancery Clerk stating that his divorce papers for Maria Louisa Godwin had been signed by the Chancery Judge, and her divorce was final.

He got up from his office and walked slowly to the Courthouse. He went to the Chancery Clerk's office and got the papers and came out of the Courthouse building and stopped on the steps and pondered. He thought, "I have known this woman now for probably 18 months. I tried all during those months to keep it on a professional level, but in spite of that, I have fallen in love with her. I don't know how this could have happened, and I know she has no idea of my feelings. I find myself being very reluctant to go to her house and tell her about the divorce as this would mean that our relationship is over."

He slowly walked down the steps and on to the street that led to Maria's apartment. He had many thoughts, but his feelings were what overwhelmed him. It seemed to him that again he was experiencing loss, and he feared what this might lead to.

He slowly went up the steps to her apartment and rang the doorbell. Maria opened the door when she realized who it was and gave him a warm smile and asked him to come in. He said, "Maria, I have your divorce papers, and your divorce is final. I don't know how to put this, but I need to tell you what all of this has done to me. I started out seeing you as an abused woman, but being with you all these months has changed how I feel toward you. I find myself now feeling love for you, and I am despaired because I know I am too old for you, and I know it is impossible for you to have any of those feelings towards me." After saying this, he turned and started walking towards the door. Maria grabbed his arm and said, "Wait a minute, Alsey. Don't leave. Let's talk about what you said." Alsey turned, and they sat down on the couch by each other. Maria said, "Alsey, you know I am very fond of you, but I never considered the fact that you might be in love with me. You are a fine, kind gentleman, and I don't think any woman would be turned off by your age, but you see, I never thought of you as a lover. I think we need to be together for a while so that I can see what my real feelings are for you. Why don't you have supper with us, William and I, and let's just see what happens while we spend time with each other as we consider what you have said."

They went about the apartment talking, and soon Maria started preparing supper. Alsey helped her, and soon they had a fine meal on the table. They ate in silence, and after dinner they cleaned up the dishes and the kitchen and went back into the living room. Alsey played with William on the floor until it was time to put him to bed.

When Maria came back, they sat on the couch together, and Maria started talking. She said, "Alsey, I have been looking at my feelings for you, and I realize that I have had thoughts about you in a romantic sense, and when I asked myself do I love you, I found myself saying, yes, yes, I do love you, Alsey. I want you to stay tonight with me and let's see how we relate to each other physically." Alsey was surprised by what she had said and immediately felt some fear.

He was twice her age, and she was only 2 years older than Amanda Ruth. Could he live up to her expectations physically? These thoughts frightened him, and he said to her, "Maria, I am much older than you, and I fear that I will not be able to satisfy you physically." Maria responded, "Alsey, I know you will be a successful lover." They embraced each other on the couch, and for the first time, kissed each other passionately.

Soon they went into Maria's bedroom and undressed. Alsey was fearful of how his body might appear to Maria. He knew that he had old skin that was wrinkled, and when he looked at her, he saw a fresh young skin. How could she accept him when she had so much more to offer? Maria didn't respond to his physical appearance. Instead, she put her arms around his waist, and they walked to the bed. They lay on their sides facing each other and talked. As they were talking, their emotions and physical desires increased so that all negative thoughts were banished, and they became passionate lovers.

When they awakened the next morning, it was obvious that they loved each other, and all they could talk about was their future together. Maria was saying, "Alsey, your daughter, Amanda Ruth, does not approve of me. She has made many comments about how she was anxious for my divorce to be over and for me to be gone. I feel like this is going to be a problem for us. I don't think that Amanda Ruth will tolerate me being in your home."

Alsey knew exactly what she was talking about. He knew that Amanda Ruth was dominating, demanding and tried to convince everyone that she was superior to them. He said, "When we marry, Amanda Ruth will have to leave our home. She has been going steady with a friend of mine, Charles David Cagwin. He has been trying to get her to set a marriage date for several years now. He is about 15 years older than she, and he is a widower. Amanda Ruth is attracted to his prominence and position, but I don't think she loves him. She uses her engagement to him as a social controlling event and not as a promise to marriage. I am going to tell her that I am going to marry you, and two women cannot manage a household. So, she will have to leave, and if she doesn't marry Charles, then she will have to live on our plantation as she cannot stay in our home."

It wasn't until February 9, 1896, that Alsey and Maria were married. At the time of their marriage, Maria was pregnant, and they would have a baby boy on September 10, 1896. This was an interesting marriage. Alsey was a conservative, serious minded person, and Maria was joyful, eager to enjoy every moment. She was a person who certainly was not conservative. She would spend money where Alsey would be very conservative.

You would have thought this would have caused problems, but Alsey was so much in love with Maria that he accepted everything she did. Their relationship was very similar to his first marriage. He literally worshipped her. On July 24, 1898, they had their second child, a baby girl, named Leah. They felt this would complete their family, and they were very happy with each other. Alsey, at this time, was **64** years old and Maria was **28** years old. They started traveling together with the children and visited places such as New York and Nova Scotia. Maria had some reservations about returning to Halifax. Geri and Luke had died shortly after Maria and Alsey's marriage, and she felt there was no one in the family that really loved her.

When they arrived at Halifax, she contacted her cousins and was surprised at how happy they were to see her. They told her that Luke and Geri had advised them that if Maria ever returned they were to treat her with love and caring. The wealth of the McGinty Firm surprised Alsey. He had no idea that Maria came from such a prominent family.

When they went to Montreal, Maria introduced Alsey to her mother and father. Her father was 68 years old, and her mother was 66 years old. She met also with her siblings, her two sisters and brother, and was surprised about how warmly they greeted her.

Alsey and Robert liked each other immediately. Maria was somewhat fearful about meeting with her mother as they had parted on such bad terms when she was 8 years old. To her surprise her mother embraced her and told her how happy she was to have her back in her life. Maria felt for the first time that she had a loving mother. They returned home in 1899, and all seemed to be going well for them.

Maria was very attracted to her daughter. She spent lots of time with her, and it was obvious that she was neglecting her sons. She encouraged her husband to spend more time with Jessie and William, but his age handicapped his ability to participate in the kind of the sports that the boys wanted to play. He tried to involve them in discussions, but all they wanted to do was to play. Maria tried to give more time to them, but her interest was obviously with Leah. When Alsey and Maria talked about this, they would end up saying, "Well, we do have some problems with age difference, but on the whole we have a good family."

It was a cold, bitter winter in the year 1904. There was some influenza at the beginning of the year, but it seemed to die out. In late January of 1904 a flu epidemic reappeared in Jonesboro. Many of their friends became seriously ill, and they thought they would escape it. On February 4, 1904, Maria became ill with the influenza. Within 24 hours Alsey was also sick with the flu. They seemed to do fairly well the next day with Alsey improving more than Maria. On February 5, Maria became more seriously ill. She started coughing blood and pus, and the doctor came and told Alsey that Maria was sick with pneumonia, and she might not survive.

On the late afternoon of February 6, Maria called Alsey into her room and said, "Alsey, I am dying. I'm leaving you with three young children. I am doing to you what your other wives have done, and I am so sorry. I love you, and I hope we will meet again in Heaven." Alsey could hardly believe what she was saying. He sat down beside the bed and held her hand. He said, "Oh, Maria, don't leave me. I can't go through another loss of my wife." Maria just looked at him and weakly smiled squeezing his hand. He was by her side for the next two hours hoping that things would change, but they didn't. Maria slowly slipped into a coma and died at 6:00 p.m. on February 6, 1904.

Alsey slowly got up from his chair beside Maria and went back into his room and lay on his bed. He asked for Charles David Cagwin to come and see him. When Charles arrived he said, "Charles, you are my dear friend. My wife has just died, and I feel like I am about to die. We have three wonderful children, and now they will have no parents. I have a large estate as you know. You have married my daughter, Amanda Ruth, and I feel she is in good hands, but I fear for my younger children. I have established a large trust and appointed you as custodian of this trust. If you should die during the course of their young lives, then Amanda Ruth will be the trustee. Will you accept this responsibility?" Charles, with tears in his eyes, said, "Oh, Alsey, I know you are terribly upset about the loss of Maria, but there is no reason for you to think about dying. You have been improving." Alsey responded, "Charles, I have no desire to live any longer. I have now buried four wives, and I have been left with the care of children that were products of those marriages. I cannot go on doing this. I have one last request of you. When I die, and it will be shortly, I want a double casket large enough to hold Maria and me. I want us to be buried side by side even in death. I do not want to be separated from her." With that, he turned on his side away from Charles and said nothing further. Charles said, "Alsey, I'll do as you request but, please, don't despair. I and your friends love you, and we will help you." Alsey said nothing and in two hours, he was dead.

CHAPTER 41

Leah Malone Thornberry was sitting in her dormitory room at Forrest Heights Girls School in St Louis, Missouri. She was 19 years old and was about to graduate with a teaching degree. She knew that her relationship with Amanda Ruth was impossible, and she would somehow have to move some place where she would have very little contact with her. She had been applying to various school districts for a teacher's job and had not been successful in locating ones that were far away from her sister. The only positive reply she got was from the Trumann Arkansas School District. This was about 30 miles from where Amanda Ruth lived. She would have much rather it had been 300 to 400 miles, but this was the best she could do at that time.

After graduation she went to Camp Gaillard, Saint Louis, Missouri, as she wanted to see her brother, Jessie. She spent a week visiting with him and met his buddy, Amos Gregory. They both liked each other instantly, and a romance was started. She had to leave to go to her job in Trumann, Arkansas, but they communicated by letters. The units that Jessie and Amos were in went overseas a short time later. Amos got a leave and came down to Trumann to be with Leah. He chose to be with her rather than his family as they were planning to be married.

It was a wonderful week for both of them and each promised to write many letters until they were reunited. It was in the last days of 1917 that Amos and Jessie went overseas. Letters came frequently from Amos to Leah and her to him. One day, no letters. A week passed and then a month and then two months. Leah was frantic. She wrote a letter to Jessie and asked him to find out what was wrong, fearing the worst.

Finally, a letter came from Jessie saying that Amos was killed January 15, 1918. He found his grave and talked to some of his buddies. Apparently, there was a severe German artillery barrage that exploded on top of his trench, and he was one of ten people killed. Leah was in a state of shock. How could she go on? This brought back a lot of memories as she pondered and grieved.

She found herself saying, "Oh, Mother, why aren't you here with me? You left me when I was just a girl of six, and now again someone I dearly loved has left me." Memories of her Mother's death flooded her. Her death then her father's death and she, Jessie, and William were all alone. People hovered around them, and a friend of her Father's, Mr. Cagwin, came and talked to them He said, "Children, I am now your new Father. I know that I can never replace your Mother and Father, but I am going to take care of you and see that you are okay until you are grown." Leah remembered him as being a kind person, and she grew to love him. He had the same problem with the two boys as Alsey had because he was as old as their Father and could not play with them the way they wanted him to, but he and Leah became very close. She remembered getting over her grief for her Mother and started again becoming the happy-go-lucky child.

In 1907, three years later, Mr. Cagwin suddenly died and who would take over but Amanda Ruth! Amanda Ruth was her half-sister, but they never got along. Leah felt that her half-sister, Amanda Ruth, saw her Mother in her and not her as a person. Amanda Ruth had no trouble telling her how her Mother had married their Father and taken him away from her. She said that Maria Louisa had seduced her Father into marriage by getting herself pregnant. She told Leah that Jessie was an early baby and that caused all of the problems that she had with her Father. This blaming colored Leah's life for the rest of her experience with Amanda Ruth. Strangely enough, Amanda Ruth loved Jessie and considered him her son, and she would take care of Jessie for all of his life.

When Leah was 17 years old, she finally was able to persuade Amanda Ruth to send her to college. She knew that college would give her a chance to train herself, so she wouldn't have to depend on Amanda Ruth. When she found the job in Trumann, she kept a big distance between her and Amanda Ruth and as she was mourning the loss of Amos, she realized that the only person in the world who could comfort her was Jessie. She didn't know how she got by the next year, but before she knew it, it was January, 1919.

She had just discharged her students for the weekend and had walked to her home in Trumann. As she opened the door, the phone was ringing. She ran to the phone hoping it was a call from Jessie as he had written he was returning from France during the month of January. Much to her disappointment, it was Amanda Ruth. Amanda Ruth said, "Leah, I have just met a very handsome soldier who has just returned from overseas. He is tall, has brown hair, and beautiful brown eyes. He is staying with his sister who lives next door to me. I think you would be interested in knowing him. Why don't you just come up Saturday and see if you like him?"

Leah didn't say much, and they hung up. She sat down at her kitchen table and thought, "I'm all alone, and I have not been dating anyone since Amos' death. I have to do something with my life other than just mourning a loss which promised more than it ever was. I think maybe this is a good opportunity to break loose from my despair and begin my life anew." Instead of waiting until Saturday, she caught a train to Jonesboro and spent the night in a local hotel. The next day she went out to her sister's house, and they both went over to the next door neighbor, and she was introduced to a handsome young soldier.

His name was Bunyon Bettendorf. They sat down on the front porch swing and talked. The whole weekend passed quickly, and she was back to Trumann. She was pleasantly surprised when Monday afternoon after school, she found Bunyon waiting for her. He told her that he had found a place to stay, and he was going to stay a week and get better acquainted. That week passed rapidly, and he had to report to his job in Monroe, Louisiana.

He was a telegrapher and worked with the Missouri Pacific Railroad. He had not been gone but a couple of days when she received a letter from him. It was a love letter. This surprised her because she did not have the feelings that he had. She answered his letter in a friendly way, but, obviously, she was not expressing any kind of love for him.

Amos was still too much in her mind. Bunn, as he preferred to be called instead of Bunyon, persisted in writing her, and she began to feel that maybe he was the best hope for her. She knew that she didn't feel for him like she felt for Amos, but she thought she would never have a relationship like that in her life. Every weekend that Bunn could get off, he would take a train to Hoxie about 28 miles from Trumann and then catch a ride into Trumann. Many times he would have a hard time finding a place to sleep and soon, Leah was letting him stay at her house. They didn't get involved sexually with each other as Leah still did not feel she wanted to marry him.

In late July, 1919, Bunn said to her, "Leah, I know I love you, and I know that you do not have the same feeling for me, and I am not going to continue to court you. This visit will be my last one with you." Leah was startled by this and suddenly felt emptiness in her chest as she considered the fact that she would not see him again. She didn't know what this meant, but she decided she would go ahead and marry him if he accepted the fact that she wasn't in love with him to the degree that he was with her.

So, they were married on September 13, 1919. It wasn't a joyous wedding, but they were kind to each other. They took up an apartment in the southwest part of Monroe, Louisiana. They quickly developed friends, and they ran around with an upper middle-class group. Leah's remaining estate helped support this, and in 1921 Leah gave birth to a baby boy named Robert. He was a healthy baby, and both were very delighted. Ten days after his birth he developed an infection in his umbilical cord, and he died a week later. Leah could not tolerate his death. She had birthed a perfectly healthy baby boy and due to the neglect of the hospital, he had died of an infection. Her despair permeated the marriage, and it was only relieved by her second pregnancy.

In February of 1923 she gave birth to a second child, a baby girl, whom she named after herself. Things began to pick up again, and there was happiness in the family again. They were in the roaring twenties then and there was much joy and dancing. Inflation was beginning, and people were becoming speculative. In 1925 another child came to the family, a baby boy named Charles and joy was in the family. They had a complete family.

Bunn started talking about the limited income of his job, and he wanted Leah to consider his farming the land that she owned outside of Trumann, Arkansas. He knew from the checks she received from the renter that this property produced big crops. He felt that his experience in farming as a boy would permit him to make those big profits, and the family would benefit from this increased income. Leah was hesitant about this and resisted his ideas until January of 1927.

They left Monroe, Louisiana, and went to Trumann, Arkansas, and set up housekeeping in the house located on her farm. They were both excited about the prospects of making a large amount of money. When spring came, Bunn went to the local Farmer's Bank and put in for a loan to put in a crop. He mortgaged her land to support the loan. By April he had the entire farm planted, and the corn and cotton were sprouting up, and it looked like they were going to have a bounteous crop.

On April 15, 1927, it started to rain and it rained, and it rained, and it rained. It rained for 35 days continuously. The St. Francis River, which ran adjacent to the farm flooded and covered the fields with water 5 feet deep. The water stayed and stayed and stayed upon the land and did not recede until December of that year. There was a total loss of the crop, and Bunn was unable to pay the note. The farm was foreclosed upon, and a significant income for Leah was lost forever.

Leah was devastated. It seemed to her that every time life was going to be good, some disaster happened. Secretly she blamed her husband, but she knew that all her neighbors lost their crops and were victims of a freakish event of nature. These thoughts began to dominate their marriage.

Bunn was aware of this change in their relationship, but they weren't a couple that would talk out their differences. They just buried it and went on with their lives knowing that somehow it was festering between them. Bunn was still trying to get a better job, and a friend of his came to him one day and asked him to be a partner in an insurance company that he was developing. He knew that Bunn had a salesman's personality, and he would be an asset in selling life insurance. So, from 1927 until 1929, they were very successful with their insurance company, and things picked up. They seemed to be happy again. They bought a new car and had a new home in the best part of Monroe, Louisiana. The purchase of the home was supported by funds from Leah's inheritance, and life seemed good again. The crash of 1929 hit them hard.

The insurance company would not support two people, and it was decided that Bunn would return to the Missouri Pacific Railroad as they were constantly asking him to return. He was given a good job at the local station and during the first few months of 1930, they did well. As the depression deepened, the railroad started running a deficit, and they started firing employees. They didn't want to lose Bunn so they allowed him to bump down. This was a process where a person with greater seniority could take a job at a lower level and displace that person. The only position that was lower than Bunn's was a station manager at Riverton, Louisiana. It was a real come down for both of them as they had to give up their beautiful home. To Leah this was another major loss of her moneys and her home. She tried not to be bitter towards Bunn, but she couldn't help herself. This was the beginning of the deterioration of their relationship.

By 1932 the railroad returned Bunn to Monroe, Louisiana, with an increase in his salary and position. He was considered at that time a very important employee and was put on a fast track for promotion. In the latter part of 1932 he was given the position of division freight and passenger agent of El Dorado, Arkansas. This was a big increase in salary, and the plan was that he would eventually go to St. Louis, the corporate headquarters. This promotion came too late in their marriage as there had been too many losses and disappointments, but they managed to somehow keep their relationship going, and it didn't seem to affect the children to any extent. Leah was very unhappy and developed many physical symptoms. She knew they were related to her despair, but she did nothing about it. Her aggressive behavior changed to a very passive state which supported her chronic depression. Bunn was aware of the fact that Leah no longer loved him, but he ignored this and because his new job was so demanding and exciting, nothing really changed in how they related.

In 1935 Bunn got into a disagreement with his immediate superior. It didn't matter that he was right because his superior had great influence on whether he would progress in his position to a job in St. Louis. This person, a Mr. England, wrote a very damaging report of his work in El Dorado, and it took Bunn off the fast track. He knew immediately that this had happened to him, and he was much despaired. So, here we now have two depressed people trying to raise two children. Neither one was willing to help the other.

In 1936 there was a lightening of the depression, and Bunn began to make more money with his passenger agent position. If he was able to develop large fares to various parts of the country, the railroad would give him a commission. A rich couple in El Dorado who knew him engaged him with a project of working out a world tour for them.

The commission for this was large enough for Bunn to take his entire family to Colorado for a two week vacation. Both he and Leah hoped that this would restart their marriage. They found, however, that it didn't change anything. Leah continued in her passive state and developed many psychosomatic conditions, one of which was pityriasis rosea. This required Bunn to take her to Little Rock for several months. She was seeing a noted dermatologist who was helping her with the symptoms of the disease. Bunn was very attentive, and he hoped this would change their relationship, but nothing changed. Leah was no longer interested in him sexually. At first he resented this, and then he decided that he would find someone else who wanted him.

When he found this person, Leah was relieved as now there was no reason to feel guilty about his lack of sex. She thought about her position and wondered why she was allowing such a disruptive force in her marriage and in her life. She knew that she was harming her children by her passiveness and depression, but for some reason she felt powerless to do anything about it. Her chronic depression had become a part of her personality, and she seemingly was comfortable with the burden it had imposed on her. She knew that her children were withdrawing from her, and it troubled her, but she did nothing.

In 1940 her daughter left for college and effectively disappeared from the family. In 1942 her son left and was not to return for a number of years.

All during World War II life was miserable for all of them. She did make one effort that was different. She got a job at a local war industry, and for several years was self-supporting. She hoped that this was the way she could escape her marriage just like her teaching had helped her escape from Amanda Ruth.

When the war ended, her job ended, and she was unable to find another one. Her old chronic depressive personality took hold of her. Although she and her husband lived in the same house, they were very lonely people.

In 1948 it seemed that both of them felt that their lives were beginning to end, and they should try to do something to change their passive depressive personalities. Bunn, at that time, had become an alcoholic and was having serious liver problems. He thought he should try to build a home for Leah and at least give her something to live in if he should die. He went to many banks in the area trying to get a loan, but his financial condition was not strong enough to support one. He had been a person who always took care of his parent family, and he appealed to his brother who was now a successful lawyer to cosign a note so he could build a house.

His brother refused, and all hope of changing anything vanished. Their daughter and son never visited them. When Charles returned from overseas, he would not come home at all. He had married a young lady while he was overseas, and they spent their leave time with her family. He did call home to tell them that he was back in the states, and when they asked if he was coming to visit them, he gave an abrupt "no" and hung up.

They realized then that all they had was themselves as their children no longer wanted to have anything to do with them. They heard that their son had gone to med school at Vanderbilt, and he was in his senior year. He graduated from med school and didn't even bother to send them a graduation announcement. Some friends told them Charles had reenlisted into the Army and was getting his internship at Brooke Army Hospital in San Antonio, Texas.

In October of 1951, Bunn awoke one morning and was not able to swallow. When he would take a drink of water, it would back up into his lungs, and he would have a terrible coughing spell. He could not swallow his saliva, and he was in difficult circumstances. They both feared that something seriously was wrong, and they rushed to a railroad hospital in Little Rock, Arkansas.

Leah called her son, Charles, and asked him to come to Little Rock and help her with his Father. Charles came with his new wife and son, Sam. For the first time, she met Lillian and Sam. Lillian was such a pretty girl, and Sam was a cute little boy. It was obvious that Lillian was in love with Charles.

During the next few days when Charles was involved with his Father's diagnosis and treatment, Lillian spent many hours with Leah. Leah found that she was a very caring person, and she found herself responding to her and her grandson. In fact, she saw Lillian as a hope for her, and Lillian was not afraid to accept that responsibility. When Bunn died postoperatively, it was Lillian who helped Leah with all the problems that evolved from his death.

Lillian had a long talk with Charles about his Mother. She said, "Charles, I think your Mother's a wonderful person, and I think you have had a bad idea about who she was and how she was. I know she's passive and has been depressed for a long time, but I find in her a woman who has had to deal with a lot of loss and despair, and I am somewhat disappointed with you that you did not recognize this and help her." Charles responded, "Lillian, I know that I have not supported my Mother, but I felt if I did reengage her, I would be swallowed up by her despair and depression. You did not live with her all the years that I did. I lived with her when I was an immature child, and I did not have the skill level that you have as an adult and when I did develop those skills, I did not want to reengage her because I did not want to tolerate her passive inability to engage life. I just wanted her out of my life forever, and I still feel that way." Lillian replied, "Charles, regardless of what you experienced as a child, you still have a Mother that is all alone, and I will not let you abandon her. I feel very strongly that we have a responsibility to help her during this period and to help her change from the type of person she is to the one she was when she was 19. I don't think you know about her experience at age 19, but I do. I know from what she told me that she was a very aggressive young woman who broke away from her hostile relationship with her half-sister and established a life for herself. She was a woman that persevered, but the burden of so many losses overcame her. You would have known this had you just talked to her." Charles replied, "Lillian, I am glad that you are willing to help my Mother, and I will be willing for us to take her with us to San Antonio, and maybe we can help her start a new life."

So, when Lillian told Leah about wanting her to come with them, Leah burst out in tears and hugged Lillian and said, "Oh, Lillian, no one has cared for me all these years, and if you had not come along, I think I would have died." They moved into larger quarters in San Antonio, and Leah had her own room and bath. Lillian was pregnant at that time with her second child.

From Leah's standpoint, Charles was being very unreasonable. He was never at home. He seemed to be compulsively driven to be a surgeon and took no care of Lillian as she struggled with her pregnancy. It disturbed Leah very much when she would see Lillian so tired that all she could do was cry. It was those times that Lillian and Leah became closely bonded to each other. When Lillian was helplessly crying in despair over her inability to keep up with her young son and her pregnancy, there was Leah taking over with young Sam and helping her with all the necessary household problems. When Charles would come home, Lillian would tell him about how much she loved Leah, but he made no attempt to understand. All he could think about was how he could get more experience in the practice of surgery.

When Lillian confronted him about what he was doing, he told her that he was trying to be efficient enough in surgery so that he could get a position in a Mash Unit in Korea. He knew that he would be assigned some duty overseas, and he didn't want to be a battalion surgeon. Lillian responded to this statement by saying, "I don't like what you just said. I think that I should be considered in this plan of yours. You are setting up yourself to be overseas when I had hopes that you would be assigned in the United States." Charles had no defense for his position and just became silent.

At the end of June, Charles completed his internship, and he did get assigned to a Mash Unit in Korea. This meant that Lillian was to go back to her family in Athens, Georgia, and Leah was to go to her daughter's home in Cincinnati, Ohio. Lillian and Leah had a very sad parting of each other, but Charles was so involved in going overseas, he noted none of this, and he was just concerned about getting the two women to the places he felt they would be safe. Both women felt that Charles was not showing any loving care for them as he departed for overseas duty.

As Leah left on the train going from San Antonio, Texas, to Cincinnati, Ohio, she knew that her daughter, Marilyn, did not want her to come there, but there was no place else to go. When she arrived at the station in Cincinnati, she had to wait in the waiting room for a period of time because her daughter was not there to greet her. She wondered about their relationship.

Memories of her Marilyn's child hood came into focus. She remembered them being at the kitchen sink in their home on sixth street in Monroe, Louisiana. They were playing while they were washing dishes. Marilyn was playing with a diamond ring on my finger. She said, "Mommy can I wear that ring." "I first said no, but she insisted, and finally I took it off. I remember that ring so well. I bought it with the last money of my father's estate. It was a four carat blue diamond ring, and I considered it my last security. Marilyn put it on her little ring finger and drew it up to her face. She did it with a quick motion, and the ring flew off into the sink. I gasped and frantically tried to catch it, but it went down the drain. The water was running, and it disappeared. I immediately got under the sink and ripped off the trap hoping to find the ring, but it was gone. A feeling of shame came over Leah as the events that followed were traumatic to both she and Leah. I remember screaming at my daughter, Marilyn, with a rage that would have frightened a gorilla. I didn't remember what I said, but it must have been terrifying to Marilyn. I could see that little girl running away from me and sobbing. How could I have been so cruel? Our relationship was never the same after that event. By the time Marilyn got into High school, she was very distant with me, and I would rarely talk with her. So here I am sitting in a large railroad passenger station waiting for a daughter that has never forgiven me, and I have never forgiven her." When Marilyn did arrive, all she said was that she was tied up with other things and could not get there until that time. Leah knew that other things were more important than she.

The next two years were disastrous for Leah, and her only happy moments were when she would receive letters from Lillian. Lillian wrote how much she missed her, and how difficult it was for her to be without her husband. She told about how she had gone to Japan to be close to where he was and how his Christmas leave had been a disastrous experience. She told Leah that she felt that Charles could not love anymore, and it was a great disappointment and concern for her.

When Leah read about Charles's lost of the ability to love, she thought about Bunn and their loveless marriage. They never had a chance in their marriage as they both brought too much despair into their relationship for any real love to develop. Why did they stay married? Her only answer was that they both were too passive to do anything. They just got into their cocoons and despaired.

When Charles and Lillian moved to the Mayo Clinic for him to continue his surgical training, Lillian wrote Leah saying that she would soon ask her to come and live with them and in September, 1956, they were finally reunited.

Lillian had insisted that Charles buy a house that would be large enough to accommodate Leah and their three children. She reported to Leah that Charles had invested in Japan businesses, and now they were receiving a large income from their investments, so money was no problem for them.

Leah would never forget the day that she arrived at the railroad station in Rochester, Minnesota, and there was Lillian waiting for her. The contrast of Lillian meeting her and her daughter's meeting her was markedly different. Lillian loved her, and her daughter tolerated her.

They went to Lillian and Charles' new home, and when she walked into the room that had been designed for her, Leah was amazed. It was a large bedroom with windows that looked out over a park area. She had a large bathroom connected to her bedroom, and she could be completely separated from the house if she so desired. Leah fell immediately in love with all of her grandchildren and helped Lillian with anything that might come up that was connected with the family.

Lillian would take Leah with her every place she went and introduced her to all of her friends. Leah's personality was changing rapidly. She began actively engaging in her contacts with other people, and Lillian's friends were charmed by her. Leah's physical appearance changed. She began to pay attention to how she dressed, and in a short time, she looked like a young 55 year old woman. They attended many parties together, Leah and Lillian, and at one party she met a middle-aged doctor by the name of Williams—Dr. James Williams. To her surprise he called her and asked her for a date. She had not thought of dating and had resigned herself to being a widow all her life. At first, she refused, but he was persistent, and before long, they were dating regularly.

It was in the summer of 1957 Leah felt a lump in her right breast. She was horrified. She couldn't talk to Lillian or anybody about what she had discovered. All she could do was regress to that old state of chronic depression and inactivity.

She knew that she was going to die of cancer as she knew this lump was a breast tumor. It was only Lillian's persistence that she told Lillian what was troubling her, and Lillian got her immediately into the hospital. Before all of this happened, James Williams had already told Leah that he was in love with her and wanted to marry her, but she had refused and told him that her first marriage was such a disaster that she didn't want to think about the possibility of another one.

When James heard about a new patient being admitted to his ward with breast cancer and learned that it was Leah, he rushed to her side. He gave her constant attention and helped her through all the decisions to be made concerning how to treat her tumor. He told her that he was not going to let anything happen to her. He said, "Leah, I lost my first wife to breast cancer, and I am not going to lose you." His caring deeply moved Leah, and she started thinking that she should try to marry again, and it would be James Williams and no one else.

She went through a radical mastectomy and a lymph node resection. The nodes had no cancer, and James told her that he felt she was cured. When he told her this, she reached up and drew him to her chest and gave him a loving kiss. She told him that his caring for her convinced her that she loved him, and she wanted to marry him as soon as possible.

They became inseparable and had many intimate talks. In one of their talks, Leah said to James, "James, you know I have lost a breast. Will this in any way affect you sexually?" James looked at her and said, "Leah, I am not in love with your breast, I am in love with you." They were married, and Leah left Charles and Lillian's home and established a home for James and her. She missed Lillian very much, but it was the children with whom she really felt the loss. Every minute she could get, she would go over and visit the children and include them in many of her activities.

The loving care of James completely changed Leah. She became aggressive and assertive. In the society they lived in, she became a leader. James was immensely proud of her and took every opportunity he could to show her off to the world, and she responded likewise. Both had been born in 1898, and when James was 65 in 1963, he retired from the Mayo Clinic, and Leah and he began traveling all over the world. Leah became quite cosmopolitan and started studying foreign languages. Since Charles was actively involved with his Japanese companies, she became fluent in Japanese and visited many of the families in Japan who were connected with Charles. James did not have the ability to learn languages, but he rejoiced in Leah's accomplishments.

By 1983 James started having problems with his heart. He had multiple, silent, small infarcts of his heart, and he was in an early state of congestive heart failure. They had to stop their traveling, and Leah was in constant attendance with James. He deteriorated slowly over the years, and by 1987, he was severely handicapped. He died that summer, but this time Leah didn't go into despair. She had gained so much in this relationship that she handled it in a very mature way. She made all of the funeral arrangements and amazed everybody about her ability to carry on when everybody knew how much she loved James. The old passive Leah was gone forever.

The last three years of Leah's life were happy years. She didn't develop any physical problems, and she spent hours with her grandchildren. She was particularly interested in Leah Lillian, the youngest child of Charles and Lillian. She loved the family that Leah L. had developed, and she felt closer to them than she did to anyone else. When she was 90 years old, she developed severe heart failure, and she became an invalid. She felt that she was dying, and she called Charles and Lillian to come to see her.

As she talked to them, she was gasping for breath, but she felt she had to say what was in her heart. She said to Charles, "Charles, I failed you when you needed me as a child. I have never been able to recapture the love that I always wanted to be between us. I know it has been hard for you to accept me in a new role, but I want you to know that I am very proud of you, and I have loved you from the moment you were born. I hope you will be able to forgive me when I was not there for you when you really needed me." Charles didn't respond to this. He just took his Mother's hand in his and squeezed it gently.

She turned to Lillian and said, "Lillian, you were the daughter I never had. It was your love of me that really saved my life. I would never have gotten to 90 if you had not come to me and been a part of my life. Thank you for giving me so much love and all those wonderful children that have made my life very happy and content. I know I am dying now, and I want you both to know that I die in peace, and I am looking forward to being with James again.

Good-bye, Charles and Lillian, I will always love you." With that she lay quietly in the bed, and her breathing became more and more difficult. She slowly lost consciousness, and she found herself dreaming. She was in a field of flowers, and there was James. He was running across the field. When he reached her and was hugging her, she stopped breathing.